PRAISE FOR KIM LAW

"*Montana Cherries* is a heartwarming yet heart-wrenching story of the heroine's struggle to accept the truth about her mother's death—and life."

—*RT Book Reviews*, 4 stars

"An entertaining romance with a well-developed plot and believable characters. The chemistry between Vega and JP is explosive and will have you rooting for the couple's success. Readers will definitely look forward to more works by this author."

—*RT Book Reviews*, 4 stars (HOT) on
Caught on Camera

"Kim Law pens a sexy, fast-paced romance."

—*New York Times* bestselling author Lori Wilde on
Caught on Camera

"A solid combination of sexy fun."

—*New York Times* bestselling author Carly Phillips on
Ex on the Beach

"*Sugar Springs* is a deeply emotional story about family ties and second chances. If you love heartwarming small towns, this is one place you'll definitely want to visit."

—*USA Today* bestselling author Hope Ramsay

"Filled with engaging characters, *Sugar Springs* is the typical everyone-knows-everyone's-business small town. Law skillfully portrays heroine Lee Ann's doubts and fears, as well as hero Cody's struggle to be a better person than he believes he can be. And Lee Ann's young nieces are a delight."

—*RT Book Reviews*, 4 stars

MONTANA HOMECOMING

ALSO BY KIM LAW

THE WILDES OF BIRCH BAY

Montana Cherries

Montana Rescue

Montana Mornings

Montana Mistletoe (novella)

Montana Dreams

Montana Promises

SUGAR SPRINGS NOVELS

Sugar Springs

Sweet Nothings

Sprinkles on Top

DEEP IN THE HEART

Hardheaded

Softhearted

THE DAVENPORTS

Caught on Camera

Caught in the Act

TURTLE ISLAND NOVELS

Ex on the Beach

Hot Buttered Yum Two

Turtle Island Doves (novella)

On the Rocks

HOLLY HILLS

"Marry Me, Cowboy" (novella), Cowboys for Christmas

Montana
HOMECOMING

Kim Law

My readers are the best, and anytime I reach out on social media, asking for help, they always come through. For this book, there were several readers specifically that helped, so I want to dedicate this one to them.

For Montana research:
Bridget Neils
Lauren Barrows

For helping me name the babies:
Marilyn Bateman Hendry
Becky Carr
Donamae Clausen Kutska

PROLOGUE

Four weeks earlier.

A *sharp prickling* sensation pinched at the base of Cord's neck as he watched the paramedic on the other side of the road. The man had stepped back, away from the SUV. His expression didn't seem right. It was blank. Strangely so.

And he was doing nothing to help Cord's mother get out of her vehicle.

Cord blinked, but the scene remained the same. His confusion grew. Then he lowered his gaze to the now-totaled sedan he'd hurried to check on and took in the pregnant woman sitting inside. She remained behind the steering wheel, seat belt removed, with a paramedic at her side. The small scratch above her eyebrow continued to dribble out a slow trickle of blood, and she also had a bruise fanning out from the base of her thumb. The airbag had caught her hand as it burst outward.

"Is she going to be okay?" Cord asked of the woman, but the man working on her didn't answer.

The paramedic continued checking her vitals, while his partner made her way back from the ambulance with a stretcher. At the sight of the

1

stretcher, Cord's heart rate increased. *The woman had to be okay. Hurting her hadn't been his mother's intention.*

He looked back to the other side of the road. His mother still wasn't out of the SUV.

And there was still no one helping her.

"Mom?" The single word was a surprise to hear, and even more of a shock to realize that he'd spoken it.

The pregnant woman looked up—she'd said her name was Bailey. She followed Cord's gaze to the opposite side of the road. "Is your mom okay?"

Cord nodded. *Of course his mom was okay. She was always okay.* But no words came.

Instead, he went back to watching. The blank-faced paramedic, who remained a short distance from the SUV, had a hand lifted to the radio clipped to his shirt, his chin dipped as if speaking into the mic.

Cord swallowed.

"Go." Bailey whispered the word, and though spoken softly, there was insistence behind it.

Cord looked at her again.

"I'm fine." She assured him with a nod, and as the paramedic stepped back, a faint smile touched her lips. She laid a hand over her belly. "We're both *fine*. Go check on your mom."

His mother was fine, too, he wanted to tell her. She'd been complaining about not being able to get the seat belt to unlock before he'd left her side. She'd yelled at him because he wouldn't get her purse off the passenger side floor so she could "fix herself" before anyone arrived.

The airbag had deployed when her car had careened into the tree, and not only had it left her covered with a fine layer of dust, but it had given her a bloody nose, as well. He'd come upon the wreck only moments after it happened.

"Go," the woman said again.

"She's fine," Cord managed, but without realizing he intended to move, his feet started toward the asphalt. The responding police officers had stopped traffic on the two-lane road—just a mile from the Wilde family home—and Cord turned his head as he reached the double yellow lines painted down the middle. A tow truck rolled slowly toward him, the driver having shifted the rig to the opposite side of the road in order to get around the line of stopped cars. The sheriff's vehicle, blue lights silently flashing, passed the truck on the shoulder. Cord's feet kept moving.

Neither the paramedic that had first attended to his mother nor the man's partner looked his way as he neared. Nor did they look at his mother.

"Mom." He said the word again, and this time when he spoke, the deputy who'd been first on scene stepped toward him.

The deputy held out a hand as if to ward off Cord's forward movement. "You're one of Mrs. Wilde's sons, right? Cord, is it?"

Birch Bay was a small town, and everyone knew of his family. "Yes."

"Son—"

Cord held up his own hand, stopping the officer from saying anything more, and shrugged away from the man's touch. The sheriff's car pulled to a stop at Cord's side.

"Cord?" the sheriff called as he stepped from the cruiser.

Cord kept walking.

"You need to stay back."

Cord heard the words, as well as the sound of the sheriff's feet hurrying through the gravel that edged the side of the road, and once again, when a hand landed on his arm, he shrugged it away. He did not need to stay back. This was what they did. His mother had an "accident," planned it so he'd be the one to find her, and he showed up to help. Just as he'd done that time.

He'd been right there. Talking to her. She'd been fine.

As his feet closed in on the still-open door, his determination somehow keeping the sheriff and his deputy at bay—or maybe he'd just blocked out anything else they might be saying—his eyes roamed over the exterior of the dark-red Suburban. The vehicle could fit all five of his siblings, along with him and his parents at the same time. It was the family vehicle his mother had been so insistent on having. The one she loved to show off around town.

3

It was also the vehicle where most times when she drove it, she did so alone. None of them wanted to be around her.

Cord finally reached the door, his vision zeroing in, blocking out everything else going on. He leaned in to ask his mother why she hadn't gotten out of the car. Only, it was no longer his mother inside the vehicle.

CHAPTER ONE

CORD SHIFTED THE TRUCK INTO A LOWER GEAR, MAKING SURE HE didn't get too close to the edge of the road, and he kept his eyes focused on the beams of his headlights. The light slashed through the dark night and the falling snow. He had no idea why he'd agreed to come. Thanksgiving had been the day before. If he'd wanted to be around his family, that's when he should have done it. Not the day after Thanksgiving when over three feet of snow was in the forecast.

He'd been going stir-crazy back in Billings, though. His partners had kicked him out of the medical practice the week before and refused to let him return. At least, not for another week. They'd insisted he needed time off—preferably with counseling. Only, he *didn't* need time off. Nor did he need counseling. And the very idea infuriated him.

He was an excellent doctor. With him not being in the office, it was his patients who would pay the price. His patients who wouldn't get to see the doctor they'd grown to trust and rely upon. All because of a few bad dreams that had the misfortune of keeping him awake a little too often.

Irritation swelled. The other partners had no right to insist he take a vacation. They'd overstepped. However, with Cord being the least senior partner—and since there *were* a couple of other general practitioners in the practice—he'd reluctantly agreed. But he *hadn't* agreed on counseling.

He gripped the wheel as his tires temporarily caught nothing but snow and kept the truck going. His brother Nate had called the night before, worried about their dad, so Cord had agreed to come home. And since he had the time off, he figured he might as well stay for the week. No need to hurry back to nothing. He'd hole up in one of the cabins on his family's property and check in on their dad first thing in the morning. And while in town, he'd also lay eyes on his very-pregnant sister and two pregnant sisters-in-law, one of which was expecting twins and all of which were due in the coming month. Then the rest of the week? He scowled. He'd do nothing. Exactly as he'd been doing at his place.

He rounded the last curve before the straight stretch that would lead to the family property, and as he'd done for the last sixteen years, he kept his gaze trained away from the tree where his mother had died. Continuing down the road, he'd barely come out of the curve when another set of headlights broke through the blizzard-like conditions. Only, their path didn't run horizontal to the road. They shot up toward the trees.

Quickly pulling to a stop, his snow tires sliding more than what made him comfortable, he cut the engine. The sedan was off the opposite side of the road, its back end buried in the ditch. He grabbed his jacket from the seat beside him and while shrugging into it, ducked his head against the wind and hurried to the car. Once there, he could make out a woman behind the wheel. Relief passed through him as he saw her thumbs moving over the glowing screen of a phone.

"Are you okay?" Cord called through the howling wind.

He clenched his hands against the cold as the woman continued tapping on her phone, and he wished he hadn't forgotten to grab his gloves and hat.

"Ma'am?" He rapped on the window with his knuckles.

The woman jerked in surprise, her shocked face whipping around to his—and then she frowned.

Crap. He knew her.

"Open your window." He motioned for her to do just that, hoping she didn't take the moment to ignore him as he'd ignored her a few months earlier.

Her window opened one inch. "I'm fine." She spoke through the narrow crack, her iced-over voice and hard eyes letting him know that she'd have preferred *anyone* come along to help her out other than him. Then the glass once again slid up.

Cord sighed. There was nothing more fun than a stubborn woman.

Unless it was a stubborn woman whom he'd had a mind-blowing weekend with—who'd then repeatedly called, obviously hoping there could be more to their time together.

He'd told her up front there couldn't be, though. And he wouldn't apologize for that.

She might be annoyed with him, but that didn't mean he'd leave her sitting in the snow on the side of the road. Especially since in the past, cell service could be flaky on this part of the highway, even without a major storm rolling through. "Is your phone working?" He held his now-very-cold hand up to his ear as if talking on a phone, then pointed to her hand.

She looked from him down at her cell which had gone dark. Then she ignored him.

"Come on, Maggie." He thumped his fist against the glass. Frustration mingled with the freezing temperatures and had him glaring down at her when she looked back up.

She glared back.

"Is it working?" he gritted out, once again jabbing his finger in the direction of her phone.

The phone screen lit up then, highlighting the mutinous expression on her face, and she pressed the screen of the cell up to the window. Multiple texts showed as having failed to send, and there were no bars on her signal. He sighed again. Then he tugged at her door handle.

Surprisingly, the door opened.

"Hey!" she shouted as snow fell in from the crease of the door. She leaned back to avoid it dumping on her.

"Come with me," he growled. He positioned himself against the door, bracing a leg on the edge of the ditch, and held out a hand to help her. The car sat at such an odd angle that she could easily fall simply trying to step out. "I'll take you up to the house and you can call someone there," he told her.

"I don't want to go to your house."

He kept his arm outstretched, his thin grip on his anger threatening to slip. "Good thing it's not *my* house then." Nor would it be the family house soon. It was currently nearing the end of renovations that would turn the home he'd grown up in into a lodge. Afterward, he and his family would spend one last Christmas there, then Nate and his wife Megan would begin renting it out to tourists.

"Well, I don't want to go with you, period," Maggie said. She remained stubbornly in the driver's seat of the car, her arms wrapped around what appeared to be a blanket bundled in her lap, and she stared straight ahead.

He wanted to slam the door and walk away. He didn't need any more hassles in his life right now, not even of the temporary kind. But after what happened a month ago, even if he *were* the type to walk away from a woman in a snowstorm, he wouldn't do it.

He'd never walk away again.

"I'm not leaving you out here in these conditions, Maggie. So quit being stubborn."

Her head whipped around again, and she repeated her insistence that she was fine. "I'll call my brother when the signal comes back."

He was freezing his ass off out there. "Doesn't your brother live an hour away?"

"It's only forty-five minutes," she informed him. "And he'll come get me."

"I'm sure he will. In the meantime, you'll freeze to death trying to get through to him." Tired of the delay, he leaned in so that his face was only inches from hers. "I'm sorry I never returned your call, Maggie. That was a shit thing for me to do, especially after saying I would. But can you please ignore that one injustice for the moment so we can both get out of here and to somewhere where there's heat?"

She scrutinized him again, as if trying to decide if her life was worth the risk, but he didn't back off. He would not leave her sitting out there, so all she was accomplishing was wasting both their time.

"Mags . . ."

"Fine," she snapped, and he'd swear he felt a flame of fire burst out of her. "But I'm calling my brother just as soon as I can."

"By all means."

She grabbed her purse from the passenger seat, looping it over her left wrist, then she suddenly slowed, taking her time to drag a cream-colored knit hat down over her hair. Next, she pulled on thick gloves that matched the hat and checked her reflection as she tucked flyaway strands of hair up underneath the brim. And when she finally turned his way again, her annoyance as clear as the "innocent" look she'd plastered on her face, he couldn't keep the snarl out of his voice.

"About *ready?*" he asked. She had to know he was freezing out there. So much snow had landed on his head he could feel the wetness seeping into his skull, not to mention inching its way under the back collar of his jacket. Yet she seemed to have zero concern for him.

She smiled brightly. "Not quite."

Her smile disappeared, and her dark eyes bore into his as she reached inside the collar of her thick coat and pulled out the ends of a scarf. She took extra time twining the length of it around her neck and covering the bottom half of her face—checking her appearance in the rearview once again—then she finally took her purse back into her right hand and held out her left to him.

She looked like the Michelin Man who mistakenly thought he was a princess as she sat there bundled from head to toe with one hand primly held out as if waiting for him to kiss it.

"Now?" he asked instead of taking the proffered hand.

Her eyes burned hot. *"Please."*

He leaned in long enough to punch the start button that she hadn't thought to turn off, then just to be annoying, he subtly dipped his head as he went to step back. He didn't let himself smile at the high-pitched squeak as the snow that had been in his hair landed on her.

He helped her out of the seat, needing both hands to assist her in maneuvering, and as he noted how awkward it was for her to find her footing, he frowned. Had something happened since he'd last seen her? Once they'd managed to clear the ditch and stand on the side of the road, though, a very important detail finally registered.

That hadn't been a bundled blanket in her lap at all. She was pregnant.

MAGGIE CROWDER DIDN'T LOOK at Cord as she picked her way through the snow and toward the man's truck. She didn't want to see the look on his face now that he had to have figured out she was pregnant. And not just pregnant, but enormously so. With *his* baby. Why the heck couldn't he have returned a phone call six months earlier? Or five months ago when she'd tried a second time? He'd texted back that time, at least, and said he'd call. But he never had.

The entire thing exasperated her. His ego, for one—no doubt he'd assumed she'd just been reaching out because she wanted to hook up again. She was also frustrated with the fact that she now had to go into this discussion in the middle of a snowstorm, when she wasn't exactly at her best. And then there was the matter that when he'd first seen it was her in the car, he'd looked as annoyed as she'd been. What had that been about? *He* wasn't the one who should be annoyed.

"You're pregnant?" The question, coming from behind, made her realize that Cord hadn't followed her into the road.

She turned back. "I am."

She couldn't bring herself to say any more. Not just yet. But as he stood there, the look on his face indicating that he saw her condition as more disease than miracle of life, she found herself with tears suddenly filling her eyes.

That made him move. "Are you okay?"

He hurried toward her, and she took two steps back, not wanting to be near him. But as she did, one of her feet slipped. She flailed, fear instantly corkscrewing through her, but Cord stopped her from falling by locking one hand around her bicep.

Heart pounding, she stared up at him. She hadn't fallen. She hadn't hurt the baby.

Her next thought was that Cord didn't look horrified any longer. Now he looked *terrified*.

Was something wrong that she hadn't realized? Had she hurt the baby, after all?

She looked down at herself, taking in Cord's hand still clasped tightly around her arm before sweeping her gaze over the rest of her body. She seemed exactly as she had before she'd run off the road. Before she'd looked up and found Cord Wilde staring in through her window at her.

She hadn't fallen, she repeated to herself. She hadn't hurt the baby.

Her pregnancy was textbook, and her son was exactly where he should be at seven and a half months. There were *no* signs her delivery would be anything but normal.

As the words calmed her, she pushed at his hand. "I told you, I'm fine. I don't need your help."

He didn't let go. "You're crying." His voice was deep.

More tears leaked out, and she swiped at them now. "Pregnant women cry. Sue me."

His hand remained firm around her arm as he lowered his gaze and took in the fullness of her stomach. He stared at her for a long moment, his breath seeming to be caught in his lungs, before he brought his gaze back up to hers.

Panic flashed through his eyes.

And then . . . anger?

Before she could process why he might be angry, all emotion cleared from his face. "You just wrecked." His tone went professional. "You could have an injury that isn't visible. You could be in labor. I need to get you to the hospital."

They stood alone in the middle of the road, snow swirling around them, the streetlights casting an eerie glow down over them, and it finally sunk in that he hadn't put two and two together. He didn't yet realize this baby was his.

"I *don't* need to go to the hospital," she assured him. She tugged at her arm again, but his clamp remained tight.

"Yes, you do. You need to be put on monitors. You could already be in labor."

She snort-laughed at that. "If only. I'm weeks away from delivering, Cord. I promise."

Disbelief slashed the line of his mouth, and he looked her up and down again. "Come on, Maggie. That can't possibly be true. You look—"

Her hackles went up. "I look *what? Fat?*"

Her brows lifted as she stared at him. She knew exactly what she looked like. She looked like she should have given birth at least two weeks before. From what she could tell, she was due to pop out the next NFL offensive lineman in exactly six weeks, and the child would likely enter the world ready to suit up and take the field.

"No. I just mean . . ." Cord seemed at a sudden loss for words.

"I know exactly what you meant. I'm huge. It's a side effect of having a baby, didn't you know? Just like the tears." She was tired of standing out in the cold. If he intended to help her, then it was time he got to it. "Can we go to the house now?"

"I'd rather take you to the hospital."

"Well, I'm not going." She stuck out her chin. "You either take me to the house or you drive away and leave me standing here."

She didn't know a whole lot about him, but she did know enough to understand that there was zero chance he'd leave her standing in the snow. Even while *not* knowing that the baby she carried was his. And that's because as a teenager, he'd once come upon his mother after she'd wrecked. She'd died before the paramedics could get to her, and all the while Cord hadn't even known she'd been seriously injured.

Maggie had heard that story as a teen. Cord had been sixteen at the time, her thirteen. And given she was also now good friends with one of his sisters-in-law and with another *soon*-to-be sister-in-law, she'd also heard Cord's name mentioned more than once in the last year and a half.

He took care of people; that's what he did. He'd gotten a medical degree and moved to Billings, and though for a long time he'd rarely come home, he now made regular visits. And he did that because his father had been diagnosed with Parkinson's disease. Because back in the spring, in the middle of a medically induced hallucination, his dad had driven a tractor headfirst into a tree.

Max Wilde had lost a leg that day, and Cord, the son with the medical degree, had taken responsibility for his care personally. He didn't do things like leave people standing in the middle of a snowstorm.

Cord finally nodded. "I'll take you to the house."

He kept a hold on her as he led her to his truck, and she scowled down at where his arm now looped through hers. She didn't comment on it, though. Because the reality was that her center of gravity was so far off that while in the snow, she'd much prefer a helping hand. She just wasn't about to tell him that.

"What are you doing here, anyway?" she grumbled as they made their way to the truck. She'd been told he wasn't coming in that weekend. And she'd been told that because she'd specifically asked. Because if he *had* been planning to come in this weekend, she wouldn't have gone to visit her parents the day before. Instead, she would have shown up unannounced at Cord's family Thanksgiving, and then she would have confronted him, making it impossible for him to ignore her yet again.

"I came in to check on Dad," he muttered. "Nate called."

That's all he said, but it told her enough. There was something he was worried about. He'd checked on his dad multiple times the weekend they'd gotten together. Max had just gone into the rehab facility after he'd lost his leg.

They reached the truck, and as he opened the passenger door, an annoying reality slammed into her. She sighed. She wouldn't be able to get in by herself. Not even if it hadn't been snowing. She couldn't possibly stretch one leg up far enough to hoist herself into that cab. At least, not without falling over backward.

Cord read the situation correctly, and with no more warning than a brief, but direct glance into her eyes and an annoyed slant to his mouth, he gripped her under both arms. The ground left her feet and she found herself hoisted up and plopped down on the seat before him. With her legs now dangling out the side of the truck, she suddenly found herself light-headed.

"Well," she murmured. She dragged her eyes off the brick-hard line of his jaw and looked around the spotless cab of the Chevy. "That's one way to do it, I suppose."

Scooting back as gracefully as she could manage, she pulled her legs into the truck and turned to face the windshield. However, instead of closing the door, Cord just stood there. When she peeked back at him, she found that he'd once again lowered his eyes to stare at her stomach. And as he continued to study her, her anger reappeared.

She hadn't seen the man since that weekend in April. She'd found out she was pregnant about five weeks after that, and it had seemed the honorable thing to let the father know. What *hadn't* seemed honorable, she'd decided at the time, was to do it over a text. Therefore, she'd sent a message and asked him to call. And he'd ignored her.

She seethed in memory. She'd reached out again a month later, more insistent that time via both text and by leaving a voice message, stating that she *needed* to talk to him. He'd responded, promising to call.

He hadn't.

And now here he was, staring at her, no doubt clueing into the situation himself, and given the stony hardness of his features, he was about to lay into her for not letting him know about the baby beforehand. And she was fully prepared to give it right back. Because she wasn't the one who'd been ignoring *him* for months!

Cold eyes rose back up to meet hers, the light blue of the irises as striking as always, but instead of laying into her, his words stupefied her. "Shouldn't the baby's father be the one you call instead of your brother?"

Her jaw dropped open. "The father?" Good Lord, the man was dense.

She continued to gape at him as if he weren't capable of filling out an application for medical school, much less the intensive years of studying to become an MD. How could he have not figured this out? He knew how these things worked.

The man had given her the best weekend of her life. He'd knocked her up in doing so. And it apparently would never cross his egotistical mind that those two things might possibly be related. How had she ever thought he was someone she'd wanted to be with?

"Just take me to the house." She shoved at his chest, done with him being in her face. "The sooner I can make that call and get away from you the better."

"I couldn't agree more."

He closed the door before she could say anything else, his gaze capturing hers briefly through the glass of the window, then with long strides, he rounded the front of the truck. Climbing in, he started the engine, immediately turned the heat to high, and without another word, pulled out onto the road.

CHAPTER TWO

CORD DID HIS BEST TO IGNORE MAGGIE AS HE DROVE. HE HAD LESS than a mile to go, and he couldn't get there fast enough. Why he was so ticked, he couldn't say. But the fact remained.

He'd been with her for one weekend. And what a weekend it had been. But when she'd proclaimed that she hadn't been with anyone in a long time, he'd believed her. Not that it mattered. He never expected women to be celibate. Just like he wasn't. But something about how she'd said that to him, just before he'd entered her for the first time . . . He'd let himself *like* knowing that.

But what the heck? Clearly, she'd been lying. As she clearly still was. Because no way did she have weeks left before her due date. She'd obviously been with someone else, and only a short time before him. She had to be due any day now. He'd guess a week at the most.

His teeth ground together. He hated liars.

And he hated how much he'd enjoyed that damned weekend.

What he didn't hate, though, was that there was no way that baby could be his. And that had been his first thought. But aside from the fact they'd used protection religiously, he just couldn't believe she wasn't ready to deliver. He also couldn't let go of the fact that he *should* be taking her to a hospital right now instead of going in the opposite direction. If only to confirm her declaration that she was fine.

"I got a signal." Her words were spoken so softly he assumed she was talking to herself. From the corner of his eye, Cord watched her hold her phone out in front of her, the screen glowing bright.

"Good. Make the call."

Her entire body tensed, and he sensed her continuing anger. But he didn't care *what* she felt. In fact, he didn't care if she felt anything at all. He just wanted her gone. He *just* wanted to get on with this forced vacation and get back to his life.

"Crap," Maggie murmured a minute later. "It won't go through."

"Try again."

"You think?" Sarcasm dripped heavy from her words. "Do you really think I need you to tell me that, Cord?"

He gave a shrug meant to annoy. "I don't know what you need. And even telling me still doesn't mean I'd know, does it? People lie." He glanced at her, making sure his glare wasn't missed.

She glared back. "What are you insinuating?"

"I'm not insinuating anything. Make the call."

Her eyes narrowed, but she didn't lift the phone back to her ear. "What do you think I'm lying about?"

"I never said I think you're lying. I just said that some people *do* lie."

He went back to focusing on the road, knowing his behavior was beyond childish, but he couldn't seem to stop himself. Seeing her pregnant had annoyed him an absurd amount.

After several seconds of what was likely more glaring being fired his way, Maggie went back to trying to get a call to go through. The driveway was within sight now, and since the house phone had never been disconnected, even throughout the renovations, there was really no need to keep trying. He'd have her to a working phone within minutes.

Neither of them pointed that out, though.

He kept slowly making his way through the piling snow, and this time, a millisecond before a sigh sounded in the cab of the truck, he heard the "unable to complete the call" message. He gave no indication he'd heard it, and when her hand lowered, he tossed a questioning glance her way. "I guess I was right, then."

Steam practically leaked from her ears. "Right about what?" She straightened and held her phone up between them. "I tried to call. Did you miss that? It isn't going through." Her voice rose with each word. "Why would I lie about making a phone call?"

"Why would you lie about anything?"

"I don't lie!" Her breaths came out hard and fast then, and one hand went to her stomach.

Shit. What was he *doing*? He went instantly into professional mode.

His gaze raked over her, taking in everything from head to toe. Her water hadn't broken, as far as he could tell, but that didn't always mean a woman wasn't in labor. And he hadn't been kidding before. She *could* be in labor and just not be aware of it. Adrenaline had a way of hiding things.

He needed to quit being a dick.

"Are you sure you feel okay, Maggie?" He kept his focus split between her and the road. "No pains? No contractions?" It would take only a minute to turn the truck around and head toward the hospital. He shouldn't have let her convince him otherwise in the first place.

The questions seemed to catch her off guard, and the tension seeped from her shoulders. She leaned back against the seat. And as had happened while she'd been standing in the middle of the road, tears once again sprang to her eyes.

"Damn it," he muttered. That was it. He was taking her to the hospital.

"No." She held up a hand, the word being choked off with tears. "No pain. No contractions. I only ran off the road. I didn't hurt anything but my ego."

"Then why are you crying?"

They were at the driveway to the house now, and he didn't hesitate. He turned in and immediately shifted into reverse. A gloved hand touched his forearm before he could start the vehicle moving backward, and he jerked his gaze to hers.

"I'm *fine*." Her soft proclamation came out sounding sad. "I promise. I'm crying simply because all these emotions have to go somewhere. If I can't yell right now, then I have to cry. And I can't yell at you for asking if I'm okay."

He stared through the darkness, unsure whether to trust that she was really okay. Things weren't always as they seemed from the outside. After raking his gaze over her yet again, he took in the curve of her cheek and the slight downturn of her lips. The glow from the moon reflecting off the snow provided the only light in the cab, and the space suddenly felt too intimate. It reminded him of sitting on the floor in her living room, the roar of the fire in front of them. Them laughing, playing cards, making smores by use of that very fireplace.

All the fight drained out of him.

"Maggie," he started, but he didn't know what else to say. He didn't know why they'd been arguing to begin with.

Just because they'd had that weekend . . .

Just because he'd liked thinking she hadn't been with anyone in a long while . . .

Eyes he knew to be a mix of pale green and gray peered back at him, and he had no clue if his read on things was correct, but it felt as if her look held hope. Only . . . hope for what? For whatever future lay ahead for her and her baby?

Or was it simply memory of a really nice weekend staring back at him?

Those two nights back in April hadn't been like others. At least, it hadn't for him. It hadn't just been about the sex. That wasn't to say there hadn't been a lot of sex. And a lot of *really* good sex. Because dang, she was hot. And as bold in bed as out of it. And adventurous. And just so darned fun to be around.

But he'd been in a weird place that weekend. Worried about his dad. Wishing he could somehow be both here but not have to leave his home several hours away, at the same time. She'd been just what he needed.

In between the rounds of sex, they'd talked. Not about anything in particular for the most part. Work, general day-to-day stuff. But he *had* shared a couple of thoughts about his dad. And because he had, because the time with her had put him so at ease that he'd confessed feelings he'd normally never speak to anyone, he'd shed some of the stress he'd been carrying. The weekend had relieved him when he'd been so concerned about his father, and he'd wanted more of it. He'd wanted more of the normalcy of all of it.

That's why he hadn't called her back over the summer. Because he'd been afraid talking to her would make him want to see her again. And then he might want to see her even yet *again*.

He put the truck into park as he sat there. He shouldn't have said he'd call her. He knew that. He'd done it to protect himself. To get her to back off. Because he knew that "they" could never be. And the last thing he'd wanted was to get either of their hopes up.

"I'm sorry I didn't call you back, Maggie."

A vat of silence sat between them. "You're not sorry."

Her gaze wouldn't let him look away.

He wanted to explain himself. They'd agreed from the beginning that it would be a one-time thing. She'd been as on-board with that as he. But suddenly he felt the need to make her understand *why* he didn't do relationships. Why he never would.

And he wanted to do that even while she sat there pregnant with someone else's baby.

He wanted to talk to her as freely as he had that weekend in April.

"You're right," he admitted instead. He wouldn't share his feelings, but he would acknowledge the truth. "I'm not sorry. Or, I *wasn't.* Not then. But if my not returning your call hurt you in any way"—if his not calling was any explanation for her tears—"then I do apologize for that. Sincerely."

She didn't have a response, and he let his gaze roam over her once again. But not in the medical way he'd done before. She was beautiful. Several tendrils of her dark-blond hair had escaped her hat, floating whimsically around her face, and her skin wore a healthy glow. She'd been gorgeous before, and pregnancy certainly hadn't diminished that fact. And she absolutely wasn't "fat," as she'd insinuated. She was healthy and vibrant. She was filled with life, and she glowed from the inside. And the man who would be by her side during all of it . . .

He brought his gaze back to hers. "Congratulations on your pregnancy. The father is a lucky man."

He spoke with honesty, not considering whether he had any right to say the words. Not *caring* if he had the right. But his words only made more tears roll down her cheeks.

He wanted to reach out and pull her in. "What is it, Mags? What's wrong?"

She wiped at both eyes, and she inched her chin higher. Her lips pursed before she spoke. "The father doesn't know about the baby, Cord. Not yet."

The words came as a shock. "Why not?"

She hadn't struck him as the type not to share something like that. She would want both baby *and* the man.

He could picture her settling down with a husband and having several kids. Living in the house she'd bought earlier that year. Fixing it up together. It was yet another reason he'd made sure not to return her call. She wore that kind of persona easily.

"Why haven't you told him?" He pushed for an answer, though he had no right to do so. At the same time, while sitting there in his truck together, her eyes now locked on his, her hand moving in small circles over her belly . . . it suddenly *felt* like his business.

It felt like he should have already known.

The thought stirred another. One that filled him with the urge to quit pushing. To turn and run instead. Had he been wrong? Was she *not* due in the coming days?

Fear seized him. She still hadn't answered his question. She just sat there, silently watching him spiral. And the longer the silence lasted, the harder his heart hammered.

He swallowed. Then he forced himself to ask the one question he never wanted to hear the answer to. "Who's the father, Maggie?"

"You are, Cord. You're the father."

CHAPTER THREE

CORD DIDN'T MOVE. MAGGIE'S WORDS REPEATED IN HIS HEAD.

You are, Cord.

You're the father.

The urge to get out of the truck was strong. To get as far away from the moment as he could. He *didn't* get out, though. He didn't move. The snow continued to fall outside. The wipers barely able to keep up before the windshield was covered again. The house sat several hundred feet off the road, a long walk from where they'd stopped. And even if he did trudge through the wind and snow to reach it, he still wouldn't be able to outrun this situation.

He was going to be a father.

Maggie was going to have his baby.

He stared out the windshield, his gaze locked on the fat wet flakes visible in the path of the headlights, as he let both those sentences swirl through his head. Neither felt right. He didn't want to be a father. He didn't want anyone to have his baby. And he always did everything in his power to keep that from happening. So then . . . *how* had it happened?

Another thought emerged. Maybe it hadn't happened at all.

Maybe she only *thought* it was his.

He dragged his gaze back inside the truck. Given how *she'd* come on to him, it was highly feasible she'd done the same with other men. But how many others? And if that were the case, how could she possibly be sure he was the one who'd fathered her baby?

He had to ask. It was the only hope he had. "Are you sure it's mine?"

Maggie's mouth twisted into anger. "Seriously, Cord? You're going to go there?"

"Hey." He held his hands up. "Any man would ask. I mean, we used condoms every time. And we used them *correctly*." *And* he had no idea how many men she'd been with before or after him.

She barked out a laugh. "Shouldn't a doctor be aware that condoms can fail?"

"That's my point, Maggie. They *didn't* fail." None of them had broken. He'd never let himself enter her, nor even touch her that way, without protection.

She pointed to her stomach. "I argue your point, Dr. Wilde. One did fail. *Obviously*."

They stared at each other then, her clearly annoyed at having her story questioned and him running through every possible scenario to make this not be true. And then he landed on an explanation that *did* make sense. And it was simple. He wasn't the father, just as he'd thought.

She just *wanted* him to be.

He sat a little straighter, his mood growing dark. "I'm just saying"—he went for calm, though calm was now the furthest thing from his mind—"that maybe it's someone *else's* baby. Maybe you weren't so careful with *another* man." He couldn't keep the accusation from his tone. "When, exactly, is your due date, Maggie?"

Her eyes snapped fire. "My due date? January sixth, you jerk. Nine months after *we* were together. I told you I hadn't been with anyone else. And I *still* haven't."

He didn't hide his doubt, and she quickly caught on.

"You bastard." She spit the word out. "That's what that lying comment was about earlier? You think I was with someone else?" A muscle twitched in her jaw. "And what? You also think that I *know* that it's someone else's baby? That I'm just trying to pass it off as yours?"

Her ire rose, her features growing as stormy as the weather outside, but he didn't break eye contact. He did, however, wonder if he might have crossed a line. Something deep inside told him to back off. To apologize.

He did neither.

"I can't say the thought hasn't crossed my mind," he deadpanned. "Because the fact is, I *don't* actually know you. We spent one weekend together. And *you* came on to me. I don't know what you did before or after that. What you could have been setting *me* up for."

Shock covered her face for three full seconds, and then hurt. "You son of a bitch."

She wrapped her fingers around the handle of the door, pulling at it before Cord could register her intentions. Then she turned faster than he would've thought possible and slid out of the truck. Her feet and halfway up her calves disappeared into the snow, but she stayed upright.

"What are you doing?" He reached across the seat, somehow thinking he could grab her and pull her back in.

"I'm getting away from you. I don't want a thing from you, Cord Wilde. You can consider this issue a *non*issue."

He growled under his breath. "Get back in the truck, Maggie." The howling wind competed with his words. "You're going to hurt yourself out there."

"I'll get back in that truck with you when hell freezes over!"

Her door slammed at the same time he jerked his open. Dammit. What was wrong with the woman? He reached her side of the truck before she could take more than a couple of steps away from it, but it quickly became apparent that she couldn't walk in this mess. Two feet from the truck, she just stood there, white clumps of snow quickly attaching to her knee-length coat. She looked utterly lost.

The sight had him gentling his voice. "Get back in the truck, Maggie." He'd take her to *her* house, which was what he should have done to begin with. It was fifteen minutes away when there wasn't a foot of snow on the ground, but he had four-wheel drive. He could make it.

"I told you"—she crossed her arms high over her chest—"I'll get back in that truck with you when hell freezes over."

His jaw clenched. "If you don't get back in the truck right now, we won't have to wait for hell. We'll both freeze to death right *here*." He opened and closed his hands into fists. He'd gotten out without gloves again. "This is *not* the time to be dramatic, Maggie."

"Dramatic?" Her eyes widened. "This isn't me being dramatic, you asshole. This is me standing my ground. I am not lying, and I won't sit quietly and be accused of such." She pointed to her protruding belly. "*This* . . . is *your* baby. Like it or not. Not that I think you even deserve to know about it at this point. And no," she went on, "before you even get the idea to suggest it, I did not *want* to get pregnant, *nor* did I do anything to damage a condom in order to trick you. My God." She scowled. "What a piece of work, you are. No wonder you don't do relationships. Because anyone in their right mind wouldn't have you!"

She kicked at the snow then, her cheeks as red as her temper was hot, and the movement caused her to wobble backward. Cord clamped a hand around her arm before she could tip over, but he didn't offer any reply to her words. He couldn't offer any because he had no clue what to say. Fear clawed at his chest like the jagged teeth of a bear trap ripping into animal flesh. Was she honestly telling the truth? He was going to be a father?

Terror engulfed him. He couldn't get mixed up with a woman in that kind of way.

"We were only together once." The words were lame, he knew, but his brain was still processing.

"There were many times during that 'once,'" she grumbled.

"Yes, but . . ." He looked down at her. He was six two, and she couldn't be more than five five, yet she looked even smaller. Almost tiny in the thick snow. She also looked legit. Like she *was* telling the truth.

He knew she was friends with Erica and Arsula, Gabe's wife and his youngest brother Jaden's fiancée. And the two women thought a lot of her. They also *cared* a lot for her. That's why he'd suggested she not mention the weekend to them back when it had first happened. He hadn't wanted Erica or Arsula to think less of him for sleeping with their friend, but he also hadn't wanted them giving Maggie a hard time for being with someone like him. But was Maggie the kind of "good" he could depend on to be honest about something this serious?

Her outburst had certainly seemed sincere.

Reality finally began to set in. He had to face this. "You really haven't been with anyone else?"

His question seemed to calm her. She shook her head, looking no more pleased than he. "I really haven't."

"And this, I suppose, is why you were trying to get ahold of me over the summer?"

She snorted at that. "I was *not* trying to get in touch with you to see if you wanted to bang one out again, Cord. I understood that wasn't an option from the multiple times you mentioned it. So no, that never even crossed my mind."

For some reason, her not wanting to see him again bugged him almost as much as the idea of her calling because she hoped to pass the baby off as his. Which made no sense at all.

He glanced at her stomach. The coat might be making it worse, but the baby seemed to be everywhere.

His baby.

Oh, God.

His stomach roiled. He was going to be a father. He didn't know what to do.

He brought his gaze back up to Maggie's. He did, however, know that he had to quit acting like a jerk. He'd gotten her pregnant, and within a matter of weeks, a baby was going to be born whether he wanted it to or not. And he had to figure out what to do about that.

MAGGIE SAT in the front seat of the truck once again, the heat blowing on high and the wipers still slapping rhythmically at the snow. She watched as Cord shoveled a path to the door of one of the cabins at the back of the Wilde property. Once he'd finally seemed to accept the truth, he'd asked again if she'd get back into the truck, and she'd almost cried with relief. She'd been freezing out there. Not to mention, her ankles and feet were swelling so badly at this point it hurt to stand.

He'd had to lift her onto the seat again, but that time, he hadn't wasted a second before stepping away and closing the door. They'd both agreed that calling her brother could wait, as the two of them obviously had a "situation" which needed discussing, then Cord had suggested that the main house wouldn't be comfortable enough. The temperature inside would have been turned low for the long weekend, and there wouldn't be any furniture to sit on. Instead, Cord drove the few hundred feet past the house to the entrance with an arched sign overhead that read Wilde Cabins and Adventures.

The Wildes had run a thriving cherry orchard for decades, but earlier that year, a fast-moving arctic blast had come through just as the trees were beginning to wake, and the sudden and drastic drop in temperature had destroyed the majority of the orchard. Since then, along with replanting a few hundred trees with plans to maintain only a portion of the orchard they once had, Cord and his five siblings had changed course, turning much of their land into a thriving tourist business. Step one had been the cabins—Wilde Cabins and Adventures. The business also provided a service to set up adventures with local and nearby companies for activities such as hiking, fishing, boating, and skiing. Or whatever the traveler had in mind.

Ten cabins had been built and open for rentals over the summer, all overlooking Flathead Lake, and starting in the new year, weddings and events would be held on the property. That was also when the main house would have rooms for rent. Nate and his wife Megan had taken over management of the business and were overseeing all the changes. The excitement about the new venture had been palpable throughout town for months. Everywhere she went, someone was always talking about it.

Maggie continued to watch Cord as he worked in the snow. He'd started at the porch, having found a shovel waiting by the front door, and was making his way to the truck. The porch light had also been on when they'd pulled up, and with it glowing behind him, she couldn't clearly decipher his features. She could make out the snow piling up on his shoulders and head, though. It was coming down so hard he had to constantly swipe it off. But at least he'd put on a hat and gloves before getting out of the truck that time.

He kept shoveling, focused like a man possessed, and she supposed he was using the time to sort through what he planned to say next. Or maybe what he would *accuse* her of next.

She scowled. He'd infuriated her earlier.

How dare he imply she'd try to scam him. And that's where he'd been headed, even if the words hadn't made it out of his mouth. He'd rather believe her the type to get pregnant by someone else and then say it was his, rather than him simply accepting that it *was* his. She'd known he wouldn't like hearing the news, but she never would have guessed he'd balk at it so ardently. Or maybe he really did have that little respect for her.

Her scowl darkened. That idea went against the memory of the weekend they'd had together. Not only had it been an excellent few days sexually, but she'd honestly thought they'd somewhat connected. Their time together had been easy and fun. It had seemed real. And no matter what she'd said when they'd been arguing earlier, deep inside, when she'd first reached out to tell Cord that he was going to be a father, she'd hoped the news might lead to more. That they could somehow end up together.

She sure didn't hope that now.

She bit down on the inside of her cheek as she replayed their earlier conversation. She wouldn't let what he thought of her affect reality. She *was* carrying his baby. Now they just had to figure out how to deal with it.

What part would he want to play in his child's life? Occasional father? Every other weekend?

Would he be willing to be there during the birth?

She attempted to push the last question from her mind as her heart began to thump harder. She was getting ahead of herself. First, he had to deal with the fact that he was going to *be* a dad. And then she could broach the subject of the actual birth.

Tears threatened again as visions of being alone in a delivery room flitted through her mind. Whether anyone was there with her or not, she could do this. She had to. And everything would turn out exactly as it was supposed to.

She rounded her palms over the curve of her belly and focused on stopping the incoming tears. This was not where she'd seen herself at this point in her life. It wasn't where she'd ever seen herself. A husband, yes. A good life, respect shared both ways . . . and *maybe* a baby. Possibly.

But doing it alone?

With neither her parents nor her brother even living in Birch Bay anymore?

Six years after they'd moved, and she still couldn't believe her parents had left town. At least her brother was only up in Whitefish. He visited occasionally and promised to do so more often after the baby was born. But that was after. She wanted someone to be in this with her now.

A knock sounded on the glass, and she jumped, not realizing

Cord had finished with the snow. He opened the door. "Want help getting out?"

No, she didn't want help. But she would accept it anyway.

She held out an arm, taking his when he offered. When she'd jumped from the truck earlier, she hadn't thought about how easily she could fall in the snow. But with the water retention and constant swelling of her ankles and feet, mixed with the growing depth of the precipitation, her mobility had seriously been impacted.

They made it to the cabin without incident, him opening the door, then stepping back for her to enter first, and the thing she noticed almost immediately was that it wasn't freezing inside.

It also wasn't exactly warm, but not freezing was good. It made her picture the shovel that had been left on the porch . . . and how the outside light had been on when they'd arrived. Either Nate or Megan must have prepared the cabin in advance.

"I'll start a fire," Cord mumbled, tugging off his gloves.

He left her standing just inside the door, and as she watched him stomp over to the fireplace, she had the thought that she liked him much better when he was in charmer mode. He'd been a charmer back in April.

He'd been a charmer all his life, from what she'd been told.

Tonight he was sour and snarly.

Keeping her coat on, she tugged her own gloves off, as well as her hat and scarf, and shook out her hair. And she ignored the man currently squatting in front of a waiting pile of stacked wood. She moved farther into the room. This was one of the one-bedroom cabins and had been decorated mostly in shades of browns and greens, as well as the theme of elks. Each cabin had a focus on a different animal. Megan had decorated the spaces, and Erica and Arsula had gushed about them to her many times.

Turning slowly, she took in the small L-shaped kitchen tucked into the back corner, as well as the open bedroom door just to its right. A blue, brown, and green plaid bedspread covered a king-sized mattress framed by a rustic log bedframe. Everything about this cabin exuded masculinity. It fit Cord.

Chunky, wood frames held artwork throughout the living space, and heavy pottery mugs and bowls lined open shelving in the kitchen. The place had a cozy, yet solid feel. Hard, like the man currently building a fire.

Like the man she'd had a crush on long before she'd ever met him in person.

She frowned again. That crush had certainly been snubbed out.

"I guess we should talk." Cord spoke from behind her, and when she turned, she found that though he'd stepped to the side of the fireplace, he hadn't moved away from it. He'd pulled his coat and hat off, and while flames flickered at his side, casting shadows across the distressed pine flooring, tiny sparks released the scent of burning wood into the room. She drew in a deep breath. The smell reminded her of winter evenings from before her grandmother had passed.

"I guess we should," she agreed. Nervousness had her clasping her hands together on the top of her belly.

"Please." He motioned to the sofa. "Have a seat. You'll be more comfortable."

Could he tell how miserable she was? "Thanks," she murmured.

She settled on the end of the oversized couch, not bothering to take her coat off, and as she sank into the cushy brown leather, a small sigh slipped past her lips. She then eyed the square-topped trunk that was being used as a coffee table. She'd love to put her feet up. Let some of the extra fluid drain somewhere besides into her ankles. But the trunk was too tall to be comfortable.

A high-pitched whine came from outside as a gust of wind whipped against the cabin walls, and the fire sputtered in the fireplace. Flames licked upward toward the open damper.

She drew in another deep breath. She didn't know where to begin.

Cord held his phone up. "I have a signal. I'll send you money for the bills you've already had to cover." He named a banking app that would allow him to make the transfer electronically. "Is five thousand okay to start?"

She stared at him. "Five thousand?"

"Yes." He tapped on his phone as he spoke. "We can work out details with a lawyer later, but I want to make sure you're covered for anything you've needed so far." He looked up from what he was doing. "Are you still working? Do I need to add more for that?"

"I'm still working," she mumbled, but her mind couldn't catch up. He seemed so calm. So . . . disassociated.

He was just going to stand there and transfer her some money and be calm?

After finding out that he was going to be a father . . . and then accusing her of lying about whose it was?

The one-eighty was mind-boggling.

She finally made herself focus. She cleared her throat. "I'm not looking for money, Cord."

"Use it for the baby." He didn't look up again until he'd tapped one last time, and within seconds of finishing, her cell phone chirped in her coat pocket. Apparently, she had a signal again, too.

She dug out her phone. A message announced that five thousand dollars would be transferred to her as soon as she entered her banking info.

"Cord," she started again, but that time when he looked at her, there was a questioning look on his face. Did he really not have a clue?

"What?" he asked.

"You're going to be a father."

He never batted an eye. "No. I got you pregnant. The two aren't the same at all."

Shock rippled through her, and her hand went back to her belly. "You don't want to have anything to do with your child?"

"I told you back in April that I don't do relationships."

Anger once again arrived, quickly edging out the shock. "I'm not asking you for a *relationship*." What an ego. "Geez. That ship has clearly sailed."

He tucked in his chin and lifted his brows at her. "That ship never existed, Maggie."

A slap across the face wouldn't have stung any worse. She'd known his stance on the subject, of course. And she'd believed him when he'd announced before they'd ever gotten together that he didn't get seriously involved. But still . . . his delivery was harsh.

Painfully so.

"But your baby," she began, only she couldn't finish her thought. He continued standing, looking as unaffected as he had since he'd first spoken.

How could he be so clinical about this?

"I *don't* do relationships," he repeated firmly, and she finally got it. Her insides dropped.

She put her second hand over her first one. "You're talking about the baby." He saw relationships with children the same as with women? "You're saying that you don't want a *relationship* with your son? Of any kind?"

Cord's entire body went still. "It's a boy?" He seemed to hold his breath.

"It is." She rubbed a hand over her son, and the baby kicked in return. "Does that matter?"

This time there was a tiny pause before Cord continued. "Of course it doesn't." He blinked, and when he opened his eyes again, he seemed to focus on the side of her head instead of her face. "I don't do relationships with anyone," he repeated. "Woman or child."

Though she wanted to remain angry, to demand he be a father to his son, it wasn't possible at the moment. Because she was overcome with confusion. He seemed suddenly even more impenetrable than before. Like a vital piece of information that she couldn't make out sat solidly hidden behind his giant wall of blankness. Had that sentence meant something other than that he didn't want to have anything to do with *this* kid?

Had there been more kids?

She narrowed her eyes. Was she simply the next in a long string of accidental pregnancies?

The instant the idea formed, however, she rejected it. He was far too careful. It had been a miracle she'd turned up pregnant as it was, what with the number of condoms used and his absolute refusal to touch her in the most intimate of ways until there had been protection solidly in place. So, no. There was no way this situation was "normal" for him.

Plus, she knew his family. Wouldn't they know if he were a serial sperm donor? Wouldn't she have heard about it from at least one of her friends?

And then she got it. That stony mask . . . his refusal to look her in the eyes any longer . . .

He was scared.

Or more aptly, he was terrified.

And she *totally* got that. Hadn't she just spent the last six months being terrified herself? Wasn't she still?

She'd struggled intensely in the beginning to let the situation sink in, instead trying to reject the idea entirely. She'd wanted to pretend it all away. So yes, she could understand the fear. And she could sympathize with it.

Thinking she'd go over to stand with Cord, that her presence might offer comfort in some small way, she moved to stand. Only, it wasn't nearly as easy to get off the couch as it had been to get onto it. She growled under her breath. Why did she have to look like a beached whale flopping around in front of this man?

"Let me help." Cord suddenly appeared at her side, hand outstretched, and danged if her tears didn't appear again.

"I'll just stay here," she grumbled, wiping at her eyes instead of taking Cord's hand. But when she unbuttoned and went to shrug out of her coat—because the fire he'd built was doing a spectacular job in the small cabin—his hands fell to her shoulders before she could protest.

She let her entire body sag, exhausted from the stress of the whole day, and allowed him to help her out of the bulky material. Besides, if she didn't let him help, she'd likely just end up flopping around in front of him some more. Only, once the coat had been removed—remaining wedged between her and the cushions since she didn't dare try pulling it out from under her—she wished she'd left the thing on. Because Cord now stared at her stomach again. And he was staring in an even more *oh-my-God* fascination than he had when he'd first realized she was pregnant.

She linked her fingers together, resting her hands atop her stretchy-shirt-covered belly, and she wished she'd worn something more voluminous. "It *is* yours," she argued, even though he hadn't protested again. "I'm only seven and a half months."

Blue eyes lifted to hers. "And you're okay? Not just now," he clarified, "but in general. You're healthy?"

The sincerity in his tone broke her. Why would this man not want a relationship with his son? "My doctor assures me that everything is fine. And no, there's not a second baby hiding in there. He's just going to be a big boy. But also, a lot of the extra weight is water retention. Same as in my feet." She held her feet out, her black leggings and Sherpa-lined boots hiding the issue. "She's keeping a close eye on things. So far, there's been nothing scary like high blood pressure due to the swelling."

Cord's gaze shifted to her feet, and as he remained standing in front of her, she felt ironically small. She was so swollen that she now wore shoes two full sizes larger than normal. Additionally, her pregnancy weight for sure wasn't contained only to her stomach. It had also crept into her hips and even farther down. And hey, let's not forget the boobs that now not only squished together where they met but seemed to spill into her underarms as well. Yet six-foot-plus, wide-shouldered, lean-hipped Cord Wilde made her feel tiny. And it was the best feeling she'd had in a long time.

She expected tears again, but they didn't come. So, she patted the couch. "Sit down, Cord. Let's talk about this."

Surprisingly, he sat.

"I know it's a lot to take in." She started the speech she'd tweaked for the last six months. "But it's *not* the end of the world. Children are miracles." She offered a tentative smile when he remained stiff on the cushion next to her. "Your family is going to have four other kids born within the next month, and I'm sure you're happy for them?"

She paused, but he didn't acknowledge her question.

"So," she pushed on, "I'm thinking, we look at this as a good thing. Our son somehow made it past the barrier of latex, so we know he'll be strong." She laughed lightly, just as she'd rehearsed. "Or maybe he's going to be analytical. He'll be able to solve puzzles. Or always find a way around anything blocking whatever path he sets out on."

She smiled again, but Cord now wore the same aloofness he'd donned earlier.

"What better way to start a life, right?" she finished, her voice cracking at the end. The tears were back.

Cord didn't want their baby.

He wouldn't be around when she went into labor.

"Cord?" she whispered. "It's your son. I know you live in Billings, but can't we work something out?" She wouldn't even mind going to Billings to deliver. She'd already discussed the possibility with her doctor, tossing out the idea of temporarily moving to the area after Christmas. Then, as her child grew older, she'd take him to visit on a regular basis if Cord didn't always have time to come to her. She wanted her baby to have a father he could always rely on.

Cord reached out and took her hand, and the move startled her. Warmth from his body enveloped her fingers, and for the briefest moment she didn't feel so alone in this. That soon ended, however, because his facial features hadn't changed.

"It is my son. I'll acknowledge that, and I'll also apologize for accusing you of lying about it earlier."

She nodded. "I appreciate the apology."

"But, Maggie"—he shook his head, the line of his mouth flattening—"I *don't* want a child in my life. And just like you have the right to *want* one, I have the right not to. And I'm sorry if that hurts you. I truly am. I'll take responsibility for my part in things, and I'll send whatever money you need. For as long as you need it. You can even quit working and stay home if you prefer to. But I . . ." He glanced away, and Maggie watched as he seemed to go through a litany of emotions. "It's *not* going to happen." He brought his gaze back to hers, his emotions once again under control. "I'm not cut out to be a father, so that's not up for debate."

He wasn't cut out to be a father? That was his reasoning?

That made no sense. She'd seen him with his nieces at Erica's wedding. She'd watched him at The Cherry Basket's grand opening back in April with his whole family. He'd be a *great* dad.

"If it's nerves bothering you," she started, "worrying about the what-ifs and all the things you've never dealt with, everyone goes through that. But Cord, you're wrong. You'd make a great—"

"I wouldn't." His face remained impassive. His eyes cold. "Some things a person simply knows."

She stared at him, trying to digest his words. Trying to see beneath them. Because she didn't buy his "knowledge" for an instant. He had to know how good he was with people. Even with her during their weekend. Though he'd made it clear they would never be a thing, at the same time, he hadn't been able to hide the fact that he naturally watched over people.

Was it the *idea* of being a parent that scared him the most? Or was it something that went deeper?

And then another thought occurred. Did it have to do with his mother?

She knew from Erica that the Wilde matriarch had been a deep-seated narcissist. The woman had played the six kids off each other from day one. And she'd *never* been the warm, caring mother she'd always presented to the world. Was that Cord's concern? That he'd be like her?

"You care about people." She couldn't imagine he'd be anything different as a parent than he was in his everyday life. "You went through years of school because you wanted to take care of people on a daily basis. You're here in Birch Bay now because you came to check on your dad. You told me that yourself. All you have to do is care and you'll be a good dad."

His abrupt bark of laughter made her flinch.

"Cord?" She squeezed the hand still wrapped around hers. Caring had to be enough. *"Please."*

He shook his head again, and inside, she started to shake. She needed to go.

She wouldn't sit there and plead with him any longer.

"I should leave." She pulled her hand free and slipped her arm into her coat. "I'll call my brother."

Cord stopped her by recapturing her hand. "The weather is too bad tonight. There's already almost a foot of snow out there."

"No. I'll . . ." She glanced at her cell phone, where it had slipped from the couch at some point and fallen to the floor. "I have a signal again. I'll call Mason. He'll come get me."

"Stay here tonight."

"What?" Panic filled her. "No. I can't do that."

"It's not safe to be out in this. For either of you. Not until it lets up." His voice was too calm, and that calmness made her more frazzled. "Stay tonight," he repeated. "You can have the bedroom, and I'll take the couch. There's a half bath out here that I can use. And tomorrow after the roads have been cleared, I'll get you to your house. We'll call a tow truck to pull your car out."

She shook her head, the movement jerky. "I *can't* go back to my house. *That's* why I was headed to Mace's tonight. My floors are being refinished. They started work on them today, and I can't be around those fumes with the baby." And she'd have gotten to her brother's place hours earlier if she hadn't changed her mind and decided to stay an extra night with her parents at their guest ranch. "My bathtub and sink are being re-glazed, too." Her voice inched higher, and she could hear the tightness creeping into it. "I don't even have a working bath. And I won't for a *week*."

She'd planned to come back to town and check into a hotel after the weekend. She was a third-grade teacher, and it didn't matter how much snow they had, chances were good schools would remain open.

Cord squeezed her hand again, the pressure enough to get her attention, and she realized she'd started taking in short gasps of air.

"Breathe." He said the word softly, following it with the action itself.

She followed suit, focusing on him, and pulled in a deep breath.

"Again," he murmured, and once again he inhaled.

Maggie did as she was told, and as she calmed, yet more tears showed up.

"You're going to be okay, Maggie." Cord swiped a finger under her eyes. "You and your baby are going to be just fine, and this situation tonight is going to be fine. Call your brother. Let him know you'll be staying here. There's food and water in the cabin. Nate stocked it with enough for a week, so we're all set. Then in the morning, we'll figure out what to do next."

She nodded. Her clothes were in the trunk of her car, but she could stay there for one night without them. She could sleep in what she was wearing. It was comfortable enough. Then tomorrow she'd leave. They'd get her car pulled out of the ditch and she would be on her way.

A final tear slipped out. She'd be on her way, and Cord Wilde would become nothing more than a distant memory in her and her son's past.

CHAPTER FOUR

THE SNOW CONTINUED THE FOLLOWING MORNING, HAVING NOT LET up at all overnight, but Cord didn't let that keep him from his plans. He'd come home to check on his father, so taking care of that was priority number one. Priority number two? That would be figuring out what to do about the woman currently tucked away inside the bedroom of the cabin. The woman who also happened to be carrying his baby.

Geez, how did his life get to this?

He took one last step in his snowshoes before he stopped. He'd reached the spot of the adjoining property that allowed sight of both the original Wilde land as well as the acreage his father and stepmother had purchased over the summer. With his dad now either confined to a wheelchair or using a prosthesis, he and Gloria had preferred the one-story house on the neighboring property. But mostly, Cord suspected, they'd jumped at the chance to be *out* of the house that still held too many memories for all of them. Some of the memories were good, but it was the accumulation of the bad that in the end, made the house better as tourist accommodations than a place any of them wanted to live.

Turning the house into a lodge had been their dad's idea. Then he'd sold a portion of the new property to Nate and Megan, where they were currently building their dream home.

Dani and Ben lived just up the road. Nick and Harper had a house in a family neighborhood in town. Gabe and Erica lived not far from downtown. And Jaden and Arsula had moved into a nice place just a couple of months ago. Everyone had returned to Birch Bay but him.

Everyone was content and settled . . . but him.

Cord turned in place, taking in as much as he could see from his vantage point. The original house sat quiet today. The workers would return on Monday to continue renovations. The trees were bare and drooping with snow. And the land . . . He kept turning, encompassing both properties, as well as the lake and the mountains reaching skyward on the far side of it. This land was likely why every time the idea had come up to sell, he and his family had chosen to keep the property. Because even with all the bad memories associated with the place, the land had a way of healing.

He wanted the land to heal him this week.

The thought struck him hard. If asked yesterday morning, he would have said that he didn't need healing. He just needed to go back to work. Back to his life the way it always had been.

Yes, he'd been on edge lately. And at the office last week, he'd snapped at Angie and brought her to tears. That wasn't like him, and he'd admitted it. He'd apologized. But he didn't need to be cast aside because of it. He simply needed to get a decent night's sleep instead of constantly waking to dreams about his mother.

They're not really about your mother, a voice whispered inside his head.

He shoved the voice aside. Maybe spending a week here would somehow lessen the dreams. Already, he hadn't had one last night.

Of course, he'd also lain awake most of the night thinking about the woman in the other room. Or, more accurately, thinking about the child growing inside the woman in the other room. Maggie had disappeared into the bedroom the night before and hadn't emerged since. Which suited him perfectly. There'd been nothing else they needed to talk about anyway. He would call a family law attorney first thing Monday and get an initial agreement started for child support, and then everything would be settled. He'd be out. He'd be as childless as he had been twelve hours before.

He blew out a breath, the air crystallizing in front of him, and gave in to the question he'd been trying to ignore since he'd first pulled up to the cabin last night. Did not wanting anything to do with his own child make him a bad person?

Probably.

He nodded, overriding his initial thought. Because of course it made him a bad person. What kind of person didn't want their own kid? But did knowing that change the facts? Did it change whether he wanted anything to do with the child or not?

This time, he closed his eyes as he silently answered. *No. It did not.* And he could be okay with that.

He didn't want to be a dad. End of story. It wasn't that he didn't like kids. Hell, he loved his nieces, and he couldn't wait to meet the new babies who would be entering their family soon. But being a father tied him to the mother. It opened him to whatever mental gyrations she might decide to put him through, whether the two of them were together or not. And that was the one promise he'd always made to himself. He would not let his emotions get tied up, only to be twisted without his consent, by *any* woman.

He could thank his mother for that lesson.

Hell, he could thank his father as well. Due to lack of having a backbone when it came to Carol Wilde, his father had helped show Cord all the ways that men—and not only children—could get hurt by the ones they were supposed to love.

Both their actions had shown that there was a very fine line between love and hate. And maybe no line at all.

Eyes open again, he stared at nothing. And he thought about the possibility of Maggie manipulating her child—*their* child—in the same fashion his mother had done to him. That she'd done to all of them. And he ground his teeth together at the idea. That was another thing he wouldn't allow. He may not want to be a father, but he *would* be one before he'd let that happen. Only, he'd be the *only* parent the child had. Maggie Crowder wouldn't be permitted in the boy's life if Cord ever received so much as a sniff that her treatment of him wasn't aboveboard. And he would know about it, too. Because he had every intention of keeping tabs.

When he spoke with an attorney about child support, he also planned to discuss lining up regular well-checks on the child, to be done by a third party. He understood that there *were* good women in the world and that excellent mothers *did* exist. These things were possible, so it stood to reason that Maggie could be one. And honestly, from what he'd learned about her over their one weekend, he couldn't see her being the type of conniving, evil person his mother had been. Still . . . people could hide their true selves. He knew that firsthand. So, he'd make certain Maggie was who she presented to the world. He'd make certain that his son would *never* live with the kind of mother he'd grown up with.

With fury continuing to rage inside him, he refocused his gaze, only then realizing that he faced the direction where Nate and Megan were building their house. Snowflakes landed on his face as he peered toward the rise that ended with the cliff overlooking the lake, and the chill of the air now left him so cold he could barely feel their touch. However, he wasn't yet ready to continue toward his father's place. Instead, he pictured the cliff without the house on it. He imagined how it had looked when Nate and Megan had exchanged vows there barely two months before. Cord had stood beside his five siblings that day, proud to be a part of his brother's celebration. At the same time, he'd also wanted to call a halt to everything. He'd wanted to speak up when the officiant had asked if anyone had reason the two of them shouldn't be married. He hadn't spoken up, though. Because he hadn't had a reason. He'd only had questions.

How did they know that what they felt was true? How did anyone?

How could his siblings believe the emotions each of them had embraced for another person was love and not something merely resembling the feeling? Something that would last only until hate replaced it?

How did they possibly trust that marrying, having kids, that making a life together wouldn't turn out so drastically different than what they each envisioned and hoped for? That's what he couldn't figure out. At the same time, even though he'd been watching and waiting for each of his siblings'—*and* his father's— marriages to crumble from the moment they'd all started, he'd equally given in to the acceptance that what they'd found seemed real. It seemed to work. Cord simply didn't understand how.

And not only *how* it worked, but how they could trust that it *might* work. That's what got him. They'd all grown up the same way. With the same woman—mother, *wife*—around. How were *they* not as broken as him?

But then, he supposed he could answer that question himself.

His jaw worked, and he could feel the earlier irritation trying to surge into more.

His siblings weren't as broken because their mother hadn't killed herself in front of any of them. She hadn't spent their lives making sure *they* always found her right after she'd done something stupid in a bid for attention. Begged them to "save her."

I knew you'd be here. I knew you'd help.

He shuddered. He hated those phrases.

He hated his mother.

He turned back toward the direction he'd come. He hated the fact there was a woman about to give birth to a child who was a part of him and that there wasn't a thing in the world he could do about it.

Anger suddenly erupted, making him hot from the inside out, and instead of thinking about the hows and the what-the-fucks that his life had turned into, he started moving again. With the additional inches of snow that had fallen overnight, there had been no possibility for him to get in his normal run that morning. Instead, he'd done a hundred pushups in the living room, had reshoveled the porch and the path to the truck, then he'd donned the snowshoes he'd grabbed before leaving his house in Billings and set out.

His dad's place sat only six hundred yards from where the cabins had been built, so it wasn't that great of a distance. However, making the trek in the snow should provide a decent burn of energy.

As his father's house came into view, though, and with anger still churning, he wished he'd brought a pair of cross-country skis instead. Without speed, he hadn't been able to get a decent grip on the gnawing bitterness that so often took up residence inside him these days.

In the distance, he could see snow piled on either side of the back sidewalk, indicating that Gloria had been out shoveling. He'd take the task over for her before he left, and that should help get himself back under control.

He made his way through the yard, concentrating on the sound of his breathing and each step pushing through the snow, and he finally let himself think about his dad. He didn't expect to discover anything wrong on this visit. Their father had been doing well with the prosthesis since he'd gotten fitted for it six weeks before. In fact, given the jolting shock it had been for his dad to go from two legs down to one, he'd been doing exceptional for the last eight months. His mood took the occasional downturn, but none of those times had lasted for more than a few days, and none were out of the ordinary for someone going through the loss of a limb.

Cord had stayed on top of all details concerning his dad's health, coming to town every two or three weeks since the accident, as well as checking in with his doctors via emails and phone calls. The initial rehab had been rough, but his dad had continually grown stronger. Then a little over two months ago the residual limb healed to the point that a prosthesis could be molded. He was doing great with it, too. Cord had visited a week after his dad received it, and he'd been pleased with the initial mobility.

Physical therapy continued, of course, to get his dad fully functional. But after all the hurdles crossed during the first few months, Cord had been even more satisfied to learn that the last medication changes had finally not only quieted the quivers from the Parkinson's into almost nonexistence, but had eliminated the hallucinogenic side effects, as well. Everything was on track. His dad was fine. Nate was simply worried since this was the first time Cord hadn't been home in over a month.

At least, that's what Cord told himself. But Nate also wasn't the type to worry over nothing.

His brother had called Thursday night, insisting a problem existed. Their dad and Gloria hadn't stayed long for Thanksgiving dinner, and he'd apparently also quit coming over to check on progress at the two houses every day.

Their dad had a golf cart with a cover he could zip closed on cold or rainy days, and ever since work had begun, he'd been driving over on almost a daily basis. The last couple of weeks, though, he hadn't been over at all. He'd insisted there was no reason for the change, only colder weather, but Nate didn't buy it. Therefore, Cord was here.

"Cord!" Gloria opened the back door when he knocked, looking as shocked as he'd expected her to be. Only Nate had known he planned to come into town. "What in the world are you doing here?"

He motioned back the way he'd come. "Decided to take a few days off. I arrived last night." Now that the house was under renovation, he always stayed in one of the cabins when he came into town. He preferred the same one each time, if available. He liked the feel of cabin number one. "I wanted some exercise this morning, so I snowshoed over to say hello."

She chuckled and looked down at his feet. "Well, come on in. Get out of the cold."

Cord took a minute to unstrap the shoes and shake the snow off before stepping inside, then he quickly shed his outerwear in the cramped back mudroom. He hung up his coat and hat and grabbed the extra socks he'd brought out of his coat pocket. As suspected, quite a bit of snow had inched its way into his boots.

"Dad around?" he asked as he ran his fingers through his flattened and damp-around-the-edges hair. He stepped into the kitchen.

"In the living room. Sitting in his favorite chair." Gloria's cheeks were flushed, confirming Cord's guess that she'd recently been outside.

"Stay in the house, Gloria. I'll finish clearing off the sidewalk before I go."

In the event his dad needed to use his wheelchair to get to his car, he had to do so by way of the sidewalk. The garage was wide enough for only a single vehicle, and though accessibility changes had been made to the house before they'd moved in, there hadn't been enough space in the garage to add a ramp.

"I'll take you up on that." She patted him on the arm and offered a small smile, and Cord looked at her thoughtfully. She seemed more tired than usual. Or was it sadness he was picking up on? Her eyes seemed to droop at the corners.

"Dad okay?" he asked quietly. Had Nate had been right? Was their dad having issues?

"He's still doing good. Your father is a strong man." She turned away, moving to the stove on the other side of the room. "Can I fix you a cup of tea to warm you up?" She looked over her shoulder. "Or coffee?"

"I'm good." He wouldn't put her out. "I'll just go visit with Dad. Don't worry about me."

"If you're sure."

He studied her again. She'd normally try to insist on fussing over whoever showed up. "I'm positive, Gloria."

"Okay, then." She motioned, nodding toward the opening that led to the living room, then she clasped her hands together in front of her. "I'll leave you two to visit."

Something was off, but Cord couldn't put his finger on it, so he gave an agreeing nod and made his way to the living room. His dad, as Gloria had said, was in his favorite recliner. It was the one that had been in the other house for as long as Cord could remember. Only, he was leaned back in it and asleep. At nine o'clock in the morning.

Cord glanced at his watch, as if confused by the time, then picked up the TV remote and lowered the volume of the show currently airing. He caught Gloria watching from the doorway, and when he glanced over, she offered another smile.

"He hasn't been sleeping well," she informed him.

"How long has that been going on?"

"I think it's the new medicine. It started about the same time."

The last tweak of his dad's medication had been done the week after Cord's previous visit, and he wordlessly berated himself for not coming home to personally check on him since. He'd let his own issues get in the way of worrying about his dad.

"I won't wake him," Cord assured her. He noted that his dad's prosthesis was on the floor beside the recliner. The wheelchair sat in the corner of the room. "I didn't sleep well last night myself," he went on. "I might just stretch out on the couch."

"Make yourself at home."

Gloria headed down the hallway, and Cord lowered to the couch. He didn't stretch out, but after changing his socks, he did drop his head to the back cushion. And as had happened so many times during the night before, the picture of a very pregnant Maggie Crowder materialized in his mind.

He kept himself from groaning out loud. If only she'd been calling over the summer for another weekend of sex.

Tunneling both hands into his hair, he closed his eyes and replayed their conversation from the night before. He didn't know why he kept beating himself up. He didn't want a kid. There was nothing more to think about. However . . . he'd never really thought about a kid of his actually growing inside another human being.

A son.

He kept his eyes closed. His father had been vocal about wanting a grandson.

There were three granddaughters in the family already, and when Harper, Erica, and Dani had all announced back in the summer that they were expecting around the same time, the idea had been tossed out to *not* find out the babies' genders. They'd decided it would be a fun way to build up the suspense to see if a grandson—or grand*sons*—would make their way into the world. But what they didn't know was that the answer to that question would now be a definite *yes*.

Or *did* they know?

Cord's eyes popped open. Maggie was friends with Erica and Arsula. Had she told them?

Clearly, they'd know she was pregnant. And from what he knew about women, they would have wanted details. Especially since Maggie wasn't married. What had she shared with them?

He slowly lowered his hands, his mind continuing to spin. If they did know about the baby, he couldn't believe he hadn't heard about it before now. His brothers would have called, if not to kick his ass for doing that to Maggie, then at least to let him know that he was going to be a dad. Wouldn't they?

His heart thundered inside his chest. What a mess.

The fact was, if his brothers *didn't* already know, he didn't dare tell them. He couldn't share that there was a baby with his DNA coming into this world whom he planned to have nothing to do with. None of them would understand. Not after finding "love" and being over the moon happy about having their own kids.

He closed his eyes again, frustration mounting, but as soon as he did, rustling came from the recliner. Turning his head where it lay on the back of the sofa, he discovered his dad fumbling with the lever to lower the footrest.

"Cord?" His dad stopped mid-action as soon as he locked eyes on Cord. He looked around as if confused. "What are you doing here? Where's Gloria?"

"I think she went into one of the bedrooms." Cord moved to get up. "I'll get her for you."

"No." His dad's gaze flicked toward the hall. He lowered the footrest with a soft thump. "Let her be. She's probably lying down."

They were both now taking extra naps?

"What are you doing here?" he asked again. "You weren't at your sister's house Thursday night."

No, he hadn't been at Dani's house. That's where the family had gotten together. He gave a shrug, not wanting to admit that Nate had called him. "I decided to get away for a few days after all. I'm staying over at the cabins."

"Is that so?" His dad picked up the glass of water on the side table but merely glanced down at it instead of taking a drink. "Anybody else out there with you?"

Cord paused with the question. "Renting, you mean?" But upon second thought, he didn't think that was what his dad actually meant. "Or staying in the cabin with *me*?"

The thought irked. After all the months of coming in every few weeks to check on the man, he immediately assumed Cord was there to shack up with someone instead of to check on him? But then, hadn't that been Cord's MO for years? He'd spent more time since leaving for college worrying about himself, building his career, and seeking the pleasures of women than coming home to visit his family.

That had changed in the spring, though.

Honestly, it had begun to change before that. As each of his siblings had settled into a new life, he'd found himself being drawn home more often. It was nice to see their happiness.

His dad studied him. "Renting," he finally answered, but Cord wasn't fooled.

"No." And he wasn't about to mention that Maggie had stayed last night. Her being there wasn't the same as what his dad had been implying anyway. It was *worse*. "Nate said a couple of the cabins had been reserved for the weekend, but when the forecast changed, pushing the snow into the area sooner than expected, the reservations got canceled. No one wanted to risk getting stuck here longer than the holiday weekend."

"Probably smart. Sounds like we're still in for another foot of it."

"Looks that way, too." Why were they talking about the weather? And why did the conversation seem so stilted?

What was he missing?

He moved to the end of the couch closest to his dad and leaned in, elbows propped on his knees, and he studied his father's face. There seemed to be a hopelessness wedged in the crevices that had been carved throughout the past year. Or maybe it was just the fact that his dad looked so much older.

And then Cord read the changes for what they likely were. His dad simply looked tired. Extremely so.

Which would explain taking a nap at nine in the morning.

"What's going on, Dad?" He reached out and touched his dad's knee. "I came to town to check on *you*, okay? Not for any other reason. I should have come on Thursday, and I didn't, so I'm here now. But then I show up and find that you're taking a nap at nine in the morning. What's up with that?"

Faded blue eyes met his, and Cord wondered if his eyes would look like that one day. Would he lose the vibrant hue he and each of his siblings had inherited, only to look as tired as their dad?

"I just didn't sleep well," his dad answered. "Nothing to worry about."

Cord didn't believe him. "Is it the medication? Gloria mentioned that you started taking naps about the time the last changes were made."

The edges of his dad's mouth pulled down. "The medication is fine. I'm just not sleeping well."

"But hadn't you been sleeping fine before?"

The only answer was a mulish stare, and Cord decided to change tactics. He sat back and took in his father as he would a patient. His coloring was fine. His breathing good. There were a couple of over-the-counter pain reliever bottles on the side table, as well as a bottle of lotion and a container of nuts. The prothesis lying on the floor appeared to be in good shape and ready to be used.

His father did *seem* okay. At least, on the outside.

Yet he wasn't sleeping well.

And he'd completely quit going over to the worksites.

Nate was right. Him not checking on progress, at least at the main house, didn't make sense. His dad had stated his desire several times to be part of the new direction the family was taking the business, and because of that desire, he'd been keeping a close eye on the renovations. He'd been working hard to return to full mobility so he could be available day one when the lodge opened. He and Gloria both intended to help at the check-in desk.

Cord then pictured Gloria standing in the kitchen when he'd first come in, her cheeks flushed. And now she was napping. Did he have it wrong? Was it not his dad they should be worried about?

"Is it Gloria?" he probed. "Is something wrong with *her*?"

His dad rubbed at the end of his amputated leg. "No. She's just tired, too. My tossing and turning keeps her up."

"Is it your leg?"

The rubbing stopped as abruptly as Cord fired the question. Wary eyes watched his.

"Is your leg hurting, Dad? Is something going on that you haven't told anyone?"

"Rubbing it is simply habit now." The reply came quick, almost as if it had been repeated before, and Cord noted that the answer hadn't been "no." Something was off with his dad's leg.

He leaned back in, putting his face directly in line with his father's, and he delivered the look he'd seen parents give unruly children. "I'm not leaving here until you tell me what's going on. Until you let me *help*. That's why I came over."

"You need to get back to work."

"Not today, I don't."

His dad looked pained, but not in the physical sense, and his hesitancy bothered Cord.

What was so bad that he wouldn't want to share it?

"What is it?" he urged. "Nate mentioned that you didn't stay at Dani's very long Thursday night. He also said you've quit visiting the jobsites."

"It's too cold to go out."

"Okay. I can understand that." The temperature had certainly taken a turn into frigid lately. "So, you're just sitting here all day doing nothing?"

"I'm still doing physical therapy."

"And how is that going?"

His dad glanced over his shoulder as if expecting Gloria to come down the hall, and when he turned back, his posture sunk. The air pushed out of his chest. "I did miss a couple of appointments recently, okay?"

"Why?"

"Because . . ." He sighed, then he reached for his pant leg.

He rolled the material up over the end of his limb, and when Cord got his first look, the bottom fell out of his stomach.

"Dad." The flesh around the scarring was swollen and covered with sores.

"Shhh," his father hissed. "Don't wake Gloria. She doesn't need to worry about this. I've been having a little trouble with my new leg, is all."

"And you're just now telling someone?" There was one place on the outside edge that was not only rubbed raw but looked like it had been bleeding. Cord hurt for the man. He knew it had to be hard to suddenly be so dependent on others. "Why wasn't this reported by your physical therapist?" he asked.

"He doesn't know about it. We're working on walking right now. I do exercises with the leg on."

Meaning, his therapist hadn't been fully checking his dad during whatever appointments he *had* actually made it to. Because no way had his dad's efforts not taken a downward turn since this issue started. And there *hadn't* been an issue the last time Cord had been home.

"I'll be talking to your therapist," he growled, angry for the unneeded pain his dad had to deal with. "Someone should have noticed this." He squatted in front of the recliner to examine the leg and gently probed at the area. "When did this start? And why haven't you told anyone? Your prosthesis needs to be adjusted."

"Telling someone is what I'm doing now."

Going back on his haunches, Cord stared up at his dad as understanding dawned. "You were waiting for me to come home before mentioning it?" And then *he* hadn't been home in over a month.

"It's just that everyone is so busy." Guilt seemed to consume his dad. "I don't want to be any more of a burden than I am. Gloria does so much. She helps me do darned near everything. She's worn down, and I won't add any more to it. And then three of your brothers are getting ready for new babies. Their wives need their husbands at home, not running me all over the place. Nate is working hard to get the house done and ready to open, and Jaden's only been on the job as a counselor for a few months. I didn't want to ask him to take time off, either. Nor do I want to ask you. I know how many days you've already been out of the office this year because of me, and there's no need to take any more."

"Then who do you expect to help you?"

His father looked lost. "I was hoping it would get better without having to bother anyone. I put lotion on it all the time."

Cord hung his head. "*Dad.* You can't fix this by yourself."

"Apparently," he grumbled. He rubbed his calloused and age-stained thumb along the edge of the worst spot. "This is from Thursday. I tucked a piece of gauze in there before we headed over to your sister's, hoping to pad the spot that always gets the worst of it. But the gauze must have slipped. I came home with this, instead."

This being the equivalent of a second-degree burn. "Has it been bleeding?" Heated red skin rimmed the edges, indicating an infection had already set in.

His dad nodded. "A little. When we got home, I got it cleaned up myself. Gloria had lunch plans with a friend on Friday, and I didn't want her to cancel."

Stubborn man.

Cord rose to his feet. If he'd come in on Thursday, *he* could have gotten this taken care yesterday. Now his dad had to wait even longer. "I'll take you to the prosthetist on Monday. Be ready to go."

"No. I'm serious, Cord. I don't want you taking more time off work because of me. I'll tell Gloria, and she can take me."

"Yes, you will tell her." He glared at his father. "Because you shouldn't have hidden it from her to begin with. She wants to be there for you, Dad. You know that. And she'll feel awful thinking you had an issue and she didn't notice." Gloria was terrific with his dad. They'd been together for seven years before they'd married almost three years ago. "I'll still take you on Monday, though. And it won't be a problem because I already have the day off. In fact"—he muttered—"I have the whole freaking week off."

His dad looked at him. "You're taking a week off?" His shock was obvious.

"Yes."

"Why?"

"Because I want to." He gave his father the same mulish stare he'd inherited. His dad wasn't the only Wilde who could be stubborn.

His father didn't believe him, though. Cord could tell. A year ago, the man wouldn't have known that about him, but over the course of the last eight months, they'd spent a lot of time together.

Far more than they had since Cord went away to college. And his dad knew he liked to work. That he took pride in being an excellent physician.

It had been difficult getting away every time Cord needed to be here, but he'd managed it. Often by being on the phone multiple times throughout the day. If one of his patients came in with an unexpected issue, his partners knew to keep him in the loop. He wanted his patients to know that he was always there for them, even if he couldn't physically be in the same location.

He wasn't there for them right now, though.

That was one of the things he and his partners had argued about after they'd asked him to take time off. After an hour of discussion that had gone nowhere, he'd finally relented and agreed to a two-week vacation. Then he'd return, and his life would resume exactly as it had been. Of course, his partners still wanted him to speak to a counselor during this break.

And, of course, he had no intention of doing so.

He stepped away from his dad, his anger back in full force. If he'd come home weeks before, he would have caught this issue in the beginning stages. Just like, if he hadn't refused to see his patient that day at the office, he'd have been on top of her issue, too.

He'd screwed up in both instances. And it hadn't been him in the end who'd gotten hurt.

He headed for the kitchen, ready to get out of there. "I'll be back later with an antibiotic cream. In the meantime, talk to your wife."

CHAPTER FIVE

MAGGIE READ OVER THE PAGE IN HER NOTEPAD AND GAVE A FINAL nod. Her birth plan was complete. At six weeks from delivery, naturally, she'd been thinking about it for some time. However, she'd never written the details down due to waiting to see if Cord would be around for the delivery. Not that his being there or *not* being there mattered as to how she wanted to deliver. She just hadn't been able to fully picture the day until now. After last night, though, her picture was complete. She would deliver alone.

She would make all decisions alone.

She lay the pen she'd been using on top of the notepad and pushed up from the table. In six weeks, she'd deliver a beautiful, healthy baby boy at the Birch Bay hospital. She'd breastfeed him from the moment she was able. She'd welcome him into the world with love, lowered lights, and soft music—preferably without an epidural, though she did reserve the right to change her mind. And after she went home, she'd be the best mother she could possibly be.

Also, she'd make sure her brother upheld his promise to be the best uncle *he* could be. Because as the baby's uncle, Mason would also be the main man in her son's life.

She wrinkled her nose. All of that would be fine and dandy if she could honestly believe every word running through her mind. Rarely did things work out exactly as planned, though. Her growing belly was proof of that.

Turning from the table, she moved to the stove. She'd been up and out of the bedroom since Cord had walked away from the house several hours before. After locking herself away the previous night, she hadn't wanted to come out today. She hadn't wanted to look into Cord's impassive face yet again. However, she'd also known that she couldn't hide away forever. She'd been in the bathroom, trying to make herself look as if she hadn't just slept in her clothes, when she'd first heard him leave through the front door.

Soon after, rhythmic scraping noises had come from outside, and she'd figured out that he'd been clearing the path to the truck again. He'd then come back in, a couple of thumps had sounded from the other room, and within seconds, the front door had opened and closed once more. Then all had gone quiet.

Maggie had remained in the middle of the small room, unmoving, straining to hear what he might do next. No sounds had come, but movement had finally caught her attention through the bedroom window. She'd crossed to watch until Cord disappeared from view. A lone, dark figure making its way through the unmarred and still-falling snow, and the sight had represented to her what she'd always known about the man himself.

He was a loner.

But he was also a caretaker.

He'd been making his way to his father's house, she was certain, and after no longer being able to see him, she'd finally come out of the room. What had been waiting for her had squeezed at her heart.

"Breakfast" had been scrawled in heavy slanted letters on a yellow sticky note, with the note attached to a package of blueberry bagels. Another note had proclaimed "cream cheese" and had been stuck to the front of the refrigerator. The last message had still been attached to the square pad of paper the others had been ripped from, a permanent marker lying to one side of it and a charcoal-gray hoodie to the other. "In case you get cold," it had said.

He'd left her breakfast and a sweatshirt.

He'd also left a fire roaring in the fireplace; thus, she hadn't gotten cold. Nor did she think the hoodie would stretch around her oversized midsection.

But oh, she'd wanted to try it.

She'd wanted to snuggle deep into the soft cotton and breathe the darned man in. He smelled better than any person she'd ever met, and she'd lay money the smell was a natural scent and not something manufactured and sold at a markup.

She glanced at the sweatshirt again, still lying on top of the table untouched, and told herself not to be moved by the thoughtfulness. It didn't change anything. Her son's father still wanted nothing to do with him, and as soon as the tow truck driver delivered her car to the cabin, she'd be on her way and out of Cord's life for good.

And if Cord didn't return before her car got there?

Well, then she'd use one of his sticky notes to leave a summary of the decisions she'd made overnight.

One: she wouldn't accept his five thousand dollars nor any other money at any other time.

Two: she wanted a legal document filed, stating that he wished to have no rights as a parent. This, she *would* let him pay for.

And three: he would lose her phone number, and she'd lose his. They would be done forever.

The decisions broke her heart for her son, but she could—and she *would*—give him a good life. She didn't need Cord's money to make that happen.

Footsteps sounded on the porch outside, but instead of allowing herself to glance in that direction, she lifted the lid off the pot of potato soup. When she'd called to see about getting her car towed to the cabin, she'd found out that it would be several hours before they could get to it. Unsurprisingly, she hadn't been the only one having problems on the roads the night before. So, she'd decided to pass the time by cooking. She'd want to eat again soon anyway. Plus, uncomfortable discussions tended to go better with food, and if anything were true in the moment, it's that any conversation she and Cord were to have would likely be uncomfortable.

The door opened and the whistle of wind rushed in. Maggie sniffed at the soup.

The door closed.

A tiny foot jabbed at her from the inside.

When no additional sounds came from the other side of the cabin—or movements from within—Maggie caved. She peeked over. Cord remained just inside the door, a perplexed look on his face as if surprised to find her standing there. He had one hand lifted to the tab of the zipper on his jacket, and his cap had been pulled low over his ears and down to his eyebrows. He appeared to be damp all over, and he had to be freezing.

"How's your dad?" She smoothed her hands over the shirt she'd now been in for over twenty-four hours.

"He's . . ." Cord finally moved, shaking his head as if emerging from a trance. He shrugged out of his jacket and headed for the fireplace. "He needs his prosthesis adjusted." He practically grunted out the words. "The thing has rubbed sores in several places, and he thought that keeping the skin soft with lotion would be a solution."

"Gloria thought lotion would be enough, too?"

Cord looked over his shoulder as he stooped, his mouth twisting into a frown, and she could read his mind as clear as day. He hadn't meant to say anything to her about his dad. He'd done the same back in April, intending to keep personal topics exactly that. But after an exhausting trip to the rehab center that Saturday, a visit in which he'd eventually admitted the pain it caused seeing his dad like that, he'd opened up. Slightly. Max Wilde had been a topic of conversation a couple of times after that, and though he'd been the only personal subject Cord *had* spoken about, that alone had provided an additional layer to what they'd been doing that weekend.

Cord was likely remembering those details right now. And most likely, refortifying his resolve to keep her at a distance.

"Gloria?" Maggie prodded. She stared him down. She could appreciate boundaries, and she acknowledged that Max and Gloria weren't a part of her family. So, Max's health wasn't *actually* any of her concern.

However, she detested being ignored simply due to someone being in a foul mood.

And she hated undeserved foul moods being directed at her.

Finally, Cord replied. But he clearly did so grudgingly. "He hadn't told Gloria."

He returned to the fire, adding another log, and the way his shoulders went rigid was a clear sign that she wouldn't be getting anything more out of him. However, as Maggie watched, even as her irritation made a valiant effort at bubbling to an eruption, she couldn't help but sense Cord's utter frustration. For a man who liked to control the situations around him, his life must seem completely chaotic at the moment. A baby . . . his father needing help that he clearly hadn't wanted to ask for . . . stuck in a cabin with *her*.

She wasn't heartless. The man was having a rough day. She could cut him some slack.

At least, a little.

"I made soup," she offered. They might as well get the conversation started so they could get it over with.

He didn't look at her.

"I also thought—" She clenched her hands into fists as he needlessly poked at the fire again, his intention to continue ignoring her made perfectly clear. And she decided on a change of plans. She wasn't in the mood to tiptoe around this guy's fragile ego, after all. "We need to talk, Cord. *Now.*"

That brought his gaze to hers.

"And don't worry. I'm not going to try to change your mind. Not if you're still set on your decision." She paused, expecting him to point out that he most definitely *was* still set on his decision . . . or maybe to insinuate that he'd had time to think things over. To reevaluate.

Instead, he said nothing, and that silence left a lump in her throat.

He rose to his full height, his eyes boring into hers, so she lifted her chin.

"I made a few of my own decisions overnight." She refused to let his attempt at intimidation by silence and steely-eyed glare rattle her. "Things you and I need to discuss, such as my expectations where you're concerned." At his raised brows, she continued, "Or the lack thereof," she finished with sarcasm.

Instead of keeping her hands gripped at her sides, she very pointedly uncurled her fingers and straightened her shoulders. Then she motioned toward the stove. "So, I made soup."

His gaze finally moved from her over to the pot still simmering on the stove. "Soup?" he said. She could read nothing into the one word.

"Truce soup."

At that, his gaze came back, and for just a second, she thought he might relax his stance. Maybe even offer a tiny smile. He did neither.

"Others call it potato soup," she added, being sure to keep her own emotionless stare in place. She flicked her gaze to the tiny pantry where she'd found the vegetables. "There were only three potatoes, and given that I also found three steaks, you probably meant to use them for baking. I made soup instead. So, what do you say? Can you drop the attitude for ten minutes while we call a truce and have a conversation?"

There was a pause before he replied. "What happens after ten minutes?"

The sigh slipped out before she could restrain it. "Whatever you want to happen, Cord. I'll go back into hiding in the bedroom until my car arrives if you wish. Or if it'll make you happier, I'll grab my things and wait in the front seat of your truck." Her glare now matched the one he'd been dishing out. "Whatever Dr. Wilde deems appropriate."

She narrowed her eyes, miffed because he'd made her lose her calm so easily. But dang, the man acted as if she'd personally set out to wrong him. When, from what she remembered, the so-called "wrongs" that had been done, had been done *personally* to each other.

"You're not going to wait in my truck," he stated.

"Fine. The bedroom it is, then." She crossed her arms over her chest. "Truce?"

Twelve feet separated them, but it suddenly felt like none. Cord's presence invaded the entire cabin, and though the smell of soup had filled the space not thirty seconds before, all she could currently breathe in was Cord.

She had to get a grip.

She had to quit thinking of him as anything but a sperm donor.

His stony façade seemed to crack just a fraction, his gaze darting away from hers for the briefest of moments before warily making its way back. His jawline tensed. "Have you told anyone else about the baby?"

It took her a minute to change subjects. "That I'm pregnant?" She looked down at herself. "Geez. It's not like it can be hidden."

His eyes traveled over her body, as well, but this time, she didn't feel as if what he saw disgusted him the way it had the night before. She didn't know exactly *what* he might be thinking, but the invisible hunk of a wall separating them seemed to crumble a tiny inch. "That I'm the father." Blue eyes locked back on hers. "Have you told any of my family that I'm the father of your baby?"

Oh. It hadn't occurred to her he wouldn't know that.

She shook her head. "I haven't." And that hadn't been easy. Erica and Arsula were two of her closest friends. It had been tough not sharing everything with them. Hard not being able to lean on them when Cord wouldn't return her call.

But if she opened up to them about her baby's parentage, they'd in turn feel obligated to share the information with Gabe and Jaden. And it wasn't her friends' places to let Cord's family know he was going to be a father. That would be Cord's decision. Or his decision *not* to inform them.

"What have you told them?" he pushed. "I know Erica and Arsula are friends."

The baby shifted, pushing down on the bottom of her uterus, and she put one hand under her belly and the other to her lower back. "They are friends, yes. But they don't know you're the father."

"Who do they think is?"

She wanted to let him know that it was none of his business what she'd told her friends. If he didn't wish to be in his son's life, then he should have no vested interest in any part of it *or* in hers. Her indignation had passed, however, and at this point she just wanted to be real. She was exhausted of everything else. "They think it's a man from out of town who I met at the grand opening of The Cherry Basket." Which *was* when the two of them had gotten together. It just hadn't been when they'd officially met.

They'd *met* two months before at Gabe and Erica's wedding. She simply hadn't managed to get his attention that day.

Cord's eyes remained distant as they continued to watch her. "And if I hadn't found you on the side of the road last night, would you have ever told *me* about the baby?"

At his question, her surprise showed. "Cord. I *tried* to tell you. More than once."

"I know that. But would you have tried *again*?" He shifted, his stiff posture suddenly seeming difficult to pull off. His throat moved as he swallowed. "Or were you finished trying?"

She didn't know what he wanted her to say. What was he getting at? "Would you have wanted me to try again?"

His eyes bore into hers, his jaw tight. Then in a blink, his expression changed. For the first time since the night before as he'd reminded her to breathe through the beginning of a panic attack, he didn't wear a glare. He tilted his head, and his eyes softened just the slightest. And she saw the man who'd spent the weekend with her back in the spring. "Please answer the question, Maggie."

What was she supposed to do when presented with a plea like that?

She nodded. "I would have tried again." Glancing at the phone, where it lay on the table, she added, "In fact, I wouldn't have only tried, this time I would've succeeded. I intended to send you a text Monday morning announcing the good news. I can show you the drafted message if you don't believe me."

His gaze shifted to the phone, his features giving nothing away, then he offered a small nod of his head. "I believe you. And I accept your offer of a truce."

CHAPTER SIX

TRUCE SOUP.

Cord stared at himself in the mirror of the steamed-over bathroom, squinting to see past the condensation rapidly reforming over the circle he'd cleared. Maggie had made truce soup. And he'd thought that was cute.

He shook his head in disgust. Maggie Crowder was nothing but a fling, and he couldn't let her get under his skin. He couldn't allow her to charm him like she had back in April. And that's exactly what she'd done. She'd been helping to clean up after the grand reopening party he and his family had thrown on the town square, but she'd also been noticeably putting herself within viewing and speaking distance of him. *Often.* Even so, he'd maintained his decision *not* to come on to his sister-in-law's friend. Just as he'd told himself during Gabe's wedding: sisters-in-law's friends were off-limits.

However, after one particularly obvious sweep of her gaze over his body followed by a groin tightening come-hither grin. . . and *then* followed by an oops-I-didn't-mean-to-trip-and-fall-right-into-your-arms move, he'd slipped and given her *his* best smile. And them getting together at that point couldn't have been stopped even if God himself had reached down and put a hand between them.

If Maggie hadn't followed her not-so-subtle move by asking if he wanted to hang out, *he* would have. Because he'd liked her, all the way back to their meeting in February. She was bold, cute, clearly had enough gumption to go after what she wanted, and her humor was more than a little off-center. She made him laugh.

Grabbing a hand towel, he swiped at the mirror again. After agreeing to a truce, he'd requested a shower before soup. He'd not only needed to warm up from the time spent outdoors, but he'd desperately desired a few minutes alone. Away from the mouthwatering smell of potatoes, broth, and onions—and away from the picture of a pregnant woman standing at the stove as he'd first come through the door.

He glowered at himself. That had not been what he'd expected to find upon returning to the cabin.

It wasn't what he ever expected to find.

Still . . . for a moment it had felt right. Homey.

Personal.

Tossing the towel into the open hamper, he pulled a clean set of clothes from his bag and dressed. He'd been in the compact bathroom for only a handful of minutes, but even so, he felt as if he were in Maggie's space. Upon entering the room, he'd noticed a single brush lying precisely along the side of the sink and a wet washcloth hung over the shower rod, and he'd almost turned around and left. He showered with women all the time. Or he showered in the same room as them, after they'd finished and stepped out. But being in this space made him uncomfortable. He told himself he hurried because he was hungry. However, he also knew he hurried because Maggie Crowder was already getting to him.

Heading back to the main part of the cabin, he cleared his mind of the gut-churning thoughts that had been going through him since the evening before and determined to remain calm and to keep things casual. To "lose the attitude," as Maggie had requested. He didn't make a habit of being a jerk to women, so he could get through this one meal, and one more discussion, without doing so.

Upon seeing him return, Maggie immediately started to rise from the table.

"Don't get up." He held out a hand. "You've done enough. I'll serve the soup."

At his words, she paused, her rear half off the seat and her long hair slipping over one shoulder. She seemed as exhausted as she had the night before.

"Put your feet up while you're at it." He nodded toward the chair nearest her. He'd noticed her ankles swelling again when he'd first come in. "Do they swell like that every day?"

Her gaze lowered to her feet. "Most days," she muttered. She plopped back down and did as he'd suggested, creating a horizontal bridge between the two seats. Then she leaned her head back and let out a weary sigh. Her eyes closed. "There's also bread in the oven."

With minimal direction, he ladled soup into the waiting bowls, grabbed the warming bread and the silverware, and had everything on the table in record time.

Once they were both settled, and after he'd returned to the fridge to retrieve a bottle of water for her and a can of soda for him, they both finally dug in. And the moan of satisfaction that slipped from his lips was both undignified and unmanly.

"Damn," he murmured.

"My momma's recipe," she offered. "She's had the soup added to the menu at the guest ranch they own."

He spooned up another bite. "Your mother is an excellent cook."

"Sometimes."

Cord looked up at the solitary word, but Maggie had her eyes downcast, focusing entirely too closely on the soup. He tried to remember if she'd mentioned anything about her parents before.

He knew that her brother lived in Whitefish. Cord had seen Mason at the grand reopening party, and that subject had come up. They knew each other because the two of them once played football on the same high school team. And if Cord remembered correctly, when the subject of Maggie's parents entered the conversation that weekend, she'd said that they'd moved away a few years ago, as well. He recalled her pointing out that she was the only one left in Birch Bay now.

"They own a guest ranch?" He tore off a hunk of bread and dipped a piece into the soup.

"They do." She still hadn't looked up from her soup. "It stays busy year-round, so they don't get home very often. That's where I was coming from yesterday when heading to Mace's." When he'd found her on the side of the road and discovered he'd gotten her pregnant.

He continued to eat his soup. He knew the point of the meal was to discuss whatever decisions she'd made the night before, but he wasn't ready to go there yet. Her car wouldn't be towed to the house for a while, so he'd prefer to keep things on a more even keel as long as possible.

"Did you ever think about moving closer to them? Especially now with the baby?"

At her side glance, he realized he'd just taken them exactly where he'd hoped to avoid. He mentally cringed. Flat in the middle of a discussion about the baby.

"No." She didn't offer anything more, so he took that as a sign that she also wasn't ready to get serious, and he quickly changed the subject.

"I called a tow truck while over at Dad's."

"What?" She paused, a spoonful of soup halfway to her mouth. "There wasn't any need for you to do that. I called one as soon as I woke up this morning."

"Which I found out when *I* called. I apparently chose the same company." He swirled a piece of bread in his bowl and scooped out a bite. "But I told you last night that I'd call," he reminded her. "So, I did."

Her gaze never wavered. "What you *actually* said last night was 'we'll call a tow truck.'" She put her spoon down. "So, *I* did. Because it's *my* car, Cord. *My* call to make. I didn't need you to do that

74

for me."

He stared at her in surprise. Tension filled her words, and Cord couldn't help but wonder if she didn't like anyone doing things for her or if it was just that she didn't want *him* doing anything?

Or was it him because of the baby?

He glanced at her belly. It probably had more to do with that. He didn't want to be in the baby's life, and no doubt she remained upset. What had she said earlier? That she wanted to talk about her expectations concerning him?

Well, he had news for her. There would be no expectations.

"I was only trying to help." He reined in his own irritation. There was zero need to turn this into an argument.

When she went back to eating instead of saying anything else, he considered letting her in on the fact that he'd also told the owner of the tow company to call *him* instead of her if there were any issues. He'd enjoy seeing what her reaction would be to that. He decided against it, however. Chances were the car would show up without a call needing to be made, and not bringing the subject up would be one less "discussion" they'd be required to have.

"Are you planning to drive on up to your brother's today?" He returned to a less combative topic, making the leap that if she couldn't go home due to fumes and having no bathtub, then she'd have to go somewhere.

"I am. Mace is at work today, though. He's an EMT. But I have a key to his place." She finished the soup, and with one fluid movement, her legs were down and she'd pushed out of the seat.

Cord gave a nod, even though she had her back to him now. She'd gone to the pantry, and he watched as she rummaged through the stockpile of food. "Sounds like a plan," he said. "I'll get the plow out as soon as I finish lunch and clear the driveway. That way you can be on your way whenever you're ready."

She turned back with a box of snack cakes in each hand. "Thank you. Dessert?"

At the shake of his head, she tucked the boxes back into the pantry. "You can have one," he told her. "Feel free to eat whatever you find."

"No, thanks." She rounded both hands over her belly and leaned back against the pantry door. "Believe it or not, I watch what I eat."

His eyes lowered to her belly again. "I wasn't implying you didn't." He watched as one hand smoothed over a tiny foot—or maybe the baby's backside—that poked out from the inside of her swollen flesh, and the image of her standing at the stove when he'd returned to the cabin once again flashed through his mind. That was his baby inside of her.

A baby he'd never intended to conceive, true, but one he now found gave his life surprising purpose. Whereas before—yeah, he'd accomplished things. Medical school, buying into a top-notch practice, purchasing a home, contributing to society via donations and volunteer work. However, the way his life had been panning out, he'd intended only to continue exactly as he had been: to be a part of his family's lives, to treat patients to the best of his ability, and then to grow old and die. No wife, no kids. Nothing lasting.

Now, however, it felt as if a part of him might go on to do something better. Or to *be* better. And with him not personally being involved in the child's life, he wouldn't run the risk of letting his son down.

He forced his eyes up to Maggie's. "Did you ever think of getting rid of him?"

The question had her chin lifting. She didn't answer immediately, and from her silence, he could assume an answer.

"I want my baby," she finally said, and the words rang with raw emotion. "Would *you* rather I'd gotten rid of it?"

He shook his head. He didn't even have to think about it. "No."

Her brows went up. Obviously, she doubted him. "Even knowing that you'll now have a child out there, whether you want anything to do with him or not?"

"I don't want anything to do with him." He didn't let himself think as he said the words; he simply repeated his decision. There was no need to rethink things. "And yes, even then."

She studied him, and though she stood several feet away, the fact that she was on her feet and he remained sitting made him want to come up out of the chair. He didn't like feeling as if he were at a disadvantage.

He didn't move, though. Instead, he felt frozen in place.

"Do you want to tell me why you'd rather I hadn't terminated?"

His breath caught at her words. She wasn't afraid to ask the tough questions; he'd give her that. She had no qualms about pushing him, whether through undesirable topics or when he used his gruffness to try to force her to back off—as he'd done the night before. He respected that. He also suspected that particular trait would play into making her a good mother. She wouldn't let the kid get away with constantly trying to pull things over on her.

But even having that boldness, she also had a softness. He'd seen both back in April. He'd *liked* both back in April. He hoped his son grew to appreciate it, as well.

And he hoped *she* loved their child with every fiber of her being. Every kid deserved that.

"I don't know why," he answered honestly, not breaking eye contact. He might be a bad person for not wanting his son to be part of his world, but at least he told the truth. And the truth was that he definitely would *not* have wanted the baby to be terminated. Just like he wouldn't have wanted to go through the rest of his life never knowing about the existence of the child.

His phone started ringing, but surprisingly, he had no urge to reach for it. The call allowed for the perfect distraction and came at the exact right moment. It would get him out of the uncomfortable conversation he'd once again inadvertently put himself in. However, he just sat there, unwilling to interrupt the moment.

Maggie interrupted it for him. "Don't you need to get that?"

When she pulled her gaze from his, looking around the room at anything and everything but him, he realized she'd grown as uncomfortable as him. He brought the phone to his ear.

"Hello?" He answered without paying attention to the caller. Instead, he watched Maggie. She'd moved to the sink and was rinsing out her bowl.

"Hi, I'm calling from Lewis's Towing and Autobody."

Maggie looked over her shoulder at him.

"I'm calling about Maggie Crowder's car," the voice continued.

"The tow company called *you*?" she whispered. Heat filled the question, and pink flooded her cheeks.

"Yes." Cord both answered Maggie and spoke into the phone at the same time. "Is the car ready to be towed?"

Steam rose from the top of Maggie's head.

"Actually, that's why I'm calling," the young man went on. "There's a slight issue."

Before anything else could be said, Maggie snatched the phone from Cord's hand and put it to her ear. The glare she offered almost made him smile. He'd known she wouldn't like him asking them to call him instead of her.

"THIS IS MAGGIE CROWDER." Maggie fumed, both at Cord and to the silent voice on the other end of the phone. "What's the issue with my car?" How dare they call Cord. She was the owner.

"Hi, Ms. Crowder. This is Logan Lewis. You probably don't remember me . . ."

Recognition dawned as the pubescent voice sounded in her ear, and Maggie closed her eyes as she tried to rein in her temper. She'd had Logan her first year of teaching. He must be helping out at his father's shop today.

"Of course I remember you, Logan." There was no need to direct anger at a mere kid. "How are you doing?"

Cord snorted under his breath as her voice changed to polite, making her want to kick him in the shins.

"I'm doing really good, Ms. Crowder. Helping Dad out today."

"I'm sure it's a busy day for everyone."

She turned her back on the man in the same room as her. A smile had landed on his lips after his snort, and it reminded her far too much of the charm he'd oozed the previous time they'd been together. That stuff was potent.

"What's going on with my car, Logan?"

Logan cleared his throat before speaking again, and along with the squeak at the end of that sound, she heard other noises in the background. People talking and clangs of metal on metal. "Well," Logan began, "Mr. Wilde asked us to check out the car before we delivered it to you."

Of course he had. She shot Cord a look, but he wasn't looking at her anymore. Instead, he'd cleared the rest of the dishes from the table and currently had the refrigerator door open, tucking the leftovers inside.

"And, I'm sorry, Ms. Crowder"—Logan cleared his throat again, his nerves at delivering bad news obvious—"but your driveshaft is bent."

"My driveshaft?" She quit watching Cord. "It's bent?"

How could her driveshaft be bent? And what exactly did that mean?

"Yes," Logan confirmed. "And your muffler and tailpipe got taken out, too. But those are smaller fixes. You apparently scraped over some rock as you slid off the road, and you hit it in just the right way to cause the damage. Or, in just the *wrong* way," he corrected, and she could feel his flush of embarrassment. "My dad has already called about getting the parts, but with it being Saturday and a holiday weekend and all, I'm sorry, Ms. Crowder, but it'll be at least the middle of the week before we can get the parts in."

"The middle of the week?" Maggie parroted. "As in Wednesday?"

Cord looked at her again.

"At *least* Wednesday," Logan corrected. "And . . . possibly a little longer." His voice went into a squeak again as he relayed the news. "With the amount of snow we're getting, Dad says the delivery might be delayed."

She didn't have time for delays. Plus, she didn't exactly have the disposable income to fix what sounded like a potentially pricey problem. She'd hoped to maintain what was left of her savings in order to take extra time off after the baby was born.

"I'm sorry, Ms. Crowder," Logan added when the silence had gone on too long.

"You're sure it isn't drivable, Logan?" The school wasn't that far from downtown. She could stay at the historic hotel on the square instead of in the less expensive one she'd intended. "I won't have far to go each day."

"Well . . . the thing is, there's a noticeable delay when turning the wheels," he answered. "It wouldn't be safe for you to drive at all."

Which meant, she was stuck. She frowned. "What about a rental?" She eyed the snow still accumulating outside the living room windows. "Does your dad happen to have any rentals on hand?"

"No, ma'am. We...um... don't do that. I could call around for you, though. If you wanted."

"Tell him no." Cord's words came from behind her, and Maggie turned to glare. She did not need Cord telling her what to do. *Or making decisions on her behalf.* "No, thank you, Logan." She did her best to telepathically fire lasers at Cord's head. "I appreciate the offer, but I wouldn't ask that of you. Could you go ahead and ask your dad to order the parts, though?"

"Yes, ma'am. Did you want to know the cost first?"

No, she really didn't want to know the cost first. As irresponsible as that may seem. She had too many other things to deal with right now. Like getting away from there . . . finding a rental car . . . seeing if there was any way to get her bathtub brought back to the house sooner so she wouldn't have to stay at a hotel for an entire week. "I've got to have a car to drive anyway, right, Logan?"

A nervous chuckle sounded in her ear. "I guess you do, Ms. Crowder. Especially with that baby coming soon."

Her free hand went to her baby, and she mimicked the laugh. "Especially with that." She closed her eyes again, wondering if the fact that a teenager she hadn't seen in years knew she was pregnant and due soon was an indication that the entire town had likely been talking about her. *Probably.* It was a small town, after all. And she was a pregnant single mother. "Have him go ahead and order the parts, Logan. And please keep me updated."

She reminded the teen of *her* phone number, then ended the call. And when she once again looked at Cord, she saw the same questions in his eyes that she knew had to be obvious in hers.

What was she supposed to do now? And how much longer would she have to rely on *him*?

"My car needs some work." She passed his phone back over.

"So I gathered."

"I, um . . ." She chewed on the inside corner of her lip. She wasn't sure what to do next. She couldn't call Mason to come get her. He was at work. And even if he *could* somehow get away long enough to help his sister out, she wouldn't want to then request he bring her right back again tomorrow. Plus, even if that did happen, it wasn't like she'd have a car to get back and forth to work with, anyway.

She looked down at her swollen ankles. Maybe this was the world's way of telling her to go ahead and start her maternity leave. It had definitely become harder to be up and down in the classroom every day. She could bunk with Mace for the next few weeks, spend Christmas with him, have the baby in Whitefish, and then come back home after her son was born. Her brother probably wouldn't mind if she took over his second bedroom for a while.

But she wasn't ready to quit working. She needed to be able to take as much time off after the delivery as possible. Plus, she now had to pay for a car repair.

Her phone rang before she could come up with a plan that might actually be viable, and both she and Cord looked toward it. Was Logan already calling back?

Maybe they'd figured out that she *could* still drive her car.

Cord picked the phone up from the kitchen table before she could get to it, bringing it the rest of the way over to her, and she saw that instead of the Lewis autobody shop, it was Erica.

"Mags!" Erica practically yelled into the phone as soon as Maggie answered.

"What?" she yelled back. She had no idea what had her friend so worked up.

"You stayed at the cabin with *Cord* last night? What's going on out there?"

Cord sat back down at the kitchen table, and as she stood in the middle of the room trying to figure out how to explain to her best friend—*who knew she'd had a thing for Cord since her high school days*—that her staying there truly had been a fluke, Cord pushed a chair away from the table with his foot.

"Sit," he mouthed, and when she didn't immediately follow his directive, he pointed to her ankles. He then lined up a second chair in front of the first one so she could not only sit but also put her feet back up.

"*Fine*," she silently mouthed. And as she sat, she immediately smiled before replying to Erica. She didn't want her friend picking up on anything being wrong. "Nothing is going on, E. It's no biggie. I ran off the road on my way to Mace's, and Cord came upon me right after it happened. There was already a foot of snow on the ground, and my car couldn't be pulled out last night, so it was too late to do much of anything else. So I came to the cabin with him. How did you know I was here, anyway?"

"Cord told us."

She immediately looked at Cord.

"Well," Erica went on, "Cord called Nate, and then Megan called me. But the question is why didn't *you* call us? You know I said you could stay here. And I meant it. For as long as you need."

She didn't take her eyes off Cord as she covered the microphone and whispered, "You called Nate to tell him that I was here?" Had he already been trying to line up a backup plan for getting rid of her?

"I called Nate because I'd gone over to see Dad. I *mentioned* that you were here."

"Is everything okay there, Mags?" Erica's tone softened into concern. "Should I send Gabe over to get you? You can just stay here, and there won't even be a need to go to your brother's. We can help you get your car towed."

She bit down on her lip. Why did everyone think she couldn't handle her issues on her own? "Thank you, but I've already arranged to have my car towed. And I'm *not* going to stay with you and Gabe. You know that."

Erica sighed in her ear. "But that's just silly. We have plenty of room, and I'm not due for another three weeks."

"And that's the last three weeks you'll have with you husband and stepdaughter before all your lives are overtaken with a new baby." She shook her head as if her friend could see her. "So no, I'm not going to do that to you. I'm not taking that time away from any of you."

"Fine. Be stubborn."

Cord snorted.

"But, Mags, will you at least call me when you get to Mason's tonight? Are you still going? It's still snowing like crazy, and you know I'll be super worried about you now. When should you get your car back, do you know?"

She pressed her lips together. She'd really hoped Erica wouldn't go there.

Swallowing, she mumbled, "Next week sometime."

"Next week?" Something thumped on the other end of the line, and Maggie imagined Erica sitting with her feet up, similar to her, before shooting up straight in surprise. "What's wrong with it?" she asked.

"I apparently bent my driveshaft. But all is okay," she continued before Erica could say anything more. "I'm going to be out of here as soon as I find a rental. I'll go on up to Mace's today and be back in town tomorrow. You know they won't close school."

"I know. But that's a lot of driving, in *a lot of snow*. In a car you aren't familiar with. Are you sure that's smart?"

Maggie pulled the phone away and stared at it. Why did everyone suddenly think she was incapable? "I am *not* a bad driver."

"Yet you found yourself stuck in a ditch last night."

Point taken. And from the look on Cord's face, he'd had the same thought. Darn these phones that were so easy to eavesdrop on. She shot a glare at Cord. Why couldn't he be polite and leave the room while she was on the phone?

"And if you do have a problem again . . . well, you're *so* pregnant, Mags. Please, just let me send Gabe for you. Stay here for one night and then go to a hotel."

Maggie wanted to be irritated with her friend. Yes, she was *so* pregnant. She looked twice as pregnant as Erica did. But still, she wasn't incompetent.

"Tell her you're going to stay here tonight."

"What?" She and Erica both spoke at the same time.

"Mags," Erica went on, "you *can't* stay there. It's *Cord*."

Cord's brows lifted.

"Of course I can stay here. He's one of the Wildes. You know they're good people. Heck, you married one of them." And why was she arguing to stay there another night? She didn't even *want* to stay there. Nor did she have a clue why Cord would suggest it.

Unless Cord was rethinking being in the baby's life . . .

If that were the case, it *might* be better to stick around a little longer.

"Of course he's a good guy," Erica agreed. "But honey, it's *Cord*. The guy you've crushed on since—"

"I am fully aware of who Cord is, E." She stood and walked away from the man in question, wishing with all her might that he wasn't there. How embarrassing that he'd heard that. "And anyway, it doesn't matter because I'm *not* staying here tonight. I have no idea why he said that. I'm going to get him to take me into town to pick up a rental, and then I'll be fine."

Cord's cell phone, with his big wide hand wrapped around it, lowered over her head and stopped in front of her eyes. A weather app displayed on it, showing the swath of snow not going anywhere fast. Then he put his mouth to her ear. "She's right. You have no business driving in this. And I'm not taking you anywhere until it stops."

A shiver shot down her body.

"What did he say?" Erica asked, but Maggie was incapable of uttering a sound.

Cord had pulled away, yet the aftereffects of his nearness hadn't gone with him. Her body remained on red alert, waiting for another heated breath against her skin. Or maybe a hot brush from those lips on her neck.

Good grief. Hormones due to pregnancy was a real thing.

She squeezed her eyes closed, willing the images from over seven months before to leave her, and continued to ignore the man.

"Are you really going to stay there again?" Erica whispered now, as if she'd finally clued in to the fact that Cord could hear every word being spoken. "Isn't he in one of the one-bedroom cabins? And you're—"

"*So* pregnant," Maggie finished drily. "Yes, I know."

"*No.* I mean . . . is your staying there wise? Your emotions are all over the place these days. I know you might have done . . . *things* with another man back in the spring, but this thing you've had for Cord . . . it—"

"*Is nothing.*" God, she was mortified. She had to end this conversation before Cord heard any more of it. And seriously, did Erica expect Maggie to put the moves on Cord in all her huge pregnancy glory if she stayed another night? *As if.* "It's never been anything, E. And it never *will* be anything. It was nothing more than a ridiculous teenage crush, so please . . . just drop it."

Erica finally quit talking, not a single sound coming from the other end of the line, and Maggie couldn't have been more grateful. Obviously, Cord had known she'd had the hots for him back in April. She'd made that fact clear the way she'd come on to him. But wanting to spend a night or two heating the sheets with a guy was far different than a crush lasting for over a decade. And probably closer to two.

She'd hoped he'd never learn about that.

"You're staying here," he said again. He still spoke from behind her, but this time he kept his distance. No mouth to the ear. No leaning in. And he said the words with a surprising amount of calm. Was he offended at the thought of her crush? Horrified, maybe?

Would he once again wonder if she'd planned the whole seduction thing and gotten pregnant on purpose?

Her never-elusive tears took that moment to fill her eyes, and continuing the conversation became impossible. "I'll be fine, E." She wiped at her cheeks. "I'll call you in the morning."

CHAPTER SEVEN

"Go," *the pregnant woman said.*

"She's fine," *Cord managed, but he started toward the asphalt. The responding police officers had stopped traffic on the two-lane road, and Cord turned his head as he reached the double yellow lines painted down the middle. A tow truck rolled slowly toward him on the wrong side of the road. The sheriff's vehicle passed the truck on the shoulder.*

Cord's feet stopped moving.

He stood in the middle of the road, knowing he had to finish crossing and get to his mother. He always had to check on his mother. But his feet wouldn't go forward.

He turned back to the pregnant woman.

"Bailey," he called out the name the woman had given him, but this time when she looked up, it wasn't Bailey sitting in the car. It was Maggie.

"Help me, Cord." Maggie reached one hand out the open door, stretching her fingers toward him. "Help the baby . . ."

She looked down at her belly then, and as she did, the back side of the car shifted. It slid at an angle, the front two tires coming up off the road.

"Maggie!" he shouted. He told his feet to move yet again, but still, they remained stuck in the middle of the road.

Chunks of the ground began disappearing behind the vehicle, dropping out of sight as if a hole had opened up, swallowing everything in its reach. The car shifted once more, one back tire hovering over the opening. A front tire spun freely.

Maggie's eyes went wide as her car continued to rock. "The baby, Cord. Please . . ."

His feet released at the same moment the car lurched for the last time, and as he lunged, reaching frantically to catch hold of any part of the vehicle, it disappeared over the cliff. A scream started low in his gut, rising up and out of him like a wounded animal. He fell to his knees.

"Cord!"

Cord heard his name being called, but he couldn't make himself look up. The car was gone. He hadn't made it in time.

He shoved away hands that reached for him.

"Cord. It was a *dream*."

He pushed again, but that time, the words began to register.

"You're dreaming. It's okay. You're safe."

The hands on his shoulders were soft. The voice gentle. Female.

He'd been dreaming. He let out a harsh breath.

Forcing his eyes open, he stared into the darkness, not seeing anything at first, but eventually Maggie's face came into focus. She was hunched over him, where he lay sprawled on the sofa, her face pale in the remaining flicker of the firelight.

"Maggie?"

"Yes." Her hand stroked over his shoulder. "It's me. You were having a bad dream."

Of course he was. Only, this dream had been even worse than his normal one. It was also the first time it hadn't progressed through what really happened. The pregnant woman had never been in any true danger. She'd only had a couple of bruises. The side of the road couldn't possibly have broken away and disappeared the way it had in his subconscious. Yet it had felt so real.

"Are you okay?" Maggie spoke softly, and Cord realized he'd

reached up to his shoulder and grabbed hold of her hand. He was squeezing it as if it were a lifeline. He'd also broken out in a sweat beneath his T-shirt.

"I'm fine." He pushed up, releasing his hold on her, and moved over on the couch. "Have a seat." She looked uncomfortable hunkered down the way she'd been.

She looked uncomfortable, period.

And she looked that way because she was swollen with *his* baby.

He gulped as the thought rolled through his mind.

Would that ever not terrify him?

He looked up at Maggie, who hadn't sat, but no longer remained hunched as she had been. She didn't seem to be in a hurry to leave. "Sit," he said again and nodded toward the couch. "Please."

He breathed a sigh of relief when she lowered onto the opposite end of the couch. As unfair as it might be, he wanted to keep her there beside him. He didn't want to be alone with his own company tonight. Not with the memories—nor with the new fear his subconscious had apparently decided to add in. And he was low enough to take advantage of Maggie's niceness by keeping her with him.

"Do you want to talk about it?" she asked.

She shifted on the seat as if trying to find a more comfortable position, and he immediately shook his head. "It was just a nightmare."

The fire had burned to mostly cinders with only two small flames continuing to fight for survival, and he stared into that movement instead of looking at Maggie. His heart beat wildly in his chest. She hadn't pushed for more, and he knew she wouldn't. He'd discovered that back in April. He'd returned to her place after checking in on his dad that Saturday afternoon, and though an initial update had poured from him, when he'd clammed up, she'd immediately changed the subject. He'd ended up helping her rip carpet out of her living room instead.

He'd liked that about her.

She also knew how to sit in silence and just "be." He appreciated that, as well.

"Did I call out your name?" The question slipped out before he thought to stop it. He remembered screaming for her in the dream.

When he looked over, Maggie simply nodded. Her eyes were hooded, as if his dream had pulled her from a deep sleep, and he found himself wanting to reach over and touch her. Not in a sexual way. Just as a connection to another person.

"I'm sorry," he muttered. He clenched his fingers into his palms. "I have odd dreams sometimes. I didn't mean to wake you."

"It's okay."

Her spine finally relaxed, and her body curved into the couch. As it did, he let his gaze drift down over her. She was so rounded and full.

The top she wore was white and stretchy, opening in a V above her chest. She wore no bra. Her bottoms were dark-blue flannel with smiley faces covering them. The waistband had to be tucked somewhere below her belly because her shirt clung in a way that if a band of elastic were positioned underneath, it would be obviously visible.

"I'm glad we were able to get your clothes," he told her. After she'd finished her conversation with Erica earlier, he'd cleared the snow from the driveway, then they'd driven into town. They'd retrieved her suitcases from her car, as well as a crammed-full bag she needed for school, and he'd watched her involuntarily cringe as she'd reviewed the estimated bill for the car.

"Me too," she murmured. Her eyes blinked closed. "I appreciate you doing that for me."

"My pleasure." He really should let her go back to bed. It was obvious how tired she was.

Instead of using common sense, though—or being anything less than self-serving—he leaned over and reached down for her feet. Her eyes cracked open, and she watched him as he moved. When he lifted her at the ankles, tugging slightly in his direction, her brows went up in surprise. But then she shifted, helping him to turn her on the couch.

She slid lower on the cushion, her belly inching closer, and when he tucked her feet securely into his lap, her eyes closed once again. A soft breath escaped from her, and this time when Cord found himself wanting to reach over and touch, it was to put his lips against hers.

He wouldn't do *that*, though. He *did* have enough control not to be that selfish. But he also didn't take his eyes off her. Her lips had swelled, along with the rest of her body, and merely looking at them made Cord want to peel her clothes away to see all the other changes. To see if she was as beautiful everywhere as were her lips.

"It wasn't a dream about you." He spoke in an almost whisper, not sure if she remained awake or not, and totally unsure why he'd brought the dream back up.

When her eyelids drifted open, he couldn't very well sit there and not say anything else.

"I dream about my mother sometimes," he explained. "The day she died. I think the stress of everything"—his eyes lowered to her belly—"of the *baby*, of . . ." He finished the next thought with a shrug. "I guess it all must have contorted together, putting you into the dream."

"Oh." She watched him through slitted lids.

Her belly moved, and his gaze shifted back to it again. The baby had kicked.

Swallowing, he dragged his gaze away from her stomach, and he absolutely did not let himself reach out and touch it.

"Do you have the dream often?" she asked. One hand went to her stomach.

"Only recently."

He saw the question in the squint of her eyes, and he knew that his answer had been telling, but he offered nothing more. What he found, though, was that just by saying that much . . . that he dreamed of his mother's death . . . the bands that continually tightened around his chest felt a little looser.

He didn't want to talk about the dream anymore. At the same time, he didn't shy away when Maggie said, "You were the first one to come upon the wreck?"

"I was."

"And you were just a kid." Her free hand lifted, as if she intended to reach for him, but it drifted back to her side. So, he reached for *it*. He wrapped his fingers arounds hers, the backs of his knuckles sliding along the side of her swollen belly, and he noted that her hand was chilled. The temperature in the room had dipped too low, but he didn't want to break the moment by getting up to stoke the fire.

He leaned over and picked up the blanket he'd likely lost while thrashing during his dream and spread it over her. After tucking the ends around her feet, he rested one hand at her ankles, enjoying the weight of her pressing down on him. Then he reached for her hand again.

"I was sixteen," he confirmed. "Not exactly a kid."

He'd been old enough he should have known better than to walk away.

"And the dreams just started again recently?"

It took him a moment to answer, even with a nod. Because that wasn't a direction he was willing to let the conversation go. "I don't want to talk about that anymore," he said, and in return, she mimicked his nod.

"Did you want to talk about something else then?" She tilted her head on the armrest as she asked the question, and he found that he did want to talk more. About anything, really. As long as it would keep her there with him.

"How about that crush that Erica mentioned?"

Her eyes went wide at his question, and he couldn't hold back the chuckle. He honestly hadn't meant to bring it up. They'd been avoiding potentially uncomfortable conversations all afternoon, and he'd told himself that teasing her about a crush would serve no purpose. He'd seen how embarrassed she'd become earlier, knowing he could overhear the conversation. Yet like what so often happened around her, his mouth opened, and words spilled out.

She did her best to look down her nose at him. "A polite man would have left the room when he realized a woman was having a conversation about him."

He really did like her. And he liked the friendship he suspected they could have. "I'm not a polite man, Maggie."

As his tone dipped, the soft timbre matching the quiet mood of the room, he took pleasure in watching the way her lashes fluttered. He'd bet her cheeks turned pink, too, but it was too dark to be certain.

"Surely you knew that from before," he added. He hadn't been at all polite the weekend they'd been together. Not in the passionate sense. He'd taken her up against the wall, over the back of the couch, and basically, every way a man could take a woman. And he'd *still* wanted more.

"Cord . . ." She let the word trail off, averting her gaze instead of saying anything more.

"I'm sorry," he apologized immediately. He hadn't meant to go there. Flirting was the last thing either of them needed to be doing right now. "Mags." He squeezed her ankle, where it lay beneath his palm, hoping she'd turn back. And when she did, he repeated his statement. "I'm *sorry*. Talking like that is inappropriate in this circumstance. It won't happen again."

She studied him as if trying to determine if he could be trusted, and though he expected her to declare that she needed to get back to bed, she didn't. Instead, she nodded. And stayed where she was.

The mood went back to quiet, and Cord found it as comforting as before. "We never talked about those expectations you mentioned."

He held his breath after making the statement. He wasn't entirely certain he was ready to hear her expectations. At the same time, the matter *had* been on his mind since that morning. But since they'd formed some kind of unspoken second truce to get through the day with the least amount of conflict as possible, the topic had never come up.

"No, we never did." She started to push to a sitting position, but he held tight to her foot.

"Stay where you are." He nodded, hoping she'd comply.

"Cord." She swallowed and again looked away. But this time she brought her gaze back on her own. "This feels . . . *wrong.*"

He played dumb. "Your lying down feels wrong?"

"Me lying down with my feet in your lap. Us together . . . like this."

He looked around then, taking in the room. A chill remained, the light from the fire barely aglow, and the snow, though it had finally stopped coming down several hours before, was plastered to every window. The moment felt as if they were cocooned inside an igloo together.

As if they were the last two people on earth.

"Still," he said. He loosened his grip on her foot and released the hand still in his. He let her know without words that if she wanted to get up, he wouldn't stop her. "I like it," he finished.

When she made no additional moves to rise, only eyed him from her end of the couch, he brought both hands back to her ankles and shifted around so that he faced her.

He nodded. "Now, tell me about these expectations."

Maggie stared at her feet. Cord's hands had slipped under the blanket and were now slowly massaging her left foot.

A freaking moan tried to slip out.

"Maggie?"

She lifted her gaze.

"The expectations?"

What was going on right now? First of all, she'd awakened from a dead sleep to her name being shouted; Cord had then "somewhat" opened up to her again; he'd *flirted*, and now he planned to massage her feet while she explained to him how she wanted absolutely nothing from him ever again.

Was she dreaming?

She had to be.

"Ooooh." She couldn't hold in the moan as Cord's thumbs stroked from her heel to the ball of her foot. It had been too long since she'd been able to do anything more than slip her shoes on, and dang it, that felt good. "What are you doing, Cord?"

She couldn't just let him do this.

His hands stilled over her sock-covered feet. "Your feet swell all the time. I thought this might feel good."

There was a question in his eyes, as well as his voice. He wasn't trying to seduce her. He seriously just thought this would be a nice thing to do.

And he hadn't been wrong. "It does feel good."

"Do you want me to stop?"

She should. Just like lying on the couch with him, this was wrong. But if this was wrong, she didn't want to be right.

"No." She shook her head. "I don't want you to stop."

"Good."

He went back to massaging, switching to her other foot, and she closed her eyes and tried to remember the decisions she'd made the night before. She hadn't brought the subject up again because the timing had never seemed right. But also because she simply hadn't had the mental fortitude to deal with it. The day had been intense all the way around, and any additional Cord-related issues had seemed more than she could handle. So, after returning from her car, she'd hidden in the bedroom.

She *had* considered suggesting Cord open one of the other cabins for her. After all, there were nine of them sitting unused. But practicality had won out. She'd only be there for one more night, and there really *wasn't* a need for Cord to have to clear another path through the snow just for her. Plus, if she'd gone to another cabin, she totally would have had to "borrow" some of Cord's food. Her baby didn't like it when she didn't eat.

So off to the bedroom she'd gone, using the excuse that she needed to work on upcoming class plans, when the reality was that she'd simply been avoiding Cord. While in there, though, she had made one final decision. And that was that she *wouldn't* have the expectation conversation, after all. Not face-to-face, anyway. Instead, she'd planned to leave a note where Cord would find it after she was gone. And then she wouldn't answer her phone if he called. Not that she actually expected him to.

"You really want to talk about that now?" she asked, doing her best not to let her eyes roll to the back of her head because of the things he continued doing to her feet.

"I do."

Fine. Then talk they would do. Because, when presented with the perfect opportunity . . .

"Expectation number one." She imagined sitting up tall and coming across as strong and in control. In reality, she kept her feet in Cord's lap. "I won't take the five thousand dollars you sent Friday night, nor do I want any other money from you ever."

His hands quit moving. "Why not?"

She gave a shrug. "I just don't. If you choose not to be in my son's life, that's fine. That's your decision, and I'm okay with it. But if so, then *don't* be in his life. In any way. I can take care of him myself."

Cord stared at her, unblinking for several seconds before responding. "But I saw how painful the car bill is going to be for you."

"What?" She did push up then. "What are you talking about?"

He stayed as he had been, still sitting with one knee propped on the couch. "When you saw the estimate for the repairs today," he explained. "I watched you cringe. I know it's going to be a painful bill for you, so take the money. It'll help."

She gawked at him. He sounded so carefree about tossing around thousands of dollars. And he'd so easily made assumptions about her. "I also cringe when I have to send in my mortgage payment every month. Handing over wads of cash isn't exactly my idea of fun. And no, I'm *not* taking the money."

His jawline tensed. "We'll circle back to that one. What's next?"

She glared. There would be no circling back. "You'll get a legal document drawn up stating that you want nothing whatsoever to do with my son's life, and thus you'll have no rights going forward. And I *will* let you pay for that."

His nostrils flared. "What if something happens to you? If you can't take care of him?"

"Then I'll arrange for help."

"What if you're a bad mother?"

The question, as well as the harsh delivery, caused her to jerk back. Did he think she would be a bad mother? She wet her lips. "Why would you say that?" It was hard not to take the question personally. Hard not to wonder if he could foresee something in her that she'd tried hard *not* to worry might be there. "Is there a reason you think I might be a bad mother, Cord?"

He didn't move an inch. "I'm just saying that bad mothers exist. I've known them." The hardness of his expression had her wanting to pull back. "There are women out there who have no business raising a baby," he continued, "much less trying to do it on their own. That's all I'm suggesting. How do you know you're not one of them?"

And then she got it. He was talking about his mother. Not necessarily about her.

She blew out a soft breath. "Are you referring to *your* mother, Cord?"

Surprise crossed his features.

"I'm friends with Erica and Arsula," she explained, as if that was all that needed to be said.

Anger tightened his jaw. "Those ladies certainly talk, don't they?"

Maggie didn't let his annoyance bother her. She shrugged. "Friends share things. But the thing is, none of us are out running around town and telling others about it."

"They told you."

He had a point. She decided to ignore it. "And before you mention the possibility of me dying," she said, "I've already thought about that. I'll have a will in place before I deliver. There will be a guardian listed."

"Who will it be?" he asked, but she hadn't decided yet. Her father didn't need that kind of responsibility on top of running the guest ranch. Her brother, perhaps?

Erica?

She swallowed. "I haven't made my final decision." She had friends from college she remained close with. "I wouldn't leave my son to just anyone, though. I promise you that."

He seemed to consider her answer, and as he did, she tried to come up with any additional objections he might have. Nothing came to mind. Which meant, there should be no reason not to draw up that document.

"No," Cord finally said. "I won't do that."

"*Cord.*" His blunt declaration surprised her, and she leaned forward as far as her stomach would allow. She wished she'd turned the light on so she could see him better. His eyes were shadowed. "Why not? You don't want anything to do with him. Why would you care?"

"I also don't want him tossed around to just anyone. Next?"

"Next?" She blinked. Did he or did he not want to have anything to do with his child?

"Yes. What's the next thing on your list?"

This wasn't at all how she'd seen this conversation going. His responses had her wondering how he'd take her third requirement, and nerves caused her subconscious to wave the caution flag. She pushed forward, however, lowering her gaze to the middle of his chest.

"When you drop me off at the rental place tomorrow, you'll lose my phone number, and I'll lose yours." She didn't mean to, but she glanced up. Her mouth had gone dry. "We'll have no reason to speak again," she croaked out. "So, no need to have the means to get in touch."

Her baby chose that moment to fire off several punches, and gratefully, she dropped her gaze again. Tears threatened, and though they'd likely spill out no matter how hard she tried to contain them, she hoped the sweep of hair falling in front her face would hide the evidence. She should have just left a note. This was too hard. And she didn't know why he was making it so.

"Maggie." He said her name softly, leaving her to wonder if the moment was hard for him, as well.

She shook her head. "We can finish talking in the morning." She somehow managed to rise from the couch on her own, keeping her face turned from Cord's as she did. "I'm going back to bed."

Cord rose behind her. "Maggie," he said again, this time more insistent. More urgent.

She didn't face him, but she also didn't walk away. Not yet. "What?"

"Stay here this week."

At that, she whipped around. *What?*

"There's no need to get a hotel," he said. His features gave nothing away. "No need for a rental either. I'll be here all week. I can take you back and forth to work."

She gaped at him. "You want me to stay here? With *you*?" She shook her head without even realizing it.

"Not *with* me," he corrected. "Just here. It makes sense. If you seriously want me to consider not sending you any more money, then I have to know that you can take care of yourself. That you can take care of the baby. Stay here. You can have the bedroom, and I'll remain on the couch."

"No." She wouldn't even consider it. She already felt bad for putting him out as it was. Doing it for the rest of the week was out of the question. Plus . . . she couldn't be in such proximity to him for that long. That would be harder than the conversation they'd just had. That would make her want him to want their baby even more.

"Then I'll send you one thousand dollars every week," he announced. "And I'll insist you accept it."

She gaped again. Was he out of his mind?

She should agree just to force him to do it. That would teach him.

"I won't put you out like that, Cord. I can pay for a hotel." Then she had another thought. It didn't solve the problem of being in his proximity, but it *would* make it easier to stay. "Unless you let *me* take the couch?"

The expression that passed over his face was comical. As if she'd caught him off guard by punching him square in the nose. "There is no way I'd ever let that happen, Maggie."

"Fine. Then I'll go to a hotel."

"No. You can stay in one of the other cabins."

The suggestion caused her to pause. It was a workable option, and if he hadn't caught her so off guard to begin with, it was one she'd have thought of herself. But why was he suddenly trying so hard *not* to get rid of her?

"You'll have your own space," he went on, "but it won't cost you anything. And I'll still be able to take you back and forth to work." He nodded, his expression both sincere and a little pleading. "Stay, Maggie. Let me do this for you. I'll talk to a lawyer Monday. You and I can work out terms that both of us are comfortable with, and at the end of the week"—his chin inched upward—"we'll do as you ask and lose each other's numbers."

CHAPTER EIGHT

"I hear Maggie Crowder is staying out at the cabins with you."

Cord looked up from his phone at his dad's statement, glancing between him and Gloria. They sat side by side, his dad in a wheelchair, in the orthopedic waiting area of the Birch Bay Medical Plaza. "Where did you hear that?"

"Nate mentioned it. He and Megan stopped by the house yesterday afternoon."

Cord frowned. His brother seemed to have picked up a bad habit of oversharing.

Nate and Megan had shown up before lunch yesterday, anxious to get Maggie settled in cabin number two, and while that had been going on, Cord had cleared a path between the two buildings. He'd also moved his truck over to park in front of her cabin. No need to make her walk in the snow any more than necessary. Then he'd shoveled the walk from it to her porch.

Megan freshened the sheets and checked on supplies while Nate had hauled in groceries, then as quickly as they'd arrived, *everyone* had disappeared. Nate, Megan, *and* Maggie.

Cord had spent the remainder of the day by himself. Exactly as he'd planned when he'd decided to come home. He'd eaten a cold sandwich for dinner, had worked on putting together some of the miniature furniture he'd brought with him—which would be part of his Christmas gifts for his two oldest nieces—and he'd found himself completely bored.

This morning, with the roads having been scraped and cleared, he'd gone for a run before daybreak. The cold air had sucked the breath out of him at first, but in the end, it was exactly what he'd needed. The time had allowed him to turn his mind to only the things he needed to accomplish that day. Take his father to see his orthopedic surgeon and prosthetist, reach out to a friend who was a family law attorney, and *not* think about Maggie. Or the baby.

The most important thing was to not think about the baby.

He'd grabbed a quick shower before hurrying back outside, intending to help Maggie to the truck, but the moment he'd opened his front door, he'd found her already waiting. *Inside* the cab. A small stepstool sat on the ground next the passenger door, and for some reason, that triangular piece of aluminum and plastic had irritated him. He hadn't minded having to lift Maggie up to the seat. And seriously, him doing that was far safer than her balancing on the small stool.

He didn't let his annoyance show, however. He'd merely gotten behind the wheel and taken her to work.

"She's not staying with *me*," Cord corrected, coming back to the conversation. "Nate got her set up in the cabin next door."

"But she *was* with you Friday and Saturday night?" This question came from Gloria, and when Cord shot her a look, she seemed as bewildered as Nate had been when he'd found out Maggie had stayed in Cord's cabin a second night.

Cord had explained that at the time, it hadn't been known she'd need to stay any longer than Sunday morning. Therefore, there'd been no need to ready another cabin. Nate had remained suspicious, however.

She's pregnant, bro. Don't be messing with her.

Cord had glowered at his younger brother. *I am* not *messing with her. I was being nice.* Exactly as he'd been when he'd suggested she stay on the property in the first place.

Good. Keep it that way.

Cord didn't need any of his brothers in his face about Maggie— nor his sister or his father and stepmother—but deep inside, he'd secretly liked knowing that someone would be watching out for her. She might need that.

"Yes," Cord replied, once again having to drag his mind back to the present. "She *did* stay with me those two nights." He ignored his father's curious stare. He'd told his dad Saturday morning that no one else had been out at the cabin. "I found her on the side of the road as I came into town Friday night." He assumed Nate had filled them in on that part, as well. "And since it was snowing so hard you couldn't see your hand in front of your face, I offered to let her stay at the cabin. Her place is being worked on, so she couldn't go home."

"Hmmm," his dad said, the sound dragging out far longer than Cord thought necessary.

"There's no 'hmmm' to it," Cord pushed back. "She needed help, and I was there."

"Sure," the older man agreed. "But . . . be careful with that one, son. She's pregnant."

Oh, sheesh. Him, too? "You think?" He scowled. "I'm not molesting the girl, Dad. I was simply helping her out."

"We know that, Cord." Gloria gave him a soft smile, reaching over to pat her husband on the thigh at the same time. "All you boys are good like that. Your dad is just a bit protective of Maggie because she's stopped by to check on him a couple of times."

The news shocked Cord. "Maggie has been to the house?"

"Yes." Gloria nodded. "With Erica and Arsula once, and another time, she stopped on her own. She brought a pie that day."

"A lemon pie."

His dad followed his words with a moaning-purr, and the sound made Cord wish he'd been able to try the pie. Her potato soup had been amazing.

"Of course," his dad mused, "she's the size of a house."

"Maxwell Wilde!" Gloria shot to her feet.

"What?" His dad seemed surprised at Gloria's shrieking. "I'm just—"

"You do not talk about a woman like that." Gloria had a finger pointing in his dad's face. *"Ever.* What in the devil is wrong with you?"

A flush crept over his father's face. "Ah, geez. I know that. I'm sorry. She just . . . *I'm* just—"

"You just, nothing," Gloria growled out. She lowered back into her seat, her stiff jawline and her narrowed eyes letting her displeasure be known. "Don't ever let me hear you talk like that again. I'm horrified." The frown pursing his stepmother's mouth, along with the hangdog look his father now sported, had Cord almost feeling sorry for the man. He'd brought it on himself, though. Cord didn't know what his dad had been thinking.

Cord went back to the text he'd spent the last twenty minutes both typing out then subsequently deleting, unsure what had him dragging his feet to get things moving with the lawyer. Meanwhile, Gloria picked up a magazine and, with a slight turn of her body, made her intention to ignore her husband clear. His dad sat in morose silence. Occasionally he'd toss out a long side-eye at Gloria, obviously hoping she'd relent and cut him a break.

Cord chuckled to himself, enjoying the time with the two of them, even if the current moment was tense. He'd been glad to see them both seemingly back to their old selves that morning.

"Poopsie . . ." his dad mumbled a few minutes later, and Cord's gaze shot back up from his phone. *Poopsie?*

Good Lord.

He had the sudden urge to be anywhere but there.

"Do not talk to me, Max Wilde." Gloria licked the tip of her finger and turned the page. "I'm not finished being upset with you yet."

Cord snickered, unable to hold the sound in, then before he

could get himself into trouble along with his dad, he rose and moved to the opposite side of the room. Plus, the distance would put him out of earshot of any more "Poopsies" his dad might toss out.

There were only two other people in the waiting room, so he found a bare spot of wall between a set of vacant chairs and leaned back. Pulling his phone back up, this time he didn't even try to send his friend a message. Instead, he tapped in Maggie's name.

He hadn't heard anything from her since dropping her off at the school that morning.

But then, he'd only dropped her off an hour and a half ago. She had a classroom full of third graders to attend to, so he would be the furthest thing from her mind. Or more aptly, he was regularly the furthest thing from her mind. Unfortunately, the same couldn't be said for him.

Her feet and ankles had been swelling again that morning.

She'd also looked tired.

He thumbed out a message.

You making it okay? Are you staying off your feet? It'll be a couple of hours between dad's appointment with his surgeon and the one with his prosthetist. Do you need anything? I could bring by lunch.

He lowered his arm before making the mistake of sending it. What was wrong with him today? First, he couldn't make himself send the message he *needed* to send. The one to get the child agreement discussions going. And now he was trying to loom over the very woman who never wanted to speak to him again?

He sighed. His actions made no sense. The baby thing had really thrown him for a loop.

And along with that, he still didn't know how he wanted to proceed. He'd spent the better part of the day before weighing every angle of each of Maggie's requests, but abiding by any of them still felt wrong.

First, she would need the money for the baby. He knew that.

Kids were expensive. And no single mother, especially on a teacher's salary, should be turning down needed funds. Plus, the last thing he wanted was to be the guy who put a woman into a financially difficult situation. Especially when there was an easy solution to keep her from getting to that point.

Then there were her other requests. One which remained a hard no, and the other . . .

He closed his eyes and thumped his head against the wall. He knew it was ridiculous to drag his feet on deleting her number, but what if he needed to get in touch with her at some point? What if she needed to get in touch with him?

He could always go to Erica or Arsula, of course. And vice versa. But that wasn't what she was asking him to agree to.

"Who do you reckon that baby's daddy is, anyway?" His dad spoke loud enough to be heard across the room.

Gloria's head snapped up. *"Max."*

"What? You know people are talking. Trying to figure out why the daddy isn't around to help out."

The other two people in the waiting room had looked up, as well.

"It is *none* of your business," Gloria hissed under her breath. She might have hoped to keep her voice low, but her words easily traveled over to Cord.

"She needs some help is all I'm saying. If not right now, when she's"—his dad's mouth pursed before continuing—"at such a *late* stage of her pregnancy, then she'll definitely need help after bringing the baby home. Mommas don't get a lot of sleep, you know?"

Gloria shook her head, her eyes not meeting her husband's, and Cord didn't say a word. He swallowed back the words that had tried to push their way up and out of him, instead.

I'm that baby's daddy, he'd wanted to proclaim.

Only, *why* would he want to say that?

The fact that Maggie hadn't shared the information with his

family was a good thing. It was the way the situation needed to be handled. He could help Maggie out without them ever having to know . . . and also, without them ever having to look at him with abject disappointment.

However, the idea that Maggie might have been protecting *him* by not telling anyone suddenly didn't sit well. And he wanted to correct it. He wanted to put a stop to any more whispering behind her back. Mostly, though, he wanted to share that the boy wouldn't have to want for anything. Cord would provide as much financial assistance as Maggie would take. He'd even hire additional help for her, if needed.

He also wanted to let his father know that he definitely *would* be getting that grandson he wanted. And that possibly Maggie would be willing to bring the boy over to visit occasionally. She seemed like a reasonable person, and she clearly cared about his dad.

He couldn't say any of that, though. Doing so would be purely selfish on his part. Not to mention, he didn't know if Maggie even wanted anyone knowing the baby was his. Possibly, *that* was the reason she hadn't told anyone. So, instead of opening his mouth and spewing words he could never take back, he lowered his gaze and lifted his hand. It was time to quit stalling and send that message.

As his thumb slid over the screen, however, he managed to hit the Send button for the message to Maggie instead. The follow-up *ding* that came from the text app seemed to ring in his ears. He was an idiot.

He'd kept Maggie close that week so they could work out child agreement issues. So she wouldn't have to worry and stress over money. Not because he felt the need to keep an eye on her. That shouldn't even be on his radar. She could manage on her own, same as she'd been doing for the last seven and a half months. She did *not* need him.

But she sure as hell wouldn't think he believed that after reading his message.

He thumped his head against the wall again. He needed a do-over for the whole day.

"Mr. Wilde?"

Cord, Gloria, and Max all looked toward the nurse as she said his dad's name.

"Right here." Gloria lifted a finger and rose to step behind Max's wheelchair. She still didn't speak to her husband, but her previous frustration seemed to disappear. Instead, her expression now returned to what Cord had witnessed when he'd gone back to the house Saturday with the prescription antibiotic cream.

His dad had finally shared that the prosthesis had been rubbing sores on his leg, and Gloria hadn't taken the news well. She blamed herself for not noticing. She said she'd suspected something was wrong, but she'd never guessed it might be the prosthesis.

They followed the nurse into the connected hallway, Cord muting his phone, and the nurse tossed a smile to each of them.

"How are you doing this morning, Mr. Wilde?" she asked.

"Well, I'm back in this darned chair, so I'm going to go ahead and say not so good."

The nurse, a tall good-looking woman with russet-brown skin, winked at Cord's dad. "Just enjoy the ride, sweetheart. They're probably jealous that it's not you pushing *them* all over the place."

His dad let out a dry chuckle. "We'll go with that story. It sounds better than reality."

The nurse patted him on the shoulder and led the three of them into an exam room, and as she took his dad's vitals, Cord stepped out of the way. His phone buzzed in his pocket, and he crossed his arms over his chest instead of pulling it out. Maggie no doubt thought he was being ridiculous, and he didn't need to see the message to confirm it.

"Everything looks good, Mr. Wilde. Dr. Borgmann will be with you in just a few minutes." The nurse tossed another wink at Cord's dad before leaving, and as the door closed behind her, Cord's phone buzzed again.

He ignored it again. It would just be the reminder that he hadn't read his message.

"I'm still not sure why we had to see Borgmann," his dad grumbled. He'd argued that morning that they only needed to see the prosthetist to get an adjustment. "You're treating the sores, and they're already a lot better."

"True," Cord agreed. "And probably we didn't need to see him. But since I'm not a specialist in this area, I wanted someone else to take a look. Dr. Borgmann sees a lot more of this than I do."

As he'd examined his father's leg again the day before, he'd determined the wound sites weren't as concerning as he'd initially feared. Nothing seemed as if they might be deep enough to allow infection to reach the bone. However, given that would be the last thing they needed, he hadn't wanted to take any chances. He'd called the surgeon over the weekend to fill him in, and he'd agreed when the doctor had suggested his dad come in that morning. Two sets of eyes were always better than one.

His phone buzzed a third time.

"You're going to request a referral to a new physical therapist, right?" Gloria asked.

"Definitely." Cord remained upset about that. No PT worth his salt should have missed this.

"Good." Gloria spoke softly. "And I'll make sure he doesn't skip any more appointments."

Cord sent her a consoling smile, hoping to share without words that no one blamed her, but she only shifted her gaze to her lap. "How about I take him to his appointments this week, Gloria?"

She glanced up. "I can do it."

"Sure. But I don't have a lot else going on anyway." He angled his head and peered down at her. "Will you please let me take him?"

His dad snorted, as if unimpressed with Cord's attempt at charm, but that time, Gloria did return his smile. Cord felt a sense of relief at the sight. His dad needed this woman. Cord might not understand love or why it actually seemed to stick for some people, but he did believe that's what was shared between these two. And he was grateful for it.

When his phone buzzed yet again, he reached for it. It occurred to him that Maggie might actually be having an issue. Had she replied, needing his help?

He motioned with his hand. "I'm going to step into the hall until the doc gets here."

Instead of finding messages from Maggie, however, there were two from his sister.

Nate said you're in town. You're with dad at the orthopedic's office?

Also, I'm still mad at you for not coming home for Mia's first birthday. What a bad uncle. I'm going to teach her to love all my other brothers more.

He couldn't help but smile at the second message. He and his other childless brothers routinely claimed to be the best uncle. Of course, with Nick now about to have his own kids—his wife Harper was the one pregnant with twins—being the best uncle probably would no longer be a top priority for him.

He tapped out a reply.

We just got back to see Borgmann, but he hasn't come in yet. And you might *try* to turn Mia against me, but when Haley sees her Christmas present, I'll definitely remain #1 with her.

He quickly followed with another message.

How are you? Doing okay?

Fat and happy.

She sent an emoji of a pregnant woman along with her message, and the tiny picture made Cord grin even wider. He was so happy for his sister. She'd had a rough time dealing with the crap their mother had dished out when they'd been younger, but her life seemed to be on track now. She'd moved home and married a good man a few years ago; she was an excellent stepmother to eight-year-old Haley, and now she was nearing the end of her second, very healthy pregnancy. He couldn't be prouder of her.

He started typing out another message. **I planned to stop by your office and see you later today. Got to pick up** . . . But he paused before finishing the sentence. Did his sister also know Maggie was at the cabins? Would she try to read something into it like his dad and Nate had?

She likely *did* know, and honestly, he wasn't sure how she'd react. But he hoped she would recognize his actions for what they were. Him simply doing a good deed.

He finished the message.

I planned to stop by and see you later today. Got to pick up Maggie Crowder from the school first, though. She's staying at one of the cabins this week. Messed up her car in the snowstorm Friday.

I heard. And come by anytime. I'll be here. But let me know what's going on with Dad, too. Should I be worried?

No. He just needs an adjustment. I'm being overly cautious, but things look fine. He's already acting more like himself. The pain is less than it was two days ago.

Good.

She then sent another quick message.

I'm glad you came home and checked on him.

This time she followed her message with three heart emojis, and he couldn't help but feel a lump right in the middle of his own heart. He was glad he'd come home, too. He wasn't glad *not* to be at work. Or the reason why he wasn't there. But it seemed right to be in Birch Bay at this moment.

CHAPTER NINE

"*Ohmygod.* I so needed fajitas tonight." Maggie loaded another tortilla with beef and toppings, carefully folding each side of the bread over, then she slid a bite into her mouth. "*Mmm,*" she moaned in pure delight. Fajitas were her favorite.

Erica and Arsula watched from their seats. Maggie could feel their gazes, even though she'd closed her eyes. Her friends had come over for dinner, toting food from their favorite restaurant, and now that the meal was nearing its end, Maggie suspected the grilling she'd been expecting would be forthcoming. Her friends didn't like the idea of her being out at the cabins, especially because she was totally dependent upon Cord for transportation.

"You seriously eat food like you're making love to it these days," Arsula observed. "Like . . . *really.*"

Maggie peeked open one eye. "Leave me alone. It's as close as I get to having sex."

She closed her eye again and finished savoring the flavors. She also thought about sex.

She'd *like* to have sex again. Pregnancy hormones and being single sucked. But even if she had someone interested in getting naked with her—and who she'd currently be willing to let *see* her naked—she wasn't sure how comfortably the deed could be accomplished with her gigantic soccer-ball belly in the way. So, if all she could manage was excellent food and even better company, she'd take that. Happily.

"Well, *I* had sex last night," Arsula announced while also loading up another tortilla. "In the car inside the garage. We couldn't even wait until we got in the house." Arsula and Jaden had purchased a home together a couple of months before, and from what Maggie understood, they regularly christened every square inch of it.

"How is that news?" she mumbled around another bite.

"Because while out for dinner, we also set a date."

Maggie and Erica halted, both with hands lifted to their mouths, before the meaning behind Arsula's words clicked. She and Jaden had set a wedding date.

Eyes going wide, all three of them erupted into squeals.

"Congratulations!" Erica shouted. She held her arms up, as did Maggie, both of them reaching for a hug, but neither having the energy to climb out of their seat to get one. Arsula laughed.

She rose from her chair. "You two are hilarious with your baby bellies."

"We're hilariously enormous." Erica smirked.

Arsula leaned down to hug Erica first, before turning to Maggie.

"When's the big date?" Maggie asked as Arsula returned to her seat.

A huge grin flashed across her face. "May twentieth."

"Of next year?" Maggie quizzed. She'd thought they were going to wait longer.

"Yes." Arsula nodded. Her teeth briefly pressed into her bottom lip, as if in attempt to contain the uncontrollable smile. "We decided there's really no reason to wait. We love each other. We already have a house together. We're talking about getting a dog. So it only seemed logical to go ahead and take the next step."

Erica grinned back at her. "Well, I, for one, will simply say thank you for not doing something crazy like deciding you want to get married in the next couple of weeks." She looked down at her nearly eight-and-a-half-month-pregnant belly. "Because, honey, I love you and all, but I would *not* want to walk down an aisle looking like this. For *anyone*. Nor be seen in any wedding photos."

Arsula giggled. "Of course I wouldn't do that to you." She took in Maggie, as well. "To *either* of you. Plus, we want to do this right. We want the whole romance of planning a wedding and all the fun that leads up to it." She paused before continuing, the smile remaining on her lips. "It's going to be out at the orchard."

Maggie sat up straighter. "You're getting married in the barn?"

"Yes." Arsula glowed. "I already have my first retreat set up at the house for next fall." Arsula was an intuitive life coach who had a knack for dream reading. "So, we thought we'd go ahead and enjoy the spoils of the new lodge in May, as well. We plan to rent it out for the wedding. We'll use the lodge and the cabins for our wedding party and out-of-town guests, then we'll do pictures both at the barn and in the section of the orchard that was the least hit with the freeze. Hopefully it'll be a normal spring next year, and the trees will be in full bloom that weekend." She sighed, the sound light and dreamy. "It's going to be so romantic."

Maggie and Erica smiled with her.

"Don't forget about the bees," Erica eventually drawled. "Bees pollinate the flowers, you know. They should make for some excellent outtakes with the pictures." She winked at Arsula, but the teasing couldn't bring their friend down.

Maggie reached across the table and squeezed Arsula's hand. "I'm so happy for you, hon. You're going to make a beautiful bride."

"And you two will be gorgeous bridesmaids."

All three of them sighed, each leaning back in their chair, and the remnants of dinner were forgotten.

Maybe this was why her friends had decided to come over tonight, and not because of Cord. It had likely been Arsula's idea. Maggie was thrilled they were getting to celebrate together.

"Okay." Erica suddenly pushed back up, shoving her leftovers to the side. She propped both elbows on the table, looking very intense about whatever it was she was about to say, and Maggie eyed the move jealously. There was no way she could lean that far forward. And certainly no way she could stretch her arms over her stomach in a similar fashion. At least, not without letting her belly droop down between her knees.

She frowned. She wished she were cute and fit in her pregnancy like Erica. Heck, even Harper, who carried twins, wasn't that much larger than Maggie. Or, at least, she hadn't been the last time Maggie had run into her. But that had been over a month ago. Harper's doctor put her on bed rest at the end of October.

"Enough about the wedding," Erica declared. "At least for the time being. We'll have plenty of time later to discuss *all* the ideas." She tossed Arsula another grin, her dimples flashing. But as quickly as the smile appeared, it disappeared. In its place appeared a solemn nod she shared only with Arsula, and the move sent an immediate streak of warning down Maggie's spine.

Her friends turned to face her.

"Now, tell us what's going on with you and Cord," Arsula instructed.

Maggie didn't move. Nor did she show any reaction. She'd reached for another bite of rice, but she hadn't yet lifted the fork to her mouth. Obviously, she'd cleared her friends of checking up on her way too soon. "Nothing is going on with me and Cord." She looked from one woman to the other. "I told you before. I ran off the road. Cord came along and helped me out, and now my car is being worked on."

She'd spoken to Erica about it again at the school the day before. The other woman had yet to take off for maternity leave, so they still saw each other every day. And Arsula had called Sunday afternoon once she'd learned what was going on.

"Cord suggested I stay here to save money thanks to the fact that I'll now have a car repair bill coming. And since Nate and Megan agreed . . ." Maggie finished with a shrug before cramming the bite of rice between her lips. She hated that she'd never felt she could confide in her friends about that weekend. She would love to unload her worries on them.

"You should stay with us," Arsula determined. "I know you don't want to be underfoot at Erica's, so stay with me."

Maggie pulled a face. "And then what? Have to worry about walking in on you and Jaden doing the nasty every time I turn around?" She shook her head. "No, thanks."

"We could keep it to a minimum."

Maggie snorted before asking, "How?" She reached for one of the remaining chips. "By doing it in the garage all week?"

Erica giggled, and Arsula fired a look her way. "You're not helping."

"I can't help it. She makes a valid point."

Maggie nibbled on her chip.

"But seriously, Mags." Erica tugged the bag of chips around so she could eat from it, too. "You staying out here with him . . . this doesn't feel right. It doesn't feel 'safe' for your mental health." She'd said similar things over the last two days.

"I'm not *staying* with him," Maggie reminded them. She looked around the cabin, making it a point to peer into each corner. "Do you see the man hiding in here anywhere?"

"Don't be a smart aleck," Arsula retorted. "You know what we mean. You're stuck out here without a car. You're relying on him to take you wherever you need to go."

"So what? He's a good guy, right? Haven't I heard both of you say that before?"

She'd definitely heard Erica say those words. And though Maggie knew that Arsula *did* think Cord was a decent guy, Arsula was also aware of the baggage he carried. She'd determined some time ago—the night she'd first heard Maggie mention how yummy she'd always thought him to be—that Cord "wasn't for her." She said her ability to know such information went along with her intuitive side. And possibly she was right. Which would matter if Maggie were trying to "be" with Cord long term. But she wasn't. She was just having his baby.

"He is a good guy," Erica agreed. "But he also loves 'spending time with women.'" She air-quoted the last part.

"And he's also a guy *you've* spent years crushing on," Arsula added.

Maggie glared at both of them. "He's also a guy who I *don't* have a crush on anymore." Dang it, she'd told them her ill-advised infatuation was gone. Why wouldn't they believe her? "And anyway," she went on. "I have *other* things to think about now. In case you haven't noticed. But also"—she pointed to her belly—"there's this. Do you really think someone looking like I do right now would be the type of girl to turn on someone like Cord?"

"While bored in a cabin in the snow and with you accessible right next door?" Arsula drolled out.

"*Arsula!*" Erica hissed, her brow furrowing. But it was too late. The words had already hit Maggie the wrong way. Tears spilled down her face.

"Oh, crap." Arsula was up and out of her chair in an instant, and she had Maggie wrapped up in her arms. "I'm so sorry," she whispered into Maggie's hair. "That wasn't a slam against you. I promise. You're beautiful, Mags." She pulled back and looked down at her. "I only hope to be half as gorgeous as you if Jaden and I ever have a kid."

That made Maggie cry even more. Arsula was a freaking bombshell. Long wavy hair, curves in all the right places—and none of them even an inch too big. Of course she would be more gorgeous than Maggie as a pregnant woman. Even if she were to carry triplets and need a shopping cart positioned underneath her belly simply to have the ability to walk around.

Everyone looked better as a pregnant woman than her.

"*Mags,*" Erica pleaded when Maggie didn't even try to rein in her tears. She reached over and captured Maggie's hand. "She didn't mean anything by it."

"I know," Maggie assured her, but her tears didn't let up. And truth be told, she didn't want to do anything to stop them. She needed a good cry. "And I'm not mad. I promise."

She just needed to shed some stress.

"Please quit crying," Arsula begged. She pulled her chair over to sit beside Maggie, then she once again reached her arms out for a hug. Maggie leaned into her and appreciated the moment. All three of them had been so busy over the last few months. So focused on the current and upcoming changes in their lives. They hadn't had moments like this nearly often enough.

"I'm really not mad," she said again, the words still coming out between her sniffles. "I know you didn't mean to say I was ugly or that Cord would be settling if he came on to me."

"Mags." Arsula stroked her hand over Maggie's hair. "*No.* Please stop it. I didn't mean any of that."

"I know. But the fact is . . . Cord *wouldn't* want me. Why would he? Just like he doesn't want his—"

She clamped her mouth shut, her eyes going wide. Oh, crap. She'd almost spilled it.

"Like he doesn't want his what?" Arsula questioned. She'd pulled back again and was once more peering down at Maggie.

"Nothing." Maggie shook her head. She couldn't think of a single thing to use as a cover.

Her heart rate skyrocketed.

"He doesn't want . . . *what?*" Erica joined in. Both of her friends now wore thoroughly confused expressions with just a hint of anger simmering under the surface. It was as if they were ready to be mad on her behalf, if needed. They just didn't know why they'd need to yet.

"Nothing," Maggie said again. She reached for another chip, but Erica tugged the bag away before she could get one. Maggie frowned at her.

"Has something already happened?" Erica questioned. "During those two nights you *did* spend at his cabin, perhaps?"

"What?" Maggie shook her head. "No. Guys, really. Of course not. Cord has been a perfect gentleman."

Of course, there *had* been that moment during the middle of Saturday night when he'd been massaging her feet. Not that he'd been doing it for any reason other than to be nice.

No matter the reason, though, it hadn't felt like pure nicety from her point of view.

She didn't mention any of that, though. Nor did she bring up the way he kept doing other things for her. Like showing up at her door that morning before she could make it out to the truck herself. He'd relented when she'd insisted on using the stool to get into the truck again, but he'd held her hand the entire time.

"Okay." The look now in Arsula's eyes indicated she was rolling another idea around in her head. "Then, has something happened in the *past* that we aren't aware of? Like . . . maybe way back at Erica's wedding?"

Maggie shook her head. "I barely even spoke to him at the wedding." She'd tried to, but he'd avoided her. She'd wanted to do that night what they'd done all weekend in April.

"Some other time, then?" Erica added, and this time Maggie sighed. She needed them to drop it.

"Please." She looked from one to the other. "Can we just stop this? What other time could there possibly have been? I spent the summer being pregnant. Did you forget that? And until now, I haven't even seen Cord in months."

Erica suddenly shifted her gaze so that she looked straight at Arsula. The line of her mouth went hard.

"What?" Arsula asked. The two of them completely ignored her.

"I saw her talking to him during the party at The Cherry Basket," Erica shared.

"I was not." The words came out too fast. Maggie tended to do that when she lied. She'd talked to Cord at every opportunity she'd been able to create that day.

"Right." Arsula lifted a finger as if it would help her to think. "I think I saw her helping him during cleanup." She turned to Maggie. "Is that right? You were helping him at the end of the day?"

Sweat formed between Maggie's breasts. These two were like a dog with a bone. "Okay, fine," she relented. Maybe by giving them a few details, they would move on to another subject. "I might have helped him a little bit. I mean, I think we took down a strand of the lights together. But really, that's all. Then I went off with . . ." Her throat squeezed tight, cutting off her words. "I went . . ." she tried again, but didn't make it any further, so she gave up.

Tears once again threatened, and the back of her throat ached. She didn't want to lie to her friends any longer. It was wrong. And it was so very hard to do. She'd lied to them the first time when she'd shared news of her pregnancy. They'd asked who the father was, and she'd made up a good-looking out-of-towner whom she'd met during the party. She'd claimed to have run into him again right before leaving for the day, and then one thing led to another.

Of course, neither of them had been able to recall seeing anyone like she'd described.

She'd then carried her fabrication forward to any other time the subject had come up. Her friends occasionally wondered if she was certain the mystery man didn't want to be a part of her son's life. Or if she didn't want to push for child support, even if he chose to remain an absentee father. But she didn't want to lie to them anymore.

She also wanted to be able to *talk* to them. She wanted to tell her friends that it completely broke her heart for Cord to refuse to have anything to do with his son. Because what if he was right and she *wasn't* a good mother?

What if it turned out that she was like *her* mother?

The tears that had threatened, now flowed free. She simply couldn't do it anymore. But the thing was, she also understood that she didn't *have* to do it. Because from the expressions now on her friends' faces, they'd put two and two together. Mixtures of both shock and wonder stared back at her.

"I'm sorry," she whispered. Her chest felt as if it might rip open with sobs.

"Why didn't you tell us?" Arsula reached for her again.

"Why has he refused to help?" Erica added.

Maggie shook her head, unable to force out any more words, and when Erica also scooted her chair over and wrapped Maggie in a hug, Maggie let her friends take the burden. They didn't push for additional details. Not yet. They simply let her cry it out. And when all the tears had finally been shed, when the pressure in her chest eased for the first time in a very long time, Maggie filled her friends in on everything.

She told them how she'd tried to contact Cord, and how he wouldn't reach back out to her. She apologized again for lying and explained why she'd made up the story of another man—she hadn't wanted to put them in an uncomfortable situation with Gabe and Jaden. She also told them about how, now that Cord *did* know, he wanted nothing whatsoever to do with the baby.

What she didn't go into were her own fears. She was too exhausted for that.

Instead, she relied on the knowledge that her friends would be there for her if, and when, she wanted to talk about anything more.

"I'm going to be in the delivery room with you," Arsula announced. And unlike the previous times she'd made that very offer, this time Maggie didn't argue. She hadn't wanted to take that moment from Arsula and Jaden. The first time to witness a birth seemed the type of experience couples should share, if at all possible. But she also didn't want to do this alone.

She didn't know if she was *strong* enough to do it alone.

She nodded. "Will you also take me to the doctor tomorrow?"

"Of course," Arsula answered without hesitation. Whatever Maggie needed, her friends would be there.

She'd mentioned the appointment to Cord, of course, since her car wouldn't yet be ready. And Cord had assured her that running her by the medical offices would be no problem. But she didn't *want*

Cord taking her to her doctor's appointment. She no longer wanted to be anywhere near the man.

His driving her to work had proved more difficult than she'd imagined. The time had been spent with small talk and them acting as if there was nothing more between them than being temporary neighbors. He'd been polite and courteous, and she'd hated every minute of it.

There had also been no additional talk of lawyers. When she'd brought it up that afternoon, he'd replied that he was still considering the best path to take, so he hadn't yet called his friend. Then he'd changed the subject.

She scrubbed the drying tears from her cheeks, taking in the expectant expressions on both her friends' faces, then she made another executive decision. She would call her own lawyer. Screw waiting on Cord.

She turned to Arsula. "Would you pick me up for work in the morning, as well?"

CHAPTER TEN

"Hey, Doc, thanks so much for seeing me." Cord held out his hand to Dr. Hamm, the man who'd been their family physician since Cord was a kid.

"Of course." Hamm clasped Cord's hand in a firm shake, then motioned into his office. The two of them entered the room together, Hamm having just come from an exam room, then Hamm continued to the opposite side of the desk. He lowered into his chair, and Cord followed suit. It was Wednesday afternoon, and there were still several patients waiting to be seen, so Cord wouldn't take up much of the doctor's time. "I can always spare time for you," the doc added, his smile genuine. "How are you doing? How's Billings?"

Ever since Doc Hamm had found out Cord intended to attend medical school, he'd taken a special interest. "It's good." Cord gave the perfunctory answer, not letting the fact that he was currently on a pressured leave alter his answer. "The practice is good. Patients are good."

Everything was fucking good, he thought. Only, he'd recently killed a patient.

"Fantastic." The doc's voice boomed. "I always knew you'd make a success of yourself."

Cord managed a nod. He didn't exactly feel successful. "Thanks, Doc. And seriously, I won't keep you long." Cord glanced behind him to the still-open door before leaning forward in his seat. "I just need to know that Jay Tatum knows his stuff."

Cord had taken his father to the new physical therapist earlier that day, and though everything Cord witnessed while there had indicated the man ran a top-notch clinic, he didn't want to take any chances.

Doc Hamm nodded. "Yes, sir. Tatum is the real deal. He's probably who we should have gotten your dad set up to see to begin with. I'd never heard any concerns with the previous PT, or I would have spoken up when Borgmann recommended him."

The fringe of white hair sweeping over the doc's forehead seemed to droop toward his eyebrows as the man's face furrowed.

"Max has been through a lot," he added. "Backsliding because of poor care isn't an issue he should have to deal with."

"I agree. And it's an issue I'll make certain doesn't happen again." Cord said the words with the assurance he felt. However, what he didn't know was how he'd manage to be on top of everything while also making up for lost time once he returned to work.

He'd get it sorted out, though. He wouldn't let his dad sit here in pain, feeling too guilty to ask for help.

"And I'll be sure to check in with him more often, as well," the doctor replied. Early days after the amputation, Doc had stopped by the house regularly. He'd also been diligent about keeping Cord up to date between visits home.

"I'd appreciate that, too, Doc. I appreciate everything you do." Right after the accident, Cord had worked with Hamm to find a neurologist who was the best fit for his dad's Parkinson's. At the same time, he'd found out the man had previously been forced to deal with the diagnosis, for the most part, on his own. Cord's dad hadn't wanted to worry the family, so he'd held on to his secret until the accident no longer made that possible. "I'll let you get back to it now."

Cord rose to leave, and they walked out of the room together, parting ways at the end of the hall. As Doc moved on to his next patient, Cord found himself standing just outside the office, in the main walkway of the medical plaza. On the opposite side of the lobby sat the Women's Pavilion. Which was where Maggie should be right now.

Which was *not* the reason he'd chosen *now* to stop by Hamm's office.

He remained in the hallway, not letting himself move toward the lobby. Maggie hadn't wanted him to take her to work that morning. Additionally, she'd changed her mind about him bringing her to her appointment today. He'd discovered a text when he'd stepped out of the shower—which had proven that her phone *did* still receive texts; she'd never replied to the one he'd sent on Monday.

When he'd hurriedly pulled on clothes and gone next door, he'd found her cabin already empty. So, he'd spent the morning checking in on Harper, instead. Her blood pressure had been up, but she also had an appointment with her OB today. Therefore, he didn't let himself worry. Her doctor would be on top of things.

Maggie, though . . . he couldn't keep from worrying. Why had she suddenly pushed him away? What had her doctor said during her appointment? Was *her* blood pressure still okay?

"Cord."

His name came from behind him, and when he turned, he found Arsula striding his way.

He grinned at his brother's fiancée. "Hey, gorgeous." Cord had met Arsula several months before his brother had, and they'd become easy friends.

"Don't 'hey, gorgeous,' me." She jabbed a finger in his chest.

"Ow." He pulled back. "What's your issue?"

"My issue?" Her hands went to her hips. "What's *your* issue is the better question. Or, more accurately, what kind of a *jerk* are you?"

"I'm not . . ." And then a sinking feeling settled. He'd seen Arsula and Erica over at the cabin the night before, so he'd assumed one of them had given her a ride to school. Likely, it had been Arsula since she was here now.

Did her attitude mean that Maggie had shared *more* than simply a car ride with her friend?

"I'm not a jerk, Arsula." He couldn't keep the annoyance from his voice. Had Maggie told her about the baby?

He wouldn't bring the subject up in the event that wasn't what had her so upset, but his gut told him he was on the right track.

"I disagree with your assessment," she tossed back. "You're apparently nothing more than a selfish, low-life, horn—" She snapped her mouth closed as a man and a woman approached, passing them in the hallway, then she dragged him over to the opposite wall. "You got her pregnant," she accused. "You got her pregnant, and you can't be bothered to do anything about it."

"Excuse me?" Anger now pulsed through him. "Not do anything about it? I don't know what she told you, but I've offered whatever amount for child support she needs. All she has to do is name a figure, and it's hers. Are you crazy, Arsula? Of course, I wouldn't leave her stranded like that. I wouldn't do that to any woman."

She snarled. "It's *your* baby, Cord. You're leaving your *baby* stranded. As *well* as Maggie."

"I am not." His jaw tensed. "I'll see to it the child has everything he needs if she'll just let me. *Everything*," he gritted out. Including a parent who didn't abuse him, he silently added. "Plus, why the *fuck* did she tell you about it? She promised me she wouldn't."

"Well, I guess her friendship with us comes before your"—her distaste shone bright as she looked him up and down—"*whatever* she has with you."

He held a hand up, his temper rising. "Us?" he asked.

"*Exactly.*" A sneer stretched her lips. "And trust me, Erica did *not* take it as well as I did." She jabbed him in the chest again. "You never should have laid a hand on her."

Cord wanted to ask whether Maggie should have laid a hand on him. Because that weekend had come about purely due to her. He didn't say that, though. The details were none of Arsula's business. "We used protection," he said instead. "We're two consenting adults, neither of which set out to be in this situation."

"Well, you may not have set out to be here, but you're right smack in the middle of it now. And the question is"—she glared at him, her dark eyes fiery—"why would you turn your back on your own son? What kind of poor excuse for a human being are you?"

The kind his mother had raised, he wanted to reply.

The kind who not only didn't save his mother when doing so had been his one purpose in the family, but the kind who'd also turned his back on a patient for the sole reason that he didn't like how she treated her children.

He was the kind of human being who had already made far too many mistakes in his life, and who didn't plan on putting himself in the position of making more. At least not at the level being in his son's life would allow.

"It's none of your business, Arsula." He wanted to step away. He wanted to walk out of the building and never look back. Get in his truck and drive to Billings at breakneck speeds. "Nor is it my brothers' business. She shouldn't have told you."

Some of her steam evaporated. "She bawled her eyes out to us last night, Cord." Her own eyes seemed to glisten now. "She hates that you don't want to be in the baby's life. Take away the fact that you won't be around to help her out, but you won't be there for your *son*. Why? I know your childhood was rough. That you—"

"No," he bit the word out. "You don't get to talk to me about my childhood. That's off-limits."

She persisted. "I've talked about it with Jaden. I understand how she was. I get it."

"I don't care *who* you've talked to. Talking about it with *me* is not allowed!"

He did step away from her then, but instead of heading to the front doors and exiting the building, he strode toward the Women's Pavilion. He wasn't mad at Maggie for sharing the information. Not logically. He knew she had a right to talk with her friends, especially concerning matters that would make her bawl her eyes out.

He shook his head at the thought and tried not to picture it. He'd never wanted to make Maggie cry.

But damn, he sure wished she *hadn't* talked. He wished . . .

He stopped walking again, once more simply standing in the middle of the hallway, his hands clenched into fists. He wished so many things, the least of which being that he was the type of man who could embrace the idea of having a child. Embrace, instead of wanting to run.

"Cord?" This time it was Maggie's voice he heard. And that voice instantly soothed him.

"Maggie." He brought his gaze to hers. She looked good today.

"What are you doing here?"

She stood in front of him in a pale-pink, long-sleeved top covered in lace and a pair of dark-washed jeans. She looked healthy and happy, and all Cord could think about was her crying her eyes out the night before. Because of him.

"I came to get you." He blinked at his own words at the same time her brows shot up.

"I'm . . ." She glanced over his shoulder, and he realized Arsula had followed him across the lobby. "I'm not ready to go." She spoke the sentence slowly. "I have another appointment to get to."

Worry prickled at him. "Is something wrong?" He looked at her belly.

"No. It's not for the baby." One hand went to her stomach, and again, her gaze flicked over his shoulder. A small line creased her forehead as her eyes shifted back. "I'm meeting with a lawyer, Cord. Arsula will make sure I get back to the cabin."

Her answer surprised him even more than his own statement had. "A lawyer?" This time it was he who looked at Arsula. "Why?" He glanced between the two women, his tone going flat.

"Because *you* apparently *haven't*," Arsula told him. He could feel her anger simmering again.

"I *haven't* because I'm still thinking about how I want to proceed," he told her.

"Are you thinking about *proceeding* by being in the baby's life?" she tossed back.

"Arsula," Maggie pleaded.

The other woman snapped her mouth closed and looked away from Cord, and he did the same.

He turned back to Maggie. "We talked about this yesterday, Maggie," he coaxed.

"No. We didn't. *I* tried to talk about it yesterday, and you averted the conversation. So, *I'm* handling it today. You don't want to be in the baby's life, and like I told you before, I'm fine with that." She shot a hard look at Arsula when the other woman made a growling noise in the back of her throat. Then she turned back to Cord. "That's your decision, and I can respect it. But my decision is that anymore 'thinking' about things ends here. There's no need to wait."

It suddenly felt as if a booming clock were ticking inside his head. "I'm not going to walk away and not provide support." He spoke softly, aware that anyone nearby could hear them. "That's unfair to you. Unfair to the baby."

"Then fine, I can deal with that. You can pay support."

Relief washed through him.

"But *I* won't be taking any of the money directly," she added.

Arsula stepped up beside them, but she didn't speak.

"What I *will* do," Maggie went on, "and this is nonnegotiable, is open a college fund. If the money is hanging you up that much, then we'll settle on an amount—and I'll even let you decide how much— and you can transfer the money into the fund each month." She licked her lips before continuing. "Then . . . you sign away your rights. Because this is *my* child, Cord." Her voice shook as she continued. "Not yours."

He nodded, unable to agree verbally. He did *not* want to do that.

At all. However, he could also see how important the issue was for her. He could still make arrangements for someone to keep an eye on the baby. She wouldn't have to know.

"And then . . ." She paused once more, and when Cord got the impression she was about to start crying again, he finished for her. "Then we never speak to each other again."

His voice ended with a shake of its own, and when she nodded in agreement, he nodded back. Neither of them said anything else because really, what else was there to say. But neither did they look away. They just stood there. Staring at each other.

At least until Arsula's words pulled their attention. "Crap on a cracker," she whispered.

Maggie jolted. "What?" She looked at her friend.

Arsula looked at him.

"*What?*" he asked, bemused.

"*Crap,*" Arsula said again, this time drawing the word out to make it two syllables. But before she could explain herself, both her phone and his dinged with an incoming text.

Arsula looked first, then her face blanched of color.

She held her screen up to them. "They're rushing Harper into an emergency C-section. She suddenly started bleeding."

CHAPTER ELEVEN

MAGGIE SAT IN THE SURGICAL WAITING ROOM WITH HARPER'S FAMILY, as well as every member of the Wilde family, her hands clenched in her lap and her panic steadily escalating. Harper could die while delivering the babies. The babies could die before they even got out. Anything could happen in that delivery room, and there wasn't a thing Harper or Nick could do to stop it!

She fervently hoped everyone would be okay.

She also wished that she'd taken Arsula's offer of using her car and gotten away before ever stepping foot inside this room.

When the texts had come in, Arsula had immediately held her keys out to Maggie, telling her to take her car and get to her other appointment. But Maggie had rejected the idea. She couldn't think about lawyers at a time like this. Harper was being rushed into surgery. So instead of leaving, she'd hurried along behind Arsula and Cord, weaving their way through the corridors that connected the medical offices to the hospital, and once here, she hadn't been able to make herself walk away.

She couldn't go anywhere until she made sure Harper was okay. That the babies survived.

She wasn't super close to either Harper or Nick, but even so, she'd felt a sense of connectedness over the last several months simply due to the fact that Harper, too, would be delivering a Wilde baby. *Babies.* With her, Erica, Dani, and Maggie all pregnant—even though Maggie was the only one to know that her baby would be a part of their family, too—she'd not been able to distance herself like she probably should have.

She'd kept up with how Max was doing in his recovery. She'd checked in on progress with Dani and Harper, though usually those checks came via either Erica or Arsula. And she'd basically watched the family from a safe distance, all while wishing she could be a part of it. And now there she was.

And there she wished she wasn't.

So many people were in the room now. They'd all converged, almost immediately. And all of them were there for each other, all having someone to rely on. While she sat by herself. Even Arsula and Erica seemed to have forgotten she'd come along. Maggie could understand that, though. Harper *was* family for them. And Harper was in danger. They *needed* to be sitting with the others, both giving and receiving comfort. And while they did that, Maggie would sit over here, spiraling in worry and wondering if *anyone* would show up for her when she delivered.

"Are you okay?" She looked to her right to find Dani approaching. She'd stepped away from her husband and their two daughters. "You look flushed," Dani added. She held the back of her hand toward Maggie's forehead, a questioning look in her eyes.

"I'm just worried," Maggie explained, but she leaned toward the other woman, letting Dani's cool fingers touch Maggie's overheated skin. "I don't always do hospitals well."

That was an understatement.

Dani lowered to the chair beside her. "Do you want me to call someone for you? Or I'm sure—"

"No." Maggie stopped her before she came up with a way to leave that would make it awkward to refuse. "Arsula offered to let me use her car, but I'd like to stay and make sure Harper's okay. If you guys don't mind, of course."

Dani studied her thoughtfully. "Of course we don't mind. You're welcome to stick around as long as you'd like. And thank you for caring."

Maggie nodded. "Sure."

Dani's blue eyes, so similar to Cord's, continued to peer back at her. "But are you sure you're okay? You're breathing as if your heart rate may be up." She nodded to Maggie's belly. "We don't need another emergency today. How about I see if a nurse can check you out?"

"I'll check her." Cord's voice came from directly behind Dani, and Dani and Maggie both looked up. He hadn't been in the room two minutes before. Instead, he'd disappeared through a Staff Only door as soon as they'd arrived, and Maggie hadn't seen him again until now.

"How's Harper?" Dani rose from her seat.

"She's doing good." The rest of the family had stopped talking, and all of them now paid rapt attention to Cord. "One of the placentas pulled away from the uterine wall," he explained, and several of the people in the waiting room sucked in sharp breaths, including Maggie. A placental abruption could be bad for both baby and mom.

"They're starting the C-section now," Cord went on. "So, we should hear more soon."

"Thank goodness they got her here in time," someone muttered, but Maggie wasn't yet convinced. She wouldn't believe it until she heard that all survived.

Dani's gaze suddenly jerked to the other side of the room, as if just remembering she no longer sat with her husband and kids. Then she looked down and offered Maggie a gentle smile.

"She's too flushed," she told Cord. "Make sure she's alright?"

"Of course."

Dani walked away, and though Cord didn't immediately take the chair his sister had vacated, he studied Maggie. Maggie didn't look up at him. She knew he was mad at her. And why wouldn't he be? She'd let Arsula ambush him earlier.

The argument out in the lobby had caught her by surprise. Arsula and Erica had promised to keep the information to themselves the night before, at least temporarily. They'd sworn they wouldn't say anything to Cord and would leave the matter in her hands. But clearly, that hadn't been the case on Arsula's part. Maggie just wished she knew what else had been said before she'd shown up.

"They figured it out on their own," she muttered. "I didn't tell them."

"I don't give a crap about that."

She looked up then, and he lowered to the seat.

"At least, not at the moment," he clarified. "I have too many other things to worry about right now." He reached for her wrist to check her pulse. "What did the doctor say earlier? Dani is right, you're too flushed."

Maggie swallowed. "She said I was fine. Everything is still on track."

"The swelling?" He reached a hand down to one of her ankles, and two fingers slipped under the hem of her jeans. He probed at the puffy skin.

"It's still there," she grumbled, and one corner of his mouth quirked up.

"Blood pressure?"

"Fine."

"Any dilation?"

She started in surprise. He truly had gone into doctor mode. She just hoped he wasn't about to check her *there*. But then again . . .

When he repeated his question with nothing more than a piercing look, she pushed the inappropriate thoughts aside. She shook her head. "Closed up tight like a chastity belt," she confirmed, and once again his mouth twitched.

"Is it a panic attack then?" He leaned in, his back to his family, and his question for her ears only.

She nodded in reply.

Few people knew she struggled with the disorder, but he'd figured it out almost immediately Friday night. She peered into his eyes. "I have it under control, though."

"You're remembering to breathe?"

"No. I'm sitting here without doing that. Thanks for the reminder."

This time it wasn't simply a twitch at the corner of his mouth, but a full-blown smile. "That's why I like you, Maggie." He was still leaning in. Still whispering. "Because you're damned funny and because you make me smile."

The Staff Only door opened then, and everyone in the room popped to attention. Nate, Gabe, and Cord stood. The person who'd come out wasn't for them, however, and as spines once again relaxed and expectant faces morphed back to grim concern, Cord returned to Maggie. He again positioned himself in a way that blocked his family from her view, and when he dropped one hand to the armrest between them, he let one finger slip lower. That finger stroked over the lace covering her arm, and a whisper of a shiver danced through her.

"What Harper is going through is scary." He spoke softly.

"I know that," she replied in kind.

"But it's not going to happen to you."

She couldn't pull her eyes off him. How could he even say that? "You have no clue what's going to happen during my delivery, Cord. No one does."

"Okay. That's fair. But the chance of placental abruption is low for a standard pregnancy. You know that, right? It's more likely with multiples. Complications of any kind are rare as long as the mother is healthy. And you keep telling me you're healthy."

"I am."

His finger kept stroking.

"But that doesn't mean something couldn't happen," she continued. "Even if the entire pregnancy goes perfectly, bad things can occur." Her breaths grew shallow. "Things that can't always be predicted. *You* know *that*. People die during delivery, Cord. People come out changed, different than when they went in. *Babies*"—she pressed her lips together, not wanting to imagine the worst, but she couldn't keep from it—"they don't always . . ."

"Hey." The single word came out hard and clipped, and when Cord touched her under the chin, she realized she'd looked down at her lap. He shook his head. "*You* are going to be fine, Maggie. I'm going to make sure of it."

"*How?*" This time it was her with the hard, clipped question.

His eyes begged for understanding. But she *didn't* understand. How *could* he make sure of it?

"You can't say that, Cord. You won't be there. You won't be able to do anything."

~

CORD DIDN'T LET his own panic show. Maggie's words were spot on. He *wouldn't* be able to help. Even if things could be different and he did intend to be in his son's life, he still wouldn't be around for the delivery. He lived in Billings. She lived here.

He knew that wasn't what she needed to hear, though. And honestly, it wasn't what he wanted to think about. But what could he say? He'd already promised something he couldn't uphold.

"Wilde family?"

Everyone jumped to their feet except Maggie and Cord. They moved only so much as to glance over at the nurse who'd stepped through the door. His and Harper's entire family now waited eagerly for news, but Cord couldn't bring himself to his feet. How was he supposed to walk away from this woman? From the baby growing inside her?

How was he supposed to protect them?

"The babies have been born," the nurse announced happily, "and they're doing just fine."

"And Harper?" Nate and Harper's mother questioned at the same time. Nate and Nick were twins, and Cord knew the minutes since the text had come in had been extra tough on him. When one brother hurt, the other always seemed to be in pain right along with him.

The nurse nodded to both of them. "Momma is fine, too. She's got two healthy babies snuggled up to her right now, and her smile is a mile wide."

The crowd sighed in relief.

"And what are they?" Cord's dad asked. "Boys or girls?"

Everyone chuckled.

"I'm sorry, but you're going to have to wait to find that out." The nurse offered a mischievous smile. "Dad asked me not to share the info. He wants to announce it himself."

The nurse disappeared after several "thanks" were offered, and as the door swung closed behind her, Jenna turned to her dad. "So, they're not going to tell us? How will we know if Pops got a grandson or not?"

Gabe rested his hand on his daughter's shoulder. "We'll find out soon enough, kiddo. Uncle Nick is excited. He didn't want to let the nurse have all the fun."

"Well, that wasn't fun at all," Jenna mumbled, and Cord watched as his oldest brother picked his daughter up and propped her on his hip. He then slid his other arm around his very pregnant wife.

"You're right," he told Jenna. "It was exceptionally boring." He kissed the top of Erica's head. "But sometimes, boring is exactly what the world needs."

Everyone went back to waiting, the level of chatter in the room inching to a higher, less-stressed pitch, and Cord returned his attention to Maggie. She'd scooted to the edge of her seat.

Cord stood. "What do you need?" He held out a hand to help her. "I can get it for you."

She grasped his hand and pulled herself up, an annoyed look passing over her face. "If I need anything, I can get it for myself. Other than to get out of a chair alone, apparently." She frowned down at the offending item. "But I don't *need* anything. I'm going to get Arsula's keys and take myself home."

The proclamation surprised him. "Why?"

She shot him a look. "Because Harper and the babies are fine. Which is the whole reason I stuck around."

She grabbed her purse and coat from the seat beside her, and he shocked himself with the realization that he didn't want her to leave. She'd been there along with the rest of them. Didn't she want to see the end result?

"You aren't going to wait and see the babies?" he asked.

"No." She shook her head as she shrugged into her coat, and when her eyes briefly met his, he saw that they were red-rimmed.

"Mags." He took a step closer. It felt like he was missing something. Snagging her hands in his, he tugged until she looked up. "Stay," he whispered. He could literally stare into her eyes all day. "See the babies," he added. "Then let me take you home."

"I'm not family," she whispered in return. "I don't want to interrupt."

His hand went to her belly, his palm covering the most rounded part of her, and both of them instantly stilled. He stared at the spot where he touched. It was so inappropriate to put his hand on her like that. To not ask, but to instead simply "invade." Yet he couldn't bring himself to pull away. At the same time, she didn't do anything to suggest he should remove his hand, either.

"You *are* family," he urged. He dragged his gaze back up to hers, finding that her eyes had rounded, making her seem as scared as he suddenly felt. "You are because of this one." He nodded down to her belly to make his point. "*Stay.* Meet the new additions. At least learn if we have boys or girls."

The baby moved under his palm then, and he swore his world tipped sideways. He stared at her belly.

"Cord." She said his name so softly that he almost didn't hear. And he most definitely didn't want to look up.

"What?" he replied, his eyes never straying from the baby's continued movements. His breathing turned raspy.

"Your entire family is watching."

CHAPTER TWELVE

THE TICK OF THE TURN SIGNAL SEEMED EXTRA LOUD AS THE TRUCK slowed at the driveway. The silence had now stretched to twenty minutes, and Maggie wasn't sure how much longer she could take it. Immediately following them getting caught with Cord's hand on her belly—and with him standing far too close for someone who should be merely the brother-in-law of a good friend—Nick had burst into the room.

He hadn't been allowed to take anyone back to see the babies yet, not until Harper had been moved out of recovery, but he did have pictures and videos to share. The babies, it turned out, were both girls. Both in the high five-pound range. And both of them had already started trying to feed.

Nick had been euphoric . . . and as Maggie had taken in all the excitement, she'd started crying.

At the sight of her tears, Cord had slid his hand to the middle of Maggie's back. He'd stroked along her spine, clearly intending to soothe, but his touch had only increased the tightness filling Maggie's chest. Being in the middle of such a supportive family made her more aware of what she wouldn't have when she delivered. Her brother had said he'd come down—but he could be working. And her parents lived several hours away. And even if they *could* get away from the demands of their guests in time to be there, she couldn't imagine her mother willing to do so. Her mother hadn't stepped foot in a hospital in twenty-two years.

Maggie understood how unfair it was to let that bother her. Her mom had dealt with a lot. But what Maggie had learned in her twenty-nine years was that logic and emotions didn't always line up.

After sharing that the babies' names would be Ellie and Emma, and once the entire group had gotten a peek at the pictures and videos, Nick had retrieved his cell phone and taken his proud self back to be with Harper. And that's when Maggie and Cord had slipped from the room. They hadn't given anyone time to return to what they'd witnessed before. Instead, Cord had nodded toward the door, silently asking if she wanted to get out of there, and she'd beaten a path out in front of him.

Since then, there had been no speaking. And Maggie wasn't sure what to make of that. Nor did she know what to make of whatever had been going on between them right before Nick appeared.

Cord considered her and their baby part of the family? She wasn't sure what that meant.

He'd also touched her.

He'd touched her *belly*.

And he'd felt their baby move.

She gulped in air. Cord had left his hand on her stomach, the awe of feeling the baby moving obvious from the stunned expression that had washed over his face, and he hadn't seemed to have a clue he'd been doing it right in front of his family.

The moment had been almost intimate. Only, they'd basically had their entire world watching.

She pulled in another deep breath. She had to know what all of that meant. Or if it meant nothing.

The cabins loomed ahead, and nerves caused a hitch in her breath. She couldn't let Cord pull up and her simply get out and go in. By the next time she saw him, he'd be acting like they were nothing more than neighbors again. Like nothing had changed. But it *had* changed. She could feel it. She just couldn't explain it.

"I'm sorry if I was in the way today." It seemed a safe place to start.

"You weren't in the way."

"Good. I enjoyed being there." It had been stressful, but she was glad she'd been a part of it.

Silence returned when she didn't say anything else, and Maggie held in a sigh. What was the man thinking?

He pulled to a stop in front of her cabin, positioning the truck so the passenger door sat closest to the cleared path, and she peered outside. The sun was just about to set on the opposite side of the lake, but its long rays continued to surround them. The snow, usually so bright, glowed warm in the afternoon light. Long shadows from distant pines reached toward them. It was a peaceful spot.

"I also apologize because your family is now going to know about the baby." She slid her hands over the bottom curve of her belly. At least she couldn't take all the blame for that one. Or . . . she couldn't take the blame for the *timing* of it. Erica and Arsula had promised to hold on to the knowledge long enough for her to warn Cord. But now that they'd caught his hand on her . . .

Well, someone was going to talk. There was no doubt in her mind.

"They would have found out anyway." At his statement, Maggie looked over. How would they have found out? *She* hadn't planned to tell them.

Before she could ask, he'd opened his door. He rounded the front of the truck, and by the time she'd gathered up her things, he was there. He always seemed to be there.

He held out an arm, giving her a steady grip as she slid down, then he took her bag from her. "Do you mind if I come in?"

"Not at all."

"Good. I'll start a fire."

She hadn't had a fire going since Nate built one when they'd moved her in on Sunday. Arsula had offered the night before, but then they'd dug into the food . . . and then Maggie had shared about Cord . . . and they'd just never gotten around to it.

"I'd appreciate it," she said now. "I love a fire."

"I remember." He walked beside her, and the silence returned. Maggie gave up trying to fill the void. She could be silent, too.

When they entered the cabin, as had happened the night he'd rescued her, Cord headed for the fireplace. The only differences from then being that he wasn't furious and this cabin was decorated with bears instead of elk.

She shrugged out of her coat, but then Cord turned back around. The fireplace behind him remained dark. Lines seemed to have been carved into his face.

"What did you mean?" he asked her. "At the hospital earlier. You said 'People come out changed, different than when they went in.' You were talking about giving birth. What did you mean?"

Oh, crap. She hadn't realized she'd said that out loud.

She shrugged. "You know, just that sometimes people . . . *change*." She glanced away. Her mother had changed.

"Like who?"

She wasn't sure she wanted to talk about this. Her past had come roaring back at her while she'd been sitting in that waiting room today. The day she'd thought her baby sister would be coming home. The look on her mother's face when she'd returned without a baby.

"Mags." Cord said her name, his voice thick and heavy. It sounded like compassion. It sounded like he cared.

Her hands started to tremble.

"How can I help?" He came back over to her.

"You can't."

"I have to." He stroked the edge of his thumb along her cheekbone, then used one finger to tilt her face up. His eyes held hers. "I can't walk away and not try to fix this. That's not who I am. And because it's you"—he gave a sardonic twist to his mouth—"it seems I can't just walk away anyway." He offered a gentle smile. "You were having a panic attack earlier. Talk to me. I know what was going on with Harper was scary. Geez, I was scared, too. I was terrified, Maggie." He whispered the last sentence as he leaned in close. It was as if he'd shared something he wouldn't tell anyone else. "But it felt more personal for you. Tell me what had you so frightened."

Terrified, she wanted to correct him. Like he'd been. She wasn't just frightened.

She couldn't easily bring herself to admit that. However, the concern shining back at her was daunting.

Should she talk about it? Would that help?

At the thought of sharing her fears, a feeling of comfort began to slip down over her. It was far from complete, but for the first time since finding out she was pregnant, she finally didn't feel like she was in this alone. Not completely.

"My mother." She bit her lip as she pictured her mother on the day she'd had to deliver a stillborn baby. "I was talking about my mother. My sister was stillborn at thirty-nine weeks. My mom was devasted."

Shock registered on Cord's face. "Oh, Jesus. I'm so sorry." He wrapped his arms around her.

She nodded, readily letting herself be swooped up in his embrace. She was sorry too.

She clung to him, her arms wrapped tight around his waist and her cheek pressed to his chest. "It was unexplained," she continued. "A total surprise. She hadn't felt the baby move for a few hours but didn't think much of it. She went in to see her doctor, and then . . ." Tears seeped from under her lashes, and she turned her head until her nose was buried against Cord's sternum. "She was induced and delivered that same day. And when she came home, she'd changed. She suffered from severe postpartum depression for a long time, but really, the depression has never left her. She hasn't been the same since."

Her mother had quit being the warm, loving person Maggie and Mason had always known, and instead had become a hollow shell of herself. If it hadn't been for her father, and her grandmother before she'd passed, Maggie didn't know where she and her brother would be. Her father had been their savior.

"She loves us." Maggie pulled back, wiping at her eyes as she looked up. "I do know that. And the bad times these days are far fewer than before. She does still struggle, though. As she has every right to. But I was seven at the time. I didn't understand it. I just saw my mother go in to have a baby, and then my mother came home and no longer loved me."

"*Mags.*"

"No." When he tried to pull her close again, she pushed out of his arms. "Don't. Now that I've started, I want to get it all out. I don't want you thinking that I sit around stressing over a stillbirth. I mean, it's in the back of my head, yes. But I also know the statistics. Today was rough because it was so real. It was scary, and it brought everything right back. But logically, I do know the chances of that happening are slim. Postpartum depression, though." She made a face at the memory. "That bitch is different. And I can't wipe that fear from my mind, no matter how hard I try. I could have a completely healthy, perfect baby boy, yet still come home changed. What if I can't love my baby like I should, Cord? What if I can't love him . . . yet *I'm* the only person he has?"

CORD STARED IN UNDERSTANDING. This was what ran through Maggie's head all the time. She thought she might not be a good mom. She worried she couldn't love their son. And then, he'd gone and pointed out that some mothers *weren't* good. He'd all but implied she could be one of them. *After* refusing to be a part of his son's life.

Arsula had been right. He really was a jerk.

"I'm going to be there for him," he blurted, and at her gasp, he reached for her hand. He needed to touch her whether she required the same kind of reassurance or not. He had to get out everything he'd been thinking on the drive home. "Don't say anything yet," he continued. "It's my turn now."

He was squeezing her hand too tightly, so he forced himself to loosen his grip. And as he did, he noticed they still stood by the front door. He'd never built that fire he'd promised.

"Let's sit." The fire could wait, but he had to get her off her feet.

Maggie followed him to the living room, looking shell-shocked and a little unsure, and after she'd settled on the couch, he lowered next to her. He took her hand again.

He wanted to be in the baby's life. That thought had been pounding through his head ever since he'd touched his hand to Maggie's belly. He wanted to be in the baby's life. But he also remained one hundred percent terrified he'd screw it up.

He couldn't just walk away, though. And he didn't know how he'd ever thought he'd be able to. Denial was a good friend, he supposed. As was fear.

He'd let fear drive too much in his life lately. Maybe for much of his life.

"I'm going to be there for him," he said again, this time in a less forceful fashion. "I'm going to be in the baby's life. If you'll still let me. I don't know how yet, or how *much*—this is all still pretty new—and no, it's not because of what you just told me. Though, I do feel like an even bigger ass now that I know I've only added to your worries."

She opened her mouth, but he touched a finger to it.

"It's still my turn," he reminded her. Then he couldn't hold back another smile. He was going to be a father. He was going to have son.

His life suddenly looked a whole lot brighter.

He slipped his fingers between hers, twining their hands together. "I'll be there for you, too, Mags. However I can be. I *want* to be there. *But . . .*" This was the part that wouldn't be easy. It was the piece he *really* hadn't figured out yet. "I can't promise to make the delivery. I live in Billings. That's a long drive. And I go back to work next week. You could have a short delivery, or it could drag out for half a day. I just don't know. But I do promise that if you'll let me know the minute labor starts, I'll head this way."

That was the part that burned. Especially now that she'd shared about her sister. How was he supposed to make sure he *could* be there when he wouldn't be *here?* Because she might say she didn't dwell on the worry of losing the baby, but there was no way that wouldn't be in her head during delivery. No way it wasn't there every single day.

"I *want* to be there for you," he repeated. "I just don't know if I can."

MAGGIE WAITED to see if he had anything more to say. He seemed to have run out of words, but she didn't want to interrupt if not. He was saying all the right things, and it made her heart want to be happy. Only, she couldn't help but wonder if he was making such promises for the right reasons. Why had he changed his mind?

"Cord?" She spoke only after he sat silent for several more seconds.

"Yes?" His warm hand remained firmly entwined with hers.

"Is it my turn now?"

He chuckled lightly, and once again the corners of his mouth tilted. Just slightly, though. He seemed to be spent. "Please."

"Is this only because I told Erica and Arsula about the baby? Because you know that your family is probably learning about everything right now?"

His eyelids dipped, and he shook his head. The movement was small. "It is *not* because of that. Though I *can* understand why you might think so." He released his grip on her and held their palms flat together. Then he studied them like he might a puzzle piece. And when his gaze finally lifted back up, she ached for the man. Because what she read inside him were all the same feelings she'd lived with for years.

He hurt. He was lonely. He needed to be loved.

"Cord?" she whispered. "I have to be sure. Make me believe."

She didn't want a father in her baby's life who felt like he was being forced to be there. That wouldn't be good for anyone.

"I do want to know my son," he told her. "I want him to be proud of me. To love me. I want to be a good dad. I want to teach him to play football and how to flirt with girls." At her smile, he continued. "But I also don't want him growing up thinking that one of his parents doesn't love *him*. That's . . ."

He let out a shaky sigh before continuing, then he reached up and cupped her jaw. His lips thinned into a flat line.

"That's something we apparently share, Maggie. A parent who wasn't always enough. And I should have considered that side of things instead of simply . . . *being scared*. I know what it feels like to believe your mother doesn't love you. To *know* she doesn't. Yet, to desperately want her love at the same time. I also know what it's like to *want* to love her. To alternate between love and hate. To wonder why you'd ever been born in the first place."

The last sentence surprised her, but she didn't interrupt.

"I get all of that, Maggie. And believe it or not, I don't wish to put that back out into the world. I want to do better. But also"—he lowered his gaze to her stomach then, and she watched him as he watched their baby kick—"I want the amazement of seeing a part of *me* grow up to be *better* than me. I want what I never thought I wanted before."

Tears released. He'd said the right things.

"Will you let me be in his life, Mags?" He brought her hand up and pressed a kiss to the backs of her fingertips. "Will you let me help you raise our son?"

"Yes," she answered without further hesitation. She took his hand and lowered it to her stomach. "I absolutely will. And if I *do* turn out like my mo—"

"You won't."

She tucked her chin in and peered over her nose at him. "If I *do* turn out like my mother, promise me that you'll see him more often. Don't leave him with me too much. If my dad hadn't been around, *especially* that first year . . ." She closed her eyes and concentrated on the feel of her hand over Cord's. Of Cord's hand on her stomach. She wasn't that confused little girl anymore. "Just promise me," she whispered.

He slipped his free hand behind her head and pressed a kiss to her forehead. "I promise."

CHAPTER THIRTEEN

THE EMPTY ROOMS OF THE UPCOMING WILDE LODGE ECHOED WITH Cord's footsteps. He'd arrived earlier than the rest of the family, but he'd also made sure not to show up before the workers left. He'd wanted a few minutes alone there. A few minutes to take in all the changes.

It still looked like the home he'd grown up in—sort of. Yet, so much of it had changed.

The common area . . . what had always been the family room, dining room, and the kitchen combined, now held a powder room, a small library of books, comfortable chairs and love seats, and an extra-long wooden table for those looking to dine in. The kitchen itself had been moved to the front of the house, and the windows in the back had been expanded to offer even more picturesque views of the lake and mountains. It was the type of accommodations visitors could easily fall in love with. However, seeing the changes also brought a surprising pang to Cord's chest.

Their home wasn't their home any longer.

Their home hadn't been *his* home for years, yet it had always been here. He'd always known he could come back if he wanted to. Now . . . for the first time, he officially felt like a non-resident of

Birch Bay. There wasn't a place for him here. He held no resentment, though. He was proud of the changes and of what this place—which had once been both home and hindrance to all of them—was being turned into. It would make people happy in the coming years, and that made him happy.

He turned toward the stairs and climbed to the second floor, then he went first to what had once been the master suite. The room spanned the back of the house, having the same views as the common area below. Only, up here, more of the lake and the land could be seen.

As he stepped out onto the deck, he breathed in a chest full of fresh air, and his gaze landed on the Ski-Doo slowly making its way between the two properties. His dad hadn't wanted to miss this meeting, and he'd insisted he could get here on his own. The sight brought a smile to Cord's mouth. His dad was back to his old self.

The rest of his family would show up soon, as well, with the exception of Nick, of course. Nick remained at the hospital with Harper and the babies, who wouldn't be released for a few more days. He would be joining via video call since Cord had requested to speak to all his siblings at the same time.

Spouses hadn't been invited. Nor had the lone fiancée. He could handle an inquisition from only so many people at once, so direct family got first dibs. He *would* give his family credit, though. They'd held off the night before. The texts and calls hadn't started until that morning. He'd avoided answering the phone, and instead of replying to texts directly, he'd suggested this meeting.

While *he* was here, Maggie would be talking with Erica and Arsula. And afterward, she planned to go home. The shop had called, saying her car was ready, so he'd taken her to pick it up. Additionally, her sink and tub had been installed today. Therefore, she no longer needed him or the cabin.

He left what would now be known as the Flathead Suite and sought out the room that had once been his. But instead of stepping across the threshold, he remained at the door. He'd been so anxious for so long to leave this place. He'd once thought all he wanted was to be on his own.

He was going to be a father now.

He would never be truly alone again.

And that, he was discovering, would be a good thing.

A clatter of noise sounded below, indicating that not only had his father made it to the house, but his brothers and sister had arrived as well. The longer they all lived here in Birch Bay, the more they seemed to move and act as a unified family unit. As the family unit his mother had once pretended to the world they were.

"Cord," Gabe called out from below.

"Up here," Cord called back. He took one more look into his old room before stepping back and closing the door. It was only him who didn't belong there anymore.

"Come down." Dani's voice floated up from the bottom of the stairs. "Gloria sent brownies, and I'm not climbing these stairs."

Cord chuckled. Dani still had two weeks before her official due date, but she'd shared that her doctor said not to be surprised if she delivered early. Erica was due at essentially the same time, and he'd heard others taking bets yesterday afternoon as to which one of them would deliver first. All hoping for two boys, of course.

"Don't eat them all before I get there." He stopped at the top of the stairs before going down. Dani stared up, a plastic container in her hands, and when he met his sister's eyes, her mouth softened into compassion.

"You okay up there?" she asked. He could hear the others milling around in the common area.

"As okay as you might expect," he admitted. His sister was the oldest, and though she only had a couple of years on him, she'd always watched out for him. She'd come home from college after their mother died to help their dad finish raising Jaden and the twins. Cord and Gabe hadn't needed all that much help at that point. They'd been sixteen and seventeen, respectively. But that hadn't stopped Dani.

While he'd been away at college, then subsequently medical school, she'd continually sent care packages. Or just the occasional funny card to let him know she was thinking about him. She'd been as much the mother he'd always wanted as she possibly could.

"Tough night?" she asked as he headed her way. One of her earlier texts had indicated they'd all assumed—given the way he'd been touching Maggie at the hospital—that he and Maggie might have had additional things to talk about.

"I've had better."

"Can I give you a hug?"

He chuckled again, the sound forlorn. Some of his brothers doled out more hugs than others, which often caused her to ask instead of to simply take. "Of course," he murmured, then he closed his eyes as his sister's arms came around him.

While she held him tight, her rounded stomach pressing into his, he thought about Maggie. He'd felt his son moving several times last night. Maggie wasn't shy about letting him touch. And every time, he'd fallen a little bit more in love.

"That's enough," he teased, pulling back. He then snatched the brownies from her hand.

"Hey!" she yelped as he hurried toward the other room.

He smiled and shoved a bite into his mouth.

"Jerk." She punched him when she caught up with him, and he held out the bowl for her to take. The rest of the family had turned, and all eyes were on him.

Nate lifted his phone, showing he already had Nick on a video call, and Cord swallowed the bite of brownie now lodged in his throat. As he opened his mouth, ready to start the conversation his family had been waiting all day to have, their dad spoke first.

"So, I *do* get a grandson, after all."

The tension that had filled the room evaporated.

"You might still get two," Gabe countered. He already had a daughter, so Cord knew Gabe hoped for a boy himself.

"Or three," Dani added. And then the comments started streaming.

"What the fuck, bro? You told her you don't want to be in the baby's life?"

"You can't just walk away. What's wrong with you?"

"When did this even happen?"

"*How* did this happen?"

"You're going to change your mind, right?"

Cord let them go on for a few more seconds, their outrage lowering with each question asked, until silence once again reigned. That's when his dad spoke again. "How long have you known?"

His dad was the only one seated. Someone had brought in a lawn chair for him.

"I just found out this week," Cord answered, and Gabe and Jaden nodded as if to corroborate his story. Cord looked at Jaden. "And I suspect, given the number of babies currently being born into this family, everyone here *knows* how it happened."

Jaden returned Cord's look with a glare, obviously taking the side of his fiancée.

"Condoms, bro," Nate muttered from beside Jaden, and Cord smirked.

"You think?" he said. "Let me share a secret with you. Condoms aren't one hundred percent."

Dani handed off the bowl of brownies, worry pulling at the edges of her mouth, and the snack passed around the group untouched. She knotted her hands together. "Erica says you don't want to be in the baby's life. *Cord . . .*" His sister's gaze implored him to make her understand. "*Why?* How could you do that to your son? To Maggie?"

"Or have you changed your mind?" Jaden fired off the question, and when Cord glanced back over at him, he added, "Arsula thinks you might have."

"Yeah? I figured Arsula was wishing me to hell right about now."

"She's doing that, too."

"Shocking." He gave his brother a bored look. Jaden was a counselor and too often thought he knew best about everything. "She let me have it at the medical plaza yesterday, by the way. Lucky for me, she didn't throw anything."

Jaden flushed. Arsula had once thrown a lamp at him, which caused him to fall down her stairs and shatter his ankle. "Leave her out of it," Jaden defended. "She's just protecting Maggie."

"I know that," Cord said, exhaustion pulling at him. He hadn't slept worth a dime last night. Nightmares had woken him every time he'd nodded off, each one causing more anxiety than the last. "And she *should* protect Maggie." He took in each member of his family. "I get it. And I deserve any of you to lay into me if you feel the need. But just know that you don't *have* to. Because I *am* changing my mind. I *have* changed it."

A smile touched his sister's mouth.

"That doesn't mean I have a clue yet how all of this is going to work. But Maggie and I will figure it out." They'd talked for a few minutes the night before, but ultimately had decided they each needed breathing room before further discussions. He *had* learned that Arsula offered to be in the delivery room though, so that took some of his worries away. Maggie wouldn't have to be alone until he could get to her. The only problem was that he wanted to be here from minute one. Both for Maggie and his son.

"We'll have to throw you a baby shower," Dani announced, and Cord laughed.

"Why would I need a baby shower?"

She looked at him as if he'd lost his head. "You need lots of things for babies, Cord. You've seen all the stuff I carry just going to the babysitter and back."

Indeed, he had. Which made him think of Maggie and her small sedan. Was her car big enough to carry everything she'd need for the baby?

"How about you just throw one for Maggie?" he suggested.

"No," Nick spoke up from the phone. "What he *needs* is to move back home."

"What?"

"Yes." Dani nodded before Cord could say anything else, as did the rest of them. "That would solve everything."

It would solve nothing, he wanted to say. He had an excellent job. He was part owner of a preeminent practice in which the other partners had sought *him* out. Not the other way around. He couldn't blow that. At least, not any more than he already had. "Are you saying I wouldn't need all that stuff if I lived here?" He tried to throw them off with a lame attempt at a joke, but it didn't go over well.

"You wouldn't if you married Maggie." This suggestion came from Jaden.

"What?" Cord said again. This conversation was rapidly getting out of control.

"You knocked her up, man. That's the honorable thing to do."

"In what century?" Cord barked out.

"In *this* one."

His dad rapped his cane on the floor. *"Boys.* We're family. This is Cord's decision. We support. We help. We don't *hurt."*

The words pulled all of them up short, in part because that was the kind of thing they'd all wished to hear from their dad when their mother was still alive, then Nick once again spoke from the phone. And this time, he did it while holding a baby in each arm. "You're not going to want to be away from him, Cord. You should give that a lot of thought. Maybe it is time for you to come home."

"HAND ME THE . . . UH . . ." Maggie's brother squinted down at the assembly instructions that lay scattered by his knee. "The number five screws," he finished.

"They're behind your left foot."

Mason reached behind him with one hand while holding the two pieces of the baby bed in place with the other. "You're not exactly helping," he complained.

"I didn't offer to let you do this for me so I could help."

She sat in the rocker recliner her colleagues had bought her for the baby's room, her feet up and her body reclined, and felt truly relaxed. She'd been back home a couple of days now, and though she hadn't seen Cord again, he'd texted several times each day. Mostly with dollar figures as a suggestion for child support. She'd declined each one, saying the number was too high. But he'd also reached out just to check on her. To see if she needed anything. And this morning he'd simply asked what she was doing today.

She'd told him that Mason was coming by and that he planned to spend the night.

"Well, I hope your lack of help doesn't mean your baby ends up sleeping on the floor." Though an excellent EMT, and in most ways a typical all-around man's man, Mason had a real issue putting furniture together. Mostly because he always tried to do it by reading only about half the instructions.

"I'm sure Baby C will sleep fine wherever I put him down."

Mason looked up. "You're still going to give him the Crowder name?"

"I . . ." She snapped her mouth closed. Mason had always called her son Baby C, so she'd taken to doing the same when talking to him, but she'd never actually been certain that's the name he'd have. She'd always planned to wait and see how Cord took the news before deciding. She didn't think now would be a good time to mention that to her brother, though. Mace hadn't exactly been thrilled to learn Cord was the guy who'd gotten her pregnant. "We haven't talked about it yet."

The expression on her brother's face turned mutinous. "He doesn't deserve to have the baby named after him."

She'd called Mason Thursday after talking to Erica and Arsula, not wanting the news to make it to him before she saw him in person. Then she'd phoned her parents. Her mother had thought Cord being the father was nice. She remembered his family always being so put together. Maggie hadn't filled her in otherwise.

Her father, however, had a different opinion. He remembered Cord, as well. And he also recalled the "ladies' man" reputation that had always swirled anytime Cord had been home between college semesters. Her dad didn't think Cord deserved her.

She hadn't pointed out that Cord didn't seem to *want* her. Nor had she let that bother her. The conversation they'd had after returning from the hospital had been strictly focused on the baby. As, she supposed, it should be. No matter that her ridiculous crush still liked to remind her on occasion that she found him oh-so-dreamy. She also found him rock solid once he set his mind to doing something. Like being there for her. She liked that.

"He didn't do anything wrong, Mace." She hadn't told her brother that Cord had at first refused to have anything to do with their son. He definitely wouldn't like that.

"What he did wrong was doing nothing to help you out for the last seven months."

She sighed. "I told you. He didn't know."

"Yeah. You also told me the asshole wouldn't call you back." He cursed as he realized that one of the two pieces he'd just forced together had been put on backwards, then he tossed the screwdriver to the floor. "I swear, I'm going to buy you a new bed that's already assembled."

He left the room, grumbling about needing something to drink, and Maggie merely smiled. She refused to let a bad attitude bring her down. Being back home had lowered her stress level. As well as learning that Cord wanted to be in the baby's life, of course. So instead of worrying about all the remaining unknowns—like what Cord being a dad was truly going to look like—she'd decided simply to enjoy the small victory. She'd return to stress later.

"I called Mom and Dad on my way down today." Mason came back into the baby's room and handed her a glass of water. He'd poured another for himself. "Dad wants to know what Cord's intentions are."

"His intentions?" Maggie snorted. "To give me all his money, I think."

She'd gotten another text right before her brother had shown up, from the same banking app Cord had used that first night. He'd apparently tried transferring the five thousand dollars to her again. Was the man made of money?

"Then take it," Mace suggested. "Whatever he'll give you. Don't let him off the hook."

"No one is letting anyone off the hook." She balanced her glass of water on her belly and smiled at her obvious skill. "But I also won't take advantage of him."

"Well, maybe you should. It seems he took advantage of you."

"You think?" She peered up at him. "Maybe *I* took advantage of him?"

That didn't make her brother happy.

"You want to hear how I took advantage, Mason?" she teased, waggling her eyebrows.

"Stop it. You know I don't."

She giggled. She and her brother had always been close, but since he'd moved out of town, she didn't see him nearly enough. She was younger by two years, and as his baby sister, she loved taunting him when it came to his protective big brother streak.

"Maybe we took advantage of each other," she goaded. "Possibly in this very room."

His jawline went stiff. "If you were this big a pain in the ass with him, I'm surprised he ever touched you."

He went back to working on the bed, and she returned to the glass she'd balanced on her belly. After taking a drink, she repositioned the water for a couple of minutes, grinning each time it stayed exactly where she'd put it, no matter which angle of her stomach she set it on. Soon, she gave up her game and let her head sink back into the headrest. She closed her eyes. It was nice to simply sit and let someone else take care of things.

Her phone dinged on the table at her side.

"Is that him?" Mason muttered.

"I don't know. I'm too relaxed to open my eyes."

The phone dinged a couple of minutes later, and she giggled when Mason grunted.

She still didn't open her eyes, though. She didn't want to see another dollar amount. When she and Cord had talked the other night, she'd agreed that since he *was* going to participate in their son's life, then he could pay child support. She would still put most of it in a college fund, but if knowing he was contributing to daily care mattered, then she'd let him contribute. But she wouldn't agree to an outlandish amount.

"How's this long-distance dad thing going to work, anyway?"

She tried to make herself smile again, knowing that Mason was likely looking at her. But she couldn't do it. She didn't have any answers. "I don't know, Mace. We haven't figured it out yet."

"Are you going to end up moving there?"

She lifted her head and looked at her brother. "No." She *had* considered offering to go to Billings for her delivery, as she'd once discussed with her doctor. Additionally, she could rent a place and live there for the first couple of months. That would give her time to adjust to being a mother, but also give Cord the opportunity to be more a part of things. In the end, though, she'd decided against it. That would feel like she'd be the one doing all the giving, and that wasn't the precedent she wanted to set. She'd be more comfortable with her own doctor here, and if Cord didn't make it in time for the delivery, then she'd at least have Arsula with her. Her biggest fear had always been more about after the delivery anyway.

"Were you wishing for a relationship?" Mason tossed out, his question catching her off guard, and her good mood slid away. She had wished for one.

She *did* wish for one, if she were being honest. As silly as that may be.

She had no clue if things could ever work between them, but she'd love to give it a try. And not because of the baby, either. If her son's parents were together, that would be great. But a relationship shouldn't be based upon that. She just really liked Cord. He made her smile. He made her tingle. And they'd gotten along so well before.

Also, there was an intensity about him, something that seemed to reach out to her. It made her want to be there for him. She couldn't explain it, but she'd felt it that first night. She'd felt like they'd connected.

So, yes. She would *love* to give it a try. She just didn't know how to approach the subject. And, if they tried and it *did* work out . . . Well, then she wouldn't have a problem moving to Billings to be with him. If she and Cord were to fall in love and wanted to be together, it wouldn't matter where they were.

Her doorbell rang before she could form a reply to her brother, and Mason held up a hand as he rose. "Stay put if you want. I'll get it. It's probably the fully assembled bed I ordered earlier," he teased.

As he left the room, she managed to push herself out of the chair, and as she did, she glanced down to see the message Cord had sent.

I'll be at your place in five minutes. Are you home?

Her eyes rounded. That was Cord at her door?

Why?

Then she heard her brother say, *"Wilde."*

Cord followed with, *"Crowder."*

She stopped moving and listened. She knew the two of them had known each other in high school, and until she'd told her brother it was Cord who'd gotten her pregnant, she'd never heard a bad word said about the man.

"Can I help you with something?" Mason asked.

"Is Maggie here?"

"Maybe."

She sighed. Her brother's protective streak hadn't come out quite like this since she'd gotten dumped by her first boyfriend because she wouldn't kiss him at the junior high dance.

"Mason," she said as she made her way to the front of the house. "Didn't you have some friends you wanted to visit while in town?"

Her brother had his arms crossed over his chest, and he didn't look away from Cord. "I can visit them later."

She shoved him to the side. "Do it *now*," she insisted. Then she looked up at Cord, who remained in the open doorway. He offered a smile, but it seemed as uncertain as she suddenly felt. The last time he'd been at her house they'd spent more time in it naked than not.

She gulped.

"Hi," he murmured.

Mason cleared his throat.

"Mason," she ground out, elbowing him as he tried to move back in. *"Please."*

"Fine." He grabbed his coat from the back of a nearby chair, then he came back and put his face in front of Cord's. "Hurt her and you'll answer to me."

Maggie rolled her eyes as he shouldered his way past Cord, then she turned back to the man who stupidly still made her toes curl. Her baby kicked inside her as if he were glad to see his daddy, too. "Would you like to come in?"

"Actually"—his smile changed from uncertain to excited—"I'd like for *you* to come out. I got something for you."

"You got something for me?" Surprise had her grinning. "What is it?" She leaned to the side, trying to peek around him, but he blocked her view.

"It's a surprise. Two of them. Get your coat and boots on and I'll show you."

She hurried to do what he'd asked, allowing him to help tug her snow boots up after she stepped into them, and when she was ready, he took her hand.

"Come on. I'm excited to show it to you."

She couldn't imagine what it could be, but she hurried along after him. He'd parked in her driveway, and he took her around to the passenger side. When he reached for the door, she paused. "Are we going somewhere?" She motioned back toward the house. "I didn't lock the door."

"No need." He squeezed her hand, and the smile on his face warmed her. "Just watch."

He opened the door, and then a chrome step slid out and then down. It was just the right height so she could step up and climb into the truck. The thoughtfulness thrilled her.

"Cord," she whispered. Her hand went to her heart.

"Now you don't need to bring a step with you." The childish glee on his face made her laugh.

"That is so sweet." She tried it out. "Thank you."

He nodded, watching her as she stepped up and down again. "That's not the best surprise, though."

"No?"

She glanced around the front seat, trying to figure out what other modifications he might have made. "What else?"

"Come on." He took her hand again, and after she'd descended, he led her behind the truck. She still hadn't spied what else this big surprise might be, but when they kept going *beyond* the truck, she quickly figured it out.

She stopped walking. "Cord. What did you do?"

A huge brand-new black SUV was parked on the street with temporary tags attached.

"I got you a new car," he announced.

"I don't ne—"

"It's big enough to hold all the baby stuff you'll need."

She let him drag her to the road, and when they got there, she saw that he hadn't just purchased the SUV, but it looked as if he'd bought every baby item he could find. There were two sizes of car seats in the back, a diaper bag, diapers, wipes, toys, clothes, blankets, bottles, burb cloths, baby monitors, and who knew what else crammed in between the car seats and stuffed in the front passenger seat. And then he lifted the rear door to show her what had been tucked away in the back. Two different models of strollers, a baby bath, more toys, a portable crib, and three mobiles.

"I didn't even know they had baby baths." He held the tub up for her to see, and she laid her hand over his arm.

"What are you doing?" she asked. This was over the top. "I don't need all of this, Cord."

"Sure. I figured you might have some of it already, but I can return what we don't need."

"I don't *need* the SUV."

Her declaration finally slowed his momentum. He took his time putting the baby tub back into the cargo space before he turned to face her once again. She read the pleading on his face before he even spoke.

"I need to do this for you, Maggie. I need to make sure you're okay."

"Of course I'm okay. With*out* all of this."

"I head back to Billings tomorrow."

That was a bit of a gut punch, but also not unexpected. His vacation time couldn't last forever. "I'll be fine," she assured him. "You don't have to worry."

"I will worry. And this will go better in the snow than your car. It'll be safer. Plus, I've already bought it. I can't take it back now."

"Cord." She peered into his eyes. She couldn't read what was going on inside his head. "What's this about? Why didn't you talk to me first?"

He took her hand in his again, only this time, he held it between both of his, then he angled his head down and looked directly into her eyes. "I've done a lot of thinking over the last couple of days, Mags. And even though I have . . . I still don't have all the answers. But I'm trying. I'll come to Birch Bay every weekend to help you out. At least for the first few months, and as often as I can after that. I'll also see if I can find a house to rent in this same neighborhood. If

I can find a place that's close enough, I can help you in the middle of the night if you'll let me. I know I won't need to take him overnight for a while—I can't imagine you'd want me driving off with him anytime soon—so this is the best I've come up with. I also know it's not nearly enough."

She stared at him. That was a *lot*. "You really think you could get away every weekend?"

"I'll do my best. Harper used to fly me home after Dad first had his accident." His sister-in-law worked for search and rescue and had her own helicopter. "I'll find a company that can do the same when the weather is clear. That way I'll be here longer instead of being on the road, driving so much. And I'll take a couple of weeks off after he's born, too. I'll also hire a nanny for when I go back to work if you want."

"Stop. Cord. No." She shook her head, her mind reeling. They remained standing at the side of the road, the back and rear doors of the SUV wide open. Cord had put a lot of thought into this. "Don't rent a place. I have a third bedroom. Stay with me." She'd had the idea earlier but hadn't decided until now if she wanted to make the offer or not. "And maybe you could come back a time or two before he's born."

Her pulse fluttered when his brows shot up. She liked being around Cord. And she especially liked protective-dad Cord.

"We should probably get used to being around each other before he's born, don't you think?" she added. "I mean, more than just . . . you know . . ." Her cheeks heated. "That one weekend."

Her voice dropped lower as the memories suddenly swamped her, and if the way his gaze dipped to her mouth was any indication, he was remembering a lot of the same things.

"You think that would work?" he asked. "Me staying here?"

He looked at her mouth again.

"I do. And I also think it's the best solution. I can pump milk before bed, and you can get up in the middle of the night to feed him if you want to. Or bring him to me if I haven't pumped."

He nodded. "I'll do that. I'd *like* to do that."

She smiled. She couldn't help it. For a man who'd recently declared he hadn't wanted a thing to do with his son, he'd certainly come around. "Then I think it's a great plan. It's a good place to start."

"Agreed." He looked back at her, not saying anything else for a minute. "Thank you, Maggie. And I guess I'll see you again on Friday." He turned her hand over, palm up. "But you have to keep the car." Without another word, he dropped the key into her hand, pressed a kiss to her forehead, and marched to his truck. She didn't try to stop him. She didn't know if she would really keep the car or not, but she loved that he'd had the idea. And she also loved that the feel of his lips now lingered on her forehead.

CHAPTER FOURTEEN

"S<small>ERIOUSLY</small>, J<small>ENNA AND</small> H<small>ALEY ARE GOING TO THINK YOU HUNG THE</small> moon when they see these things." Maggie's voice was muffled due to leaning so close into one of his nieces' dollhouses. She had a piece of pink-and-white-striped wallpaper, cut to size, and was carefully applying it to a bedroom wall.

"That's the plan." Cord sat at her kitchen table beside her, working on the furniture pieces he had yet to complete. The dollhouses were almost four feet tall, and he'd had them custom-made. He'd wanted to be hands-on with part of it, though, so he'd taken on the furniture. It had been Maggie's idea to add the wallpaper. He'd sent her pictures of the dollhouses earlier in the week when they'd been texting back and forth.

They'd texted a lot that week. They'd also talked on video calls a couple of times.

And she'd sent him links to the two ultrasounds that had been done during the pregnancy. He was officially in love with his little boy.

He still had reservations, of course. He didn't want to screw things up; he didn't want to let his son down. And the distance between here and his job wasn't small, so that would present a whole other set of challenges. But he wanted to try. His siblings had figured things out. Surely he could, too.

His siblings had also figured out relationships, the voice in his head said. But he wasn't quite ready to go there. Best to keep a distance. Don't hand over all the power.

"I would have killed to have something like this when I was a kid," Maggie murmured.

He liked that she wanted to help out. And he liked watching how hard she was focusing to be sure and get things just right.

"I'll buy you one if you want," he offered, and she laughed.

"Given the amount of stuff currently crammed into this house due to you, I believe that you would. But no, thank you." She peeked over at him. "I've outgrown playing with dolls."

He caught himself doing nothing more than smiling at her and forced himself back to the task at hand. He held a tiny piano between two fingers that needed legs attached.

He'd shown up a couple of hours before, laden down with takeout food and the dollhouses. He needed to work on them here or they wouldn't be finished in time for Christmas, and Maggie had loved the idea. It also gave them something to do in the event his being here felt awkward. So far it hadn't.

"How was work this week?" Maggie had pulled the backing off another piece of wallpaper and was concentrating intently on lining it up. "Were they glad to have you back?"

"Yeah," he answered. They *had* been glad to see him. They'd also watched him like a hawk. Waiting to see if he'd yell at anyone again. He'd turned away a patient six weeks ago when she'd tried to come in after closing. She'd claimed lower right abdominal pain. He'd been the only doctor still in the office, and he'd had their receptionist, Angie, suggest she needed to go to the nearest ER if the pain persisted. Then he hadn't thought anything else about it.

That patient had died from sepsis that weekend. With a ruptured appendix.

And he hadn't slept well since.

He had managed not to lose his cool at the office that week, though. And it had been surprisingly easy. He still had the dream more nights than not, but something about it didn't leave him feeling as frightened anymore. Also, he had other things on his mind these days. Things that made him happy.

Maggie sat back in her seat. "Do you wish we were having a girl?"

The question surprised him. "Of course not. Dad is over the moon that he's going to have a grandson."

"Yeah, but how does *this* dad feel?" She pointed at him as she said "this dad," and his heart thumped.

"This dad is thrilled." *With everything*, he wanted to add. He was simply thrilled to be having a baby. And he didn't know how that had happened. Two weeks ago, he'd found out he'd gotten her pregnant, and he'd been certain his world couldn't get any worse. The job he'd worked so hard for was being threatened; a baby would be hanging over his head. He'd just wanted his world to return to the way it had always been. But then he'd felt his son kick.

And then he'd gone back by the hospital and held Nick and Harper's twins in his arms.

And he hadn't been able to think of anything other than his own baby since.

Well, he did think about Maggie. Probably too often, in fact. He almost wished things could be different between them. His coming to her place tonight had, strangely, felt like coming home. And he wasn't quite sure what to make of that. He *was* glad to be here, though. With her. It felt good, and he'd looked forward to getting back here all week.

"What are we going to name him?" That had also been in his head a lot that week.

Maggie grinned. "I wondered how long it would take you to bring that up." She rose from the table, putting her hands to her lower back. "I hadn't decided yet." She leaned back, stretching out her spine. "Have you had any thoughts?"

He'd had a lot of thoughts. "Are you okay?" he asked instead of sharing any name ideas. "Is your back hurting?" He rose, as well.

"I just need to sit some other way for a while. I can't bend over like that for very long."

"Let's go to the living room." He could work on the furniture anytime. "You probably need to put your feet up anyway."

She chuckled wryly. "I always need to put my feet up."

They made their way into the adjoining space, and as he'd done when he'd first arrived that evening, he took in the changes that had been made to the place since the first time he'd been there. Along with the floors being refinished, a soft gray hue had replaced the faded tan color that had been on the walls, and a Christmas tree sat decorated in the corner. Lights had also been strung across the porch and glowed in through the closed blinds of the front windows. She'd told him that Mason had hung the lights for her last weekend, as well as helped her put up the tree.

"The floors look amazing," he offered. "As does the fireplace." The fireplace mantle had been replaced with a simple rustic wooden block of wood instead of the original, more ornate frame.

"Thank you." She lowered to the couch with a weary sigh. "I'd planned on trying to refinish the floors myself. I'd been looking forward to it, in fact."

"I remember." He'd helped her pull up the carpet when he'd been there before, and she'd talked about everything she'd read regarding how to refinish floors. "I guess it would be harder to do once the baby is here."

"Exactly." She nudged her head toward the couch cushion beside her, and he realized he still stood. "Grab the remote if you want to watch a movie or something." She patted her belly. "Now that I'm down, I don't want to get back up."

"I'd love to watch a movie." He snagged the remote off the coffee table and sat down next to her.

Scrolling through the movies available with her streaming service, they decided on a comedy, and before he let himself think too hard about what he was doing, he had Maggie stretched out on the couch with her head resting on his thigh. She'd turned on her side so she could see the TV and wasn't looking at him. But he watched her.

This could be different.

He did his best to ignore the voice, but it persisted.

She *could be different.*

He didn't want to believe that. What if he let himself wish for more and she *did* turn out like his mom? What if she treated their son the way that patient had treated hers? Always parading them around to show the world what a great little family they were, yet never once paying attention to them.

He didn't want that for himself, and he didn't want it for his son.

This could be different, his subconscious said again, right as Maggie shifted to snuggle in just a little bit closer.

He reached out his arm and rested it over her side, his hand wrapping around to the front of her belly, and she turned her head to smile up at him. "Thank you for keeping the SUV," he told her. They'd talked about it several times over the past week, and she'd finally relented. Her keeping it made him feel better, knowing she would be safer when he couldn't be here.

"Thank you for wanting me to have it." Her lashes dipped briefly, and he could see the pulse point in her neck pounding rapidly. "And thank you for coming over tonight. I'm really glad you're here."

He was glad, too. He didn't say it, though. He was too busy telling himself not to fall for this woman.

～

"MOM." *Cord said his mother's name again, and the deputy who'd been first on scene stepped toward him.*

The deputy held out a hand. "You're one of Mrs. Wilde's sons, right? Cord, is it?"

"Yes."

Cord held up his own hand, stopping the officer from saying anything more, and shrugged away from the man's touch. The sheriff's car pulled to a stop at Cord's side.

"Cord?" the sheriff called as he stepped from the cruiser, but Cord picked up speed.

"You need to stay back."

Cord heard the words, and once again, when a hand landed on his arm, he shrugged it away. He did not need to stay back. He had to hurry. There was no time to waste.

He started running, but he couldn't pick up speed. Everything moved in slow motion.

Finally . . . somehow *. . . he reached the SUV. The door stood open. Only, the vehicle color was no longer dark red. It had changed to black.*

"Mom?" he asked, but he didn't go to the door. Something was wrong with this dream. This wasn't right.

He looked back to the other side of the road. The pregnant lady still sat in her car. It was still Bailey. Not Maggie. The dream was back to normal. Only . . . he turned back to the SUV. The color was wrong.

"Maggie," he whispered. It couldn't be her in there.

"Help me, Cord."

"Maggie!" He lunged toward the vehicle, but once again, his feet wouldn't move. "Maggie!"

"Cord?" Maggie roused herself awake, hearing her name whispered in the room. Where was she?

She blinked into the darkness, the Christmas tree and the muted colors shining through the front blinds the only light in the room. She was still on the couch. Still curled up next to Cord.

"Maggie!"

She jerked upright as he yelled and immediately reached out to shake him.

"Wake up, Cord. It's a dream."

"Maggie!"

It took a few more shakes, but he finally calmed. Finally opened his eyes. He seemed as disoriented as she'd been just a moment before, looking around the room in almost a panic. Then his gaze swung to hers.

"Maggie?" The red, green, and blue lights from the tree made the blue of his eyes seem to glitter. He looked around once again, then a long hot breath slid from his lungs. "I was dreaming again."

"Yes." She nodded, not sure what to do. She straightened on the couch but stayed sitting next to him. His hand slid over to capture hers.

"I'm sorry." His voice came out hoarse. She'd fallen asleep before the movie had finished, and he must have turned off the TV instead of waking her. He'd fallen asleep sitting up.

"There's no need to be sorry." She covered their hands with her free one. "Do you want to talk about it, though?" The last time she'd asked, he'd said no—but then he'd proceeded to share a few details anyway. She'd hurt for him that night. After all these years, he still dreamed about his mother's wreck. That had to be stressful. "Was it about your mother again?" she reached up and caressed his cheek, the stubble of whiskers comforting under her fingertips. "Maybe talking would help."

He studied her in the quiet darkness. It would be his call, but she wanted him to know she was there for him.

"Or I could make you a cup of tea," she offered. He might prefer a few minutes alone.

"It *was* about my mother," he croaked out, and she nodded, more than willing to stay put.

She pulled in a breath. "And I showed up in it again?"

He sighed and ran a hand through his hair. "You show up in all of them now, Maggie. *Every one.*" He captured the hand still on his jaw. "And in them, I can never save you."

"Save me?" That wasn't what she'd expected to hear. "What do I need saving from?"

His gaze moved away from hers, shifting to the tree, but she doubted he actually saw any of the brightly colored decorations. He seemed to be deep inside his own head instead. "You might need saving from *me*," he whispered.

CHAPTER FIFTEEN

CORD HEARD HIS OWN WORDS, BUT HE COULDN'T BELIEVE HE'D SPOKEN them. He didn't talk about such things. What had this woman done to him? And how could he make it stop?

"Why would I need saving from you, Cord?"

She didn't sound offended. Nor did she come across as clinical, as if trying to decipher the dream. She sounded honestly curious.

He shook his head at first, not wanting her to see his fears, but he knew that wasn't fair. He kept waking this woman by shouting her name. He shouldn't keep sweeping it under the rug. He wouldn't change his mind and speak to a counselor, as his colleagues had suggested yet again, but maybe if he talked to Maggie . . . Maybe that would push some of his fears back where they belonged. Way down deep in his psyche where they'd never again see the light of day.

He shook his head once more. What the hell did he have to lose by talking about it at this point? "I fail people, Maggie." He blew out another breath. "That's what you need to be saved from. I fail people, and I don't want to fail you and the baby. I let my mother down. I let a recent patient down. I let *Harper* down."

"Wait. What?" The confusion on her face was obvious. "How did you let Harper down?"

179

Damn it. He shouldn't have brought up Harper. He shouldn't be talking about delivery scares with Maggie at all. He suspected she wouldn't let him bypass this point, though. Not since he'd already said his sister-in-law's name. He gentled his voice, but he didn't let himself adjust his words. As always, he spoke truthfully. "She could have died that day, Maggie." He squeezed her hand in his. "You know that. She and the babies *both* could have."

"Yes." She watched him carefully. "And thank goodness they didn't. But Cord . . . what does that have to do with you?"

"I was there that morning," he explained. "I was at Harper and Nick's house. I *knew* her blood pressure was up."

She still didn't look at him as if she got it. She still looked at him as if he weren't a monster. The furrow on her brow remained. "I don't understand. Was she bleeding when you saw her?"

"No. Not yet. But—"

"Not yet?" Her confusion immediately cleared. "Then what are you talking about? There's no 'but' to it. Harper's scare isn't on you. Plus, didn't I hear that she'd had a doctor's appointment that day, too? And *that's* when she started bleeding? While waiting to see her own doctor?"

That *was* when she'd started bleeding. "Yes," he agreed, holding up a finger as he went to explain. "But I should have—

"Stop it. No. You shouldn't have done anything. You were visiting your sister-in-law."

"I'm a doctor, Maggie." He was a doctor first and foremost.

"Yes, but Harper was going to *her* doctor that day. Was her blood pressure already at a dangerous level that morning?"

She was making sense. Cord could see that. But the fact remained that he'd been there. He should have done better for his family. "Not dangerous yet, no."

Maggie sat up straighter, her hand pulling away as she shifted, but once she'd settled, he reclaimed it. "Okay," she continued. "Then answer me this. If she *hadn't* had an appointment scheduled for that day, would you have done anything different because of her blood pressure?"

"Yes. I would have insisted she go in to see her doctor."

She lifted her other hand, palm up. "Then there you go. Like I said. It's not on you. Just like your mother's death isn't on you, either. You were a kid, Cord. I've heard the story many times. She had a car accident."

He really hadn't been prepared to argue these points. "You don't know what you're talking about, Maggie."

She studied him as if trying to understand. Her head tilted, and her brow furrowed once again. Her gaze softened. "Explain it to me, then. Let me help. Whatever is causing these nightmares, I want to help you through it. Whatever you need."

What he needed was love, he thought. Though he had no idea where the idea had come from. Love was the last thing he needed. Love didn't last. And it overlapped with hate.

He freaking hated his mother.

He told himself to get up and walk away. To end the conversation. Talking *wouldn't* help. Telling Maggie *wouldn't* solve anything.

But he didn't get up. He kept hold of her hand instead. And then he opened his mouth and explained.

"My mother didn't just have an accident." He wanted to look away from her, but he couldn't force himself to do it. "She *caused* the accident."

"You mean, they ruled it her fault?" She nodded as if she'd known that.

"Yes. They did rule it her fault. But no, that's not what I'm saying. I'm saying that she had the accident on *purpose*. I don't think she meant to involve another person, however. But she did intentionally swerve, most likely intending to miss the tree entirely and simply land in the ditch. She *caused* the accident. On *purpose*."

He could tell she still didn't understand. And why would she? She hadn't grown up with a narcissistic mother. Clearly, her mother hadn't been perfect, and she'd harmed Maggie in other ways. But at least she hadn't intentionally tried to screw with her head.

Maggie looked blank. "Why would she have wanted to wreck, Cord? I don't get it."

"Because she wanted attention. Because that's what she did. It's what *we* did."

"We?"

He was ready to be done with this conversation. "Yes." His voice lowered to almost a whisper. He was so tired of living with the anger and frustration from that one moment in time. So tired of knowing he should have done better. *"We,"* he said again. "Her and me. Dani had moved to New York by then; Gabe and I were doing our own things in the afternoons with school, and she apparently decided on that day it wasn't worth her time to mentally mess with Nick, Nate, or Jaden. It was my turn. When she wanted attention, she sometimes finagled 'accidents.' Like the time she almost cut off her finger with a kitchen knife. Or the time she swallowed a bottle of pills."

Maggie's eyes widened. "*OhmyGod*, Cord. She could have died either of those times. I had no idea."

"No, she wouldn't have died either of those times. That's the point. That would never have happened because she did all these things right when she knew I would find her. She knew I'd be coming through that section of the road that day. At that time. I had an appointment north of town fifteen minutes later, and I'd been coming from the school. She knew I would be there. And she couldn't have timed it more perfectly, either. I came around the curve within seconds of the wreck happening. Only, she somehow missed that another car was also coming from the opposite direction."

Horror began to fill Maggie's eyes as understanding finally dawned. She put her hand to her mouth. "Do you know this for a fact?"

"Yes, I do. First of all, that was my role in the family. I was there to save her. But also, she was awake and fully aware when I found her. She was mad because the other car wasn't supposed to be there. Mad, I would assume, because having another person potentially hurt would take some of the attention off her. *Not* mad—or feeling *bad*—because she'd run into an innocent person."

She watched him carefully. "You went over to check on the other car after speaking to your mother?"

"Right. It was a pregnant woman in that car. And that's how *you've* shown up in the dreams—at least until tonight. That pregnant woman turns into you, and then the car—" He choked off his words. He didn't want to keep going.

Maggie's soft hand caressed over his jaw again and turned his face back to hers. "Don't stop," she pleaded. "Finish telling me. The car what?"

"The car went over the damned cliff, Maggie." He couldn't stop the words. They barreled out of him as if unable to stay inside any longer. "Yet, there was and there *is* no cliff at that spot. I check every time I pass by it now. But you were in that car. You were calling for me to save you and the baby. And the cliff broke away and the car went over. *You* went over." His voice had inched higher, as well as his pulse.

"*Shhh . . .*" She touched her fingertips to his lips. "It was a dream. You know that."

He captured her hand again and held it to his cheek. "I do know that. Yet, I keep having it. Over and over. And then just now . . ."

He stopped and looked away. He didn't want to think about it, much less say it out loud.

"Tell me," she coaxed.

"Maggie . . ." He pleaded with her. "You know nothing good was in the dream. And it was about *you*. Why would you want to hear that?"

She held firm. "Because *you* need to talk about it. I don't need to have Arsula's dream reading abilities to understand that, Cord.

You're stressed about me, about the baby, so we've come into your nightmares."

"Yes. *Clearly.* I understand that's what's going on, too. But knowing it doesn't keep it from happening."

"Then tell me the rest of it." She offered him a gentle smile, and the darned thing eased his racing heart. "Maybe we can figure this out together."

He hated her seeing the darkness inside him. At the same time, it felt good having someone to share this with. And if talking about it managed to help . . .

"Tell me," she whispered.

He reached out and caressed *her* jaw then. He hadn't touched her anywhere but her hands and belly since that weekend back in April, and as his palm slid over her smooth skin, he wanted to pull her in for a kiss. He closed his eyes instead.

"The pregnant woman didn't change in the dream tonight," he started. His other hand remained wrapped tightly around hers. "I thought I'd gotten past it. You weren't in the woman's car, so even in my dream, I thought I'd escaped having to see you fall over that cliff. But then I got back over to my mother's vehicle. Exactly as I did in real life. Only, it suddenly wasn't *her* SUV sitting there. It was the one parked outside that I got for you. And you were in it. I couldn't get to you, though. I was right there. Two feet from the door. And you were calling for me. But I couldn't help. Even though I knew how it was going to end. I knew what I would find inside if I didn't get there soon enough."

He felt something damp on his cheek, and it took a minute to realize it was tears. *His* tears. He opened his eyes, finding Maggie still right there in front of him, still ready to listen to every word he was willing to share. He couldn't stop now.

"I let people down," he told her again. "I let my mother die that day. I had a patient recently who wanted me to see her after the office closed. She'd reminded me of my mother in the past—the way she treated her kids, the way she made up reasons to make other people think she was sick so they would feel sorry for her—and I refused to see her. That's why the dreams have started again. I had the receptionist tell her to go to the ER instead of me giving her five minutes of my time. Only, she *didn't* go to the ER. She went back home, and her appendix ruptured. She developed sepsis that weekend, and her organs started shutting down. She died before they could save her, Maggie. So I'm terrified. I'm terrified that I'm going to let you and our baby down, too. I don't know how . . . or *when*. But that's what I do. I have all the skills in the world in the medical field, but when it really matters . . . I *fail*."

Her lips closed over his as soon as he ran out of words, and at first he didn't move. He didn't breathe. He didn't want to lead her on.

He didn't want to *want* her.

But then he couldn't help but move. Her lips were warm and soft against his. Just like *she* was warm and soft. And she was offering him the kind of understanding that no other person in the world had ever offered.

He slid his hand to the back of her head and slanted his lips over hers, and he stroked inside her mouth as her moan mingled with his. He wanted to devour her. He wanted to never stop kissing her.

"Maggie." He pulled back, allowing only a breath of distance between them. "Should we be doing this?" He'd promised her before that he wouldn't flirt with her again. And he hadn't. He'd done his best not to think about her as anything more than the mother of his son. But she *felt* like more. And this felt like so much more than flirting.

"I do think we should be doing it. I don't know what might come of it, but I like you, Cord. A *lot*. And I think you like me." She pressed another kiss to his lips before pulling back. "And I *really* like kissing you." She smiled again, at first with a mischievous lift to her lips before they gentled as they had before. "I know you're scared of relationships. I know they terrify you, probably for all the reasons you just laid out that you fear you're going to let me down. Which I *don't* believe will happen, by the way. But I do understand your fears. I believe they're real. That said . . . I don't believe you have to fear this. You don't have to fear *us*. I think you and I could be really good together, Cord Wilde."

He peered back at her. They were still face-to-face, and he felt as if he couldn't pull in another breath. She wanted him to give *them* a shot? As in, a real relationship?

Could he dare hope?

His entire family had figured it out, he reminded himself. And they'd come from the same messed-up reality that he had.

He *wanted* to hope.

He wanted to make a family with this woman.

Tossing caution aside, he pulled in another breath. And when his lungs were filled, when he could envision nothing more than him and the woman sitting before him—along with the son who was currently tucked safely between them—he finally let himself smile.

Every part of him destressed in that one instant, and the path he was about to embark upon felt like the right direction to take. "I want to try, Maggie. I want to try to make an us."

CHAPTER SIXTEEN

I WANT TO TRY TO MAKE AN US.

Maggie continued to let Cord's words replay through her mind several days later as she, Erica, and Arsula did some last-minute Christmas shopping. She hadn't shared the changes that had come from hers and Cord's weekend yet. She'd been holding the newness of it close instead. But she was ready to talk. She needed her friends to know what was going on, and she hoped for their support.

"How about this for Gloria?" She held up a pretty cashmere sweater for them to see. She'd decided she wanted to get gifts for Max and Gloria, as well as all the kids that would soon be her baby's cousins. She could drop them off at the house sometime next week.

Erica fingered the soft wool. "That green color would look great on her. It'll bring out her eyes."

"Agreed," Arsula added.

Maggie nodded. "That's what I thought, too."

She tucked the sweater into the bag she'd picked up as they'd come into the store and led the three of them to the men's section. Erica had visited her OB that day and found out she'd started dilating. She wasn't in labor yet, but given her due date was at the end of the week, the news hadn't surprised anyone. Apparently, Dani was in the same situation. It was going to be a race to see who delivered first.

"So how was it with Cord over the weekend?" Arsula asked. She didn't look away from the belt she'd picked up, but Maggie could hear the pointedness of the question.

"It was fine with Cord."

"And he stayed at your place all weekend?" Erica questioned from her other side. She, too, seemed overly focused on a pair of socks she now held. Her friends had apparently decided to grill her before Maggie could even bring the subject up. Which wasn't surprising. They'd been checking in with her every few days, asking how things were going.

She'd let them know the week before about the decision for Cord to stay at her place, both before and after the baby came. And she'd also brought them over to the house to show them the SUV. After much discussion, they'd helped convince her to keep the vehicle. It *would* be safer for the baby—and obviously, Cord could afford it. And as for the room full of baby paraphernalia that had come with it . . . other than the duplicates of what she'd already had, she'd agreed to keep most of those items, too. The idea of Cord out shopping for so much baby stuff had been too cute for her to want to send it all back.

"He *did* stay with me all weekend," Maggie answered. Then she turned her attention to a table full of pullovers that might be a good present for Max. She fake-ignored her friends just as they'd been doing to her.

"Ms. Crowder! Mrs. Wilde!"

Two young girls and their mother spotted them from the other side of the table, and Maggie and Erica greeted all three.

"Hey, girls." Maggie had taught the oldest the year before, and Erica had her sister in class this year.

"We're out shopping, too!" They each held up shiny bags with red and silver ribbon trailing over the sides. "I was just asking Mom if you'd had your baby yet, Mrs. Wilde."

Erica put her hand on her belly. "Not yet, Talia. It should be soon, though."

The mother's eyes lit up. "That's good to hear. I hope all goes smoothly." Erica had gone on maternity leave the week before. The mother shifted her gaze to Maggie. "And how are you doing, Ms. Crowder? I hear you're still working."

"I am until this Friday." School would let out for the holidays on Friday, and though she wasn't due until after the kids would return, she'd decided early on not to go back until after the baby arrived.

The adults all talked for a few more minutes, the girls humming under their breaths to the festive music being played over the store's speakers, and when Maggie, Erica, and Arsula were alone once again, Erica put down the socks she'd still been holding.

She turned to Maggie. "Okay, *spill*. We got interrupted before, but what I was going to say is that something is different with you the last few days. We can tell. You're . . . almost annoyingly happy."

Arsula faced her, as well. "Are you going to tell us, yet again, that Cord's staying over at your place is purely innocent?"

Maggie felt as if she'd suddenly come under fire. This was the purpose for the day, however. And she *had* told them that before. But that was before Cord showed up Friday night.

"No," she finally answered. "I am *not* going to tell you that. Because actually"—she broke into a wide grin, turning to face Erica, only, instead of including both of them—"things *did* change over the weekend. We're . . ." She didn't know how to explain it other than to simply say, "Dating."

Erica's smile went as wide as Maggie's. "I knew it."

Maggie grimaced. "You don't think it's a mistake?" She could feel Arsula behind her, watching her carefully, but she didn't dare look back. She needed to know what Erica thought before facing her other friend.

"I think it's sweet," Erica assured her. She squeezed Maggie's hand. "You two are cute together."

Maggie tried to contain her giddiness. "Really?"

Erica chuckled. "*Really*. You two will be good for each other, too. So, tell us everything. What's going on?"

Maggie couldn't tell them everything until she dealt with Arsula. She cautiously turned to her other friend. "I know you don't think Cord and I should be together," she began, but before she could say anything else, Arsula waved her off.

"Don't worry about that. I changed my mind."

Maggie's jaw fell open. "You what?"

Arsula gave a grudging nod, and Erica snickered behind Maggie. "I've been waiting for her to tell you," Erica whispered.

Maggie stepped back so she could take in both women at once. "What are you two talking about?" She zeroed in on Arsula. "Since when do you *not* think Cord 'isn't the man for me'?" That had been mentioned more than once over the course of their friendship. "I thought your intuition told you he had too much baggage for me."

She waved her hand again. "So, I was wrong. It happens."

Erica snickered again.

"Plus," Arsula continued. "Knowing who's made for each other and who isn't has always been more my mom's thing than mine. I think it boiled down to the fact that I didn't *want* you to get mixed up with him because yes, he does come with so much baggage."

A lot more than they knew, Maggie thought.

"But that was before I saw you two together."

Arsula had seen them together?

Did she mean that night at the hospital? Arsula had been furious with Cord at that point. Maggie couldn't imagine she'd "seen" anything from him simply putting his hand on Maggie's stomach. Plus, his back had been to them at the time.

She racked her brain, trying to recall any other time Arsula might be referring to, but she came up with nothing. She and Cord hadn't gone out over the weekend at all. Instead, after waking in the middle of the night and talking about his dream—as well as all the things she still hadn't managed to convince Cord he shouldn't feel responsible for—they'd spent Saturday and Sunday being super low-key.

They'd cooked meals together, shared stories from their pasts, worked on the dollhouses, and he'd helped her put together the changing table that matched the baby bed. It had been delivered that week. He'd also ordered a wooden rocker for her living room, declaring they'd need to be able to rock the baby in more than one room. It had been a really great weekend.

And there had been more kissing, too.

She grinned at the memory. Being eight months pregnant . . . she supposed it *was* possible to do more than some heavy petting. But it was really nice simply to have this kind of time to spend together. There was something to be said for a nice slow burn.

"Good grief, look at that smile."

Maggie pulled her attention back from the weekend and shot Arsula a guilty look. "I can't help it. It was a good weekend. And don't tell me you haven't worn the same expression because of Jaden plenty of times."

"Well, yeah. But I would assume the sexual gymnastics that puts that kind of grin on my face aren't quite possible for you two right now." She sent a pointed look to Maggie's belly.

Maggie returned a smirk. "Stop teasing me." She went back to the table and picked up a couple of the pullovers. "And no, Cord and I are not *doing it*, if that's what you're asking. We're just getting to know each other better."

"And making out," Erica correctly guessed, and Maggie blushed.

"A few kisses," she admitted. "That's all." Then she returned to the original topic. She glanced back over at Arsula. "But what did you mean? When did you see the two of us together? We never left the house this weekend."

Arsula pointed to the burgundy shirt for Max. "At the medical plaza the day the twins were born."

Maggie eyed her. "You changed your mind from seeing him put his hand on my stomach?"

"Not then. *Before* that. While we were still over at the doctors' offices."

Maggie tried to recall what had been said while they'd been in the lobby of the Women's Pavilion. That had been right before they'd gotten the call about Harper. She'd run into Cord . . . he'd apparently been arguing with Arsula . . . and then she'd told him she had a meeting with a lawyer.

A meeting which she'd never made it to, but that wasn't a current priority.

She couldn't figure it out. "What changed your mind?"

Arsula finally broke out her own smile, only hers came across as a little dreamy. "The way he looked at you when he said you two would never speak again."

Maggie remembered that moment. They'd been coming to an agreement about her original requests. She'd agreed to a college account that he could fund. He'd agreed to sign away his rights. And then, she'd been about to cry as she'd tried to repeat her last request. Cord had finished the sentence for her.

Then we never speak to each other again.

The whole lobby had seemed to disappear as she'd stood there. His not being in their lives hadn't broken her heart for her *son* that day, but instead for *her*. Cord was a special man, whether he knew it or not, and she hadn't wanted him to walk away.

"You wore the same look he did, by the way."

"I did?"

"Absolutely."

Erica slipped an arm through Maggie's and leaned into her. "You aren't the only one with a crush, Mags," she whispered. "We think that boy has feelings."

Maggie didn't want to get her hopes up too high. "You're sure?" she asked Arsula. "You could see that?" She'd begun to think the same thing over the weekend, but with them getting together because she was pregnant, it was hard to determine if he really wanted to be with *her* or if he was just doing it for the baby.

"I could definitely see that," Arsula assured her. "And I could also see that he didn't want to agree to what you'd asked of him."

Maggie remembered more of that moment. He'd only nodded when she'd reminded him that she wanted him to sign away his rights. He hadn't agreed out loud. Had he already been doubting his decision?

"You said crap on a cracker," she recalled. Then she chuckled. "Out of the blue. I had no clue what you'd seen or what had shocked you, then we got interrupted about Harper before you could explain it. Was that why?"

"It was." She leaned in on Maggie's other side and tilted her head until it rested on Maggie's shoulder. "I felt like I was watching one of my best friends talking to the man she *is* supposed to be with," she whispered.

Pleasure washed through Maggie. She knew Arsula was likely just saying what she thought Maggie would want to hear, but she *really* did want to hear it. She'd originally thought her crush was just that. A crush. She hadn't been with a guy in a long time when they'd gotten together back in the spring, and a weekend with him had seemed like the perfect solution. Only, she'd seriously enjoyed their time together. And now that they were "dating," it had only gotten better. He reminded her, in some ways, of her father. He watched out for her. And he could be so darn sweet.

"He's a good man," she said to her friends.

They both nodded.

"He is," Erica agreed out loud. "I've known him a lot longer than Gabe and I have been together. I met him back in college, the *first* time Gabe and I dated. Their mom really messed him up, though, hon." She squeezed Maggie's arm where she still had hers looped through it. "Keep that in mind. She messed all of them up, but to hear Gabe tell it, I think she had a special knack for getting into Cord's head."

Maggie thought about Cord saying that his role in the family was to save his mom.

"I'm glad I never met her," she said.

"Me, too," they both agreed.

"He is worth fighting for," Erica continued, "just keep in mind that it may take him a while to admit how much he cares. Cord has some hard walls to scale, and I think he needs to scale them as much as he needs someone else willing to do so with him. So, if this is real . . . all I'm saying is, don't give up on him. Any of the Wildes are worth fighting for."

~

MAGGIE'S front door opened Friday night before Cord could get all the way to it, and Maggie's smiling face poked out.

"You're here early!" Joy filled her features.

"It's supposed to be clear all weekend, so I chartered a helicopter."

"I'm so glad." She stepped back, opening the door wider and hurriedly motioning him inside. "Come in. I want to show you something. I just finished."

Her excitement was contagious. He stepped inside the door. "Can I steal a kiss first?"

At his question, she immediately stopped. She slowly turned back, her bottom lip caught between her teeth, and he let himself admit what he'd been trying to avoid thinking about all week. He'd missed her like crazy.

"You want to kiss . . . *me?*" she teased. Her eyes sparkled with delight.

"I'd *like* to do a hell of a lot more than kiss you," he declared. Then he swept his gaze over her form, watching as her fingers clenched at her sides. He would love to roam his hands all over every luscious curve, even if that's all they could do. He stepped closer and pushed the door closed with his foot. "Did you miss me this week, Maggie?"

Her eyes glazed over. "I most certainly did."

"Good."

She went up on her toes before he could lean in and slid her hands into his hair. "Kiss me, Cord," she whispered against his lips. "Kiss me like you did the first time you ever walked into this house."

He growled under his breath as memories assailed him, and he ground his mouth to hers.

He tugged her close, careful not to hold her too tight, but he wanted to feel her pressed against his body. Once he had her tucked in, her curves aligned alongside his strength, he went caveman and plundered. They kissed for several minutes like that, standing right there, two feet inside the door, until both of them were out of breath. And when he pulled back, she wore the type of smile he loved to see the most.

"Hello," he officially greeted her. "It's nice to see you again."

She laughed lightly, looking flustered and thoroughly disoriented, and he told himself that seeing her reaction almost made up for not being able to be there in person over the last five days.

"Now . . ." He took her hand. *"What was it you wanted to show me?"*

She looked confused for a moment, as if still thinking about the kiss instead of whatever she'd had on her mind, and he couldn't help but pull her back in for another round. She was just too cute. And somehow, he was just too smitten.

"Cord," she whispered when he released her the second time. Her voice had turned husky, and it managed to scrape itself all the way into the depths of his soul. "I'm . . . uh . . ." She looked down at herself, her hands motioning up and down in front of her belly, and she blew out a frustrated breath.

"Over eight months pregnant?" he guessed.

"Exactly."

"I know that." He waggled his brows at her. "And you're sexy as hell."

She chuckled as if she didn't quite believe him, so he took her hands and held them out to her sides.

"Do you want to know what I see when I look at you, Mags?"

She gulped. "I don't know if I do or not. I mean . . . I'm already far too turned on as it is." She licked her lips and continued. "And the point I was trying to make before. About my state of pregnancy. Is that . . ." Her gorgeous eyes pleaded with him, and he could see her uncertainty. Not about her physical ability to be intimate, he didn't think, though that was likely in question, as well. But her doubt likely centered more around what he might think if he saw her without clothes. She would look a lot different than she had before. "I just don't know, Cord."

He cupped her chin and pressed another quick kiss to her lips. "I'm not pushing for anything more, Mags. I love kissing you. Kissing you is enough. Of *course*. But I'm also not going to lie and say that I wouldn't like to stroke my hands all over your gorgeous body. What man wouldn't want to?"

She gulped again, and then she turned without another word and headed to the kitchen.

He chuckled behind her, enjoying the moment more than any other since he'd driven away from her earlier that week. They'd talked every night on the phone, usually via video call, and he'd also ended up texting her multiple times throughout each day. He hadn't really known how he'd feel about this whole relationship thing when he'd first agreed to it, but surprisingly, he'd found that he liked it. He also figured that if he ever was going to try a real relationship, it should be with someone who made him laugh and who turned him on. And Maggie did both. She also simply left him feeling good. Being around her caused happiness. And it didn't hurt, of course, that she happened to be carrying his baby. Which had upped her sex appeal even more than what it had been back in April.

He followed along behind her. "What is this you've got to show me?"

"It's a surprise."

She took him into the kitchen, where the two dollhouses

remained and motioned toward the table with a little "ta-da." Only, he had no clue what he was supposed to be seeing. They looked the same to him.

"Did you add more wallpaper?" he asked.

"No, silly. We finished that last weekend. Lean in. Take a closer peek inside the rooms."

He edged in, scanning over the three stories of each house, and then he finally saw it. The windows of each room now had tiny curtains hanging from them. "You found curtains?"

"I *made* curtains. And I made several extra pairs for each." She opened one of the two metal cookie tins sitting beside the houses to reveal a variety of additional curtains tucked inside, all of differing colors and sizes. "They attach with Velcro." She picked up a small panel to show him. "That way the girls can easily change them out to update the look of the rooms. I thought they might like it."

When she turned her face back up to his, looking quite proud of herself and likely assuming he'd thank her for the extra effort she'd gone to, he didn't have words.

"Cord?" She frowned when he remained silent. "Oh, dang. Did I mess up? Did you have something else planned?" She put the lid back on the tin. "I'm sorry."

"No," he finally managed. *"No,"* he said again, this time cupping her face in his hands.

Making tiny dollhouse curtains was something akin to what his sister might do. His sister, who was a *great* mother. It wasn't anything *his* mother would ever have done. If his mother ever went out of her way to create anything that others might deem special, then she did it for the express purpose of making sure *others* saw it. Not simply because it would have made him or any of his siblings happy.

"They're perfect," he whispered, unable to fully express what he was feeling. "Amazing." Then he kissed her again. Not passionately this time. Not like he had when he'd first come in. But he kissed her with as much feeling, just the same. This woman was going to make an excellent mother. And she was going to be the mother of *his* son.

When he pulled back that time, he read the confusion in her eyes. She'd felt the intensity of the kiss, too, he knew, and she wanted to know what it meant. But he didn't say anything. He didn't know what it meant. Or maybe he did.

It meant that he had no clue how he was going to be away from her and their son every day. He had no clue how he was supposed to do this. His job meant a great deal to him, and he'd worked extremely hard to get noticed by such a top-tier practice. He couldn't just walk away from it. Especially not now that he was back in everyone's good graces. The dreams had subsided that week, and his colleagues had quickly picked up on his less tense mood. Life was back to normal in Billings. The job was good. His life was great. How was he supposed to consider giving all of that up?

Might *she* consider giving up her life here and moving for him?

"Cord?"

"Thank you," he blurted out before she could ask about the kiss. He stepped back from her and nodded to the houses. "Jenna and Haley are absolutely going to love the curtains. Without a doubt. Just keep in mind, though," he teased, "Mia, and now Emma and Ellie, will be coming along in a few years, expecting their own dollhouses with custom-made curtains, as well. You know who they'll be hitting up for those."

He smiled, feeling the hint of fakeness to it and hoping she couldn't tell. And then he realized what he'd just implied. That Maggie would still be around several years from now as the next group of Wilde children got older. But would she? As *more* than just his son's mom?

Would he really be willing to let her be?

"I'll keep that in mind." She eyed him carefully, and he did his best to swallow his nerves. He didn't want her asking questions he didn't know the answers to yet.

"Do you want to go out to dinner? My treat." He felt like he was botching everything.

"There's no need. I made lasagna before you got here. Why don't we have some of that, and while we eat you can tell me what that kiss was about?"

CHAPTER SEVENTEEN

CORD HADN'T YET TOLD HER WHAT THAT KISS HAD BEEN ABOUT. OR why he'd acted so strangely when Maggie had shown him the curtains. And he hadn't done so because right after they'd sat down to eat, their cell phones had gone off.

Erica's water broke. They're admitting her to the hospital.

They'd both whooped with excitement, dinner—and the impending conversation—no longer a priority, and had quickly headed out. First babies could take a while to make their entrance, of course, but neither of them had wanted to wait at the house to hear more. Nor had any other member of Cord's family. Everyone had arrived at virtually the same time, with the exception of Harper and the twins. Within the first hour of waiting, though, more excitement had happened when *Dani's* water also broke. Haley and Mia had been reshuffled to other members of the family, and a nurse hurried out with a wheelchair.

It was Saturday morning now. Most of the family had gone home the night before when things progressed slowly for both women, but everyone was back now, including Erica's family from Silver Creek. Even Harper and the twins had shown up with Nick. Arsula and Jaden were currently snuggling the babies, making the kind of cute cooing noises that had Maggie wondering if they were also thinking of kids as well as planning a wedding, and according to the latest updates on the two deliveries, Dani and Erica both seemed to be nearing the end of labor.

"Do you have any sixes?" Jenna asked Maggie. Maggie sat across from the little girl, a small end table between them, and Haley had settled on the floor, perpendicular to them. They all held a hand of cards.

Maggie peeked over her cards, grinning at Gabe's daughter instead answering the question, then she laughed along with Haley as the other girl clued in and started to giggle.

"Say it," Haley whispered from the floor. "Say it, Ms. Crowder."

Maggie winked at the girl before cutting her eyes back to Jenna. "Go fish!" she mock-shouted.

Jenna groaned and dropped her head. "No fair. I haven't won any games yet."

"That's because you don't have any skills," Haley informed her cousin.

Maggie merely eyed Jenna, then sent a playful pointed gaze to the stack of cards sitting in the middle of the table.

"Fine," Jenna grumbled. She reached for a card, but her eyes lit up as soon as she got a look at it. "I got a six!" She held the card up for them to see. "I get another turn."

"No fair." It was Haley's turn to complain. "*I* needed that six." She slapped a hand to her mouth as soon as she realized what she'd said, and her eyes went wide. *"Oops,"* she mumbled behind her fingers.

Jenna cackled before saying the other girl's name. *"Haley . . .* do *you* have any sixes?"

"Good grief," Haley mumbled and handed over two of her cards. Jenna preened as she took the cards and turned all four of her sixes facedown, and that time, Maggie laughed along with *her.* The girls were a lot of fun.

They continued playing, Maggie enjoying her time hanging out with the two of them, but from the corner of her eye, she kept an eye on Cord. Since he'd returned from Dani's room a little earlier, he'd been sitting with his dad and Gloria. He currently held one-year-old Mia in his arms, her chubby cheeks crinkling with a smile every time he wiggled his fingers somewhere on her body and tickled her.

"Ms. Crowder," Haley said, pulling Maggie's attention back to the game. "It's your turn."

"Oh. Sorry about that."

Haley met Jenna's gaze knowingly. "She was looking at Uncle Cord again." They both rolled their eyes and made gagging faces.

"She looks at him the same way he looks at her," Jenna added.

Maggie chuckled along with the girls, but inside, she wanted to question what *they* saw when Cord looked at her. Not that they'd be able to fully articulate the emotions, she suspected. But Jenna's comment reminded her of what Arsula had said when they'd been shopping earlier that week. Arsula had changed her opinion of Cord being the right guy for Maggie simply because of the way he'd looked at her.

And apparently, she looked at him the same. If that was the case, did that mean that he was falling for *her* like she was *him*?

If his kissing the evening before was anything to go by, then he definitely had some feelings. *Sweet Jesus.* She could have let that man keep kissing her forever. Of course, then he'd talked about wanting to rub his hands all over her . . . and she'd *totally* noticed the way he'd been looking at her *then*. Pretty much the way she'd looked at him back in April when she'd so determinedly sought him out.

Hungry.

Lustful.

Determined.

"Ms. Crowder," Jenna drew Maggie's name out. "You still didn't take your turn."

"Oh." Embarrassment filled her. She pulled her gaze away from Cord yet again and played another couple of rounds before she caught herself once more checking out the man she wished she were brave enough to get naked with.

She'd asked her doctor about having sex while at her appointment that week. She was over eight months along now, and forgetting the logistics for the moment, she'd wanted to know if it would be safe for her and the baby. Just in case. Not that the additional two pounds she'd put on in the last seven days added another tick in the "yes" column. Her doctor had assured her, however, that if *she* felt like doing it then she was good to go. She had no high-risk issues that would stem any extracurricular activity.

But what would Cord think if she let him see her changed body?

Would he be as turned on as he'd been the first time?

Would he still want to put his hands all over her?

She realized she was looking at him again when his eyes met hers, and when he subtly pointed toward the door with a question in his eyes, she immediately nodded. Whatever he wanted, she was there for it.

"She's going to leave us," Jenna told the other girl before Maggie could figure out how to graciously depart. "I just saw Uncle Cord ask her."

Maggie almost laughed. The man wasn't subtle enough to be overlooked by his niece.

"That's okay," Haley determined. "I can continue beating you even if she isn't here."

Maggie assured the girls that she'd play with them again, then she looked back over at Cord. He still held Mia in his arms, but as he'd watched her, his eyes had darkened and the lines of his face suddenly seemed harder. It was as if he'd been inside her mind, knowing all the X-rated thoughts that had been stirring around in there.

Cord handed Mia off to Gloria, then he and Maggie rose at the same time and walked out the door together. Once clear of the room, he dragged her around another corner, then he backed her against a wall. He leaned in, one hand flattening to the wall beside her head and the other clasping her hand down by her hip. And when his mouth went to her neck instead of her mouth, she moaned —both in protest and in pleasure.

"Cord," she whispered as he nuzzled his way up to her ear. "Are you sure this is smart?" She panted out a breath. "Someone could see us."

If her words penetrated, he didn't let on. Instead, he released her hand and gripped her chin with his fingers. He angled her face away from his searching mouth and let his lips continue to nuzzle and suckle along her skin. His ministrations had her ultra-sensitive nipples tightening into such hard points that she didn't know if she wanted to rip his clothes off or rip *hers* off so the material of her bra would quit rubbing against them. The situation would almost be funny if she weren't melting into a puddle of desire.

"What are you doing?" she breathed out the question as she heard footsteps not far away.

"I'm pretty sure you know exactly what I'm doing." His voice was rough, and the sound of it caused a shiver to trek down her body. "We've done this before, remember?"

Oh, she remembered, all right. That's why her belly now announced her arrival well before others even realized she'd entered a room.

Cord released her chin, his hand dropping away, and the backs of his fingers skimmed over the outer edge of her breast. Then he slowly lifted his mouth from her heated skin. He remained leaning in, that one hand still against the wall. And when he didn't make any additional move to touch her, she cautiously turned her face to his. Her breaths came in short pants.

"That was . . . *nice*," she croaked.

He smiled like the devil that he was. "That's what you get for sitting in a room full of my family and thinking dirty thoughts."

She gulped as he confirmed her previous impression. The man *had* been inside her head. Or, at least, he'd read her thoughts. "I don't have a clue what you're talking about," she denied.

"Oh, sweetheart." The backs of his fingers slid along the outside edge of her breast once again. "You are such a bad liar." He leaned back in and put his mouth to her ear. "What were you thinking about in there, Maggie?"

Another shiver racked her body. No way was she going to admit her thoughts. At least, not right here. Another set of footsteps sounded close by. "I was thinking that you remind me of my father," she lied.

She could feel his mouth curve into a smile. "I don't think so."

She nodded, her head moving in a quick up and down. "Yes. That's absolutely what I was thinking." Then she had to rack her brain to come up with something believable to convince him. "You were playing with Mia . . . looking all fatherly. He was a good dad, you know? Just like you're going to be."

He pulled back and looked at her. The glint in his eyes had shifted from teasing to serious, but his words remained light. "I am *not* your father, Maggie Crowder. Make no mistake about that."

She couldn't keep the smile from her lips. "Oh, I'm very aware that." She lowered her gaze to his mouth, and very intentionally caught her bottom lip between her teeth. "*Nor* would I want you to be," she added in a murmur. And when she lifted her eyes back up to his, she felt another piece of her heart break off. This man did things to her that she didn't want him to ever stop doing. "You're also sweet," she told him, reaching up to caress his jaw. "My dad has always been sweet. Both to my mom and to me."

The teasing slipped from Cord's expression. "You think I'm *sweet?*" He seemed serious.

"I do."

He continued to peer down at her. "I feel like I should be offended by that, but for some reason, I'm not. I kind of like it."

"You should like it. You're a special man, Cord Wilde."

He kissed her then, right there where other people were walking by and where anyone who wanted to take a peek could see. And it wasn't a chaste peck on the cheek. He held her face in his hands, and he made love to her mouth in the same way she remembered him cherishing her entire body back in the spring. It also made her think of how he'd kissed her the night before. Not when he'd first arrived, but after she'd shown him the curtains. He'd kissed her then as if he treasured everything about her that made her unique. And he'd kissed her as if he never wanted to let go.

When they both came up for air, he didn't look away. His eyes had grown dark. "Come with me to my family's Christmas," he whispered. "If you aren't going out of town to see *your* family, of course. We're going to—"

"I'd love to," she interrupted. She didn't need to hear any more. She'd been hoping he'd ask ever since Arsula and Erica had mentioned that the entire family would be spending the night at the Wilde house. Each child would stay in the room they'd grown up in —with the exception of Nick and Nate, who'd shared a room— along with their spouses.

She wasn't Cord's spouse, but she took the invitation to mean that they'd spend the night together.

"Good." Cord lowered his gaze to her lips. "That would be perfect. You being there . . . Then you can make certain to get credit for the curtains."

"And the wallpaper," she added. "We can't forget the wallpaper."

She didn't think they were just talking about curtains and wallpaper. She wasn't, at least. He'd said her being there would be perfect, and she couldn't agree more. Being with him was the only place she wanted to be. And whatever happened between the two of them in his childhood bedroom . . . Well . . .

Cord dragged his gaze back to hers. "The wallpaper," he agreed. And then he smiled.

She loved his smile.

"You're going to make an exceptional mother, Maggie."

The words caught her by surprise, jarring her by coming out of nowhere, but the sentiment meant the world to her. He knew her ability as a mother was something she continually worried about. "You think?"

He nodded. "I know. I've always known, but when I saw the curtains . . . "

He brought her hands up and kissed the backs of her fingertips, and this time when his gaze found hers, there was no heat. Only emotion. "My mother would have *never* done anything like that," he told her. "Not for any of us, but certainly not for someone else's nieces. Unless there was a benefit to her, of course. But you so selflessly give. You—" He stopped talking, seeming to need to think about his words before continuing. "That's what I was thinking Friday night, Maggie. When you showed me the curtains. That you were going to make an exceptional mother, and that I'm so lucky because you're going to be the mother of *my* son. Nothing could make me happier. And that's what that kiss was about. All those feelings were jumbled up inside me, and the only way I could show you was with the kiss."

When his words ran out, he remained standing with her backed against a wall, and what she saw staring back at her were all the same things she felt. "And you're going to make an exceptional dad," she whispered. Her eyes grew damp. "We're going to make one hell of a team."

He kissed her again then. Slow at first, worshipping her lips. But passion quickly became the theme of the moment, and when he tunneled his fingers into her hair, she couldn't hold in the moan of pleasure that rippled through her. She was crazy about this man. And she thought he might just be feeling the same.

When he once again pulled away from her, they both looked up toward the ceiling at the same time. A soft lullaby was coming through the hospital's speaker. A baby had just been born.

CORD STOOD at the doorway to the hospital room, remaining quiet so as not to be noticed. The lullaby had sounded, and within a couple of minutes everyone on the family group text had received both a picture and an announcement. Ivy Rochelle Wilde had entered the world at 10:07 a.m. weighing seven pounds five ounces. Gabe and Erica had had a girl.

Maggie was in the hospital room with Erica, Gabe, and Jenna now. She'd initially stayed in the background, allowing both families to visit with the new baby, but now it was her turn to spend time with her friend. Gabe stood off to the side, the pride on his face unable to be missed. Nor could Cord keep from seeing the love. On either parents' face. But it was Maggie who Cord couldn't pull his attention from.

Maggie held the pink-faced baby in her arms, the tiny thing snuggled in tight above her belly, and Cord couldn't help but think that it would be their baby in her arms soon. And that he would be the one exuding the roomful of pride.

He couldn't wait to meet the child they'd made. He couldn't wait to see where his and Maggie's relationship could go.

"That's one good-looking family," his dad said as he stepped to Cord's side.

"It is." Cord had little else to say. His entire family had changed so drastically over the last three years, and it seemed that he was now right in there with them. None of them could have predicted the paths they'd all taken.

"You ready to have one of your own?"

Cord looked over at his dad's serious tone. The two of them rarely had long, deep conversations, but it felt like one coming on now.

"I am ready." That was only a small fib.

His dad watched the room instead of looking at Cord. "And you think you're going to be okay driving away from them every week?"

Leave it to his father to get right to the point.

Cord still had no idea how he was going to do that. "My job is in Billings, Dad."

"So get a new job."

Cord closed his eyes instead of letting out a sigh. "That's easier said than done." It was also easier for everyone else to say than for him to *want* to do.

"Horse crap." His dad still didn't look at him. "Your priorities are screwed up. This is what life is about right here." He nodded toward the others in the room, and Cord could hear soft murmurs coming from Erica as she spoke to Ivy. "Family. Kids." His dad paused again before adding, "A wife who loves and respects you."

As his father's gravelly voice washed over Cord, it wasn't a potential wife for *him* he thought about, but the wife his dad once had. And as he looked at the past from a different perspective for the first time, he also felt bad for his dad for the first time. At least, bad as it pertained to living with Carol Wilde.

For so long, Cord had merely thought of his father as being complicit with his mom's behavior. The man had never done much to try to stop it. Instead, he'd simply rolled over and let her run roughshod over him, as well as the rest of them. But hearing his words now, Cord suddenly saw a glimpse of his dad's life in a different light. The man had produced six children with the woman. They'd been together for two decades. Had he ever truly felt love from her? And if not, how must that have hurt? How must it have bothered him that he couldn't be a better father?

At least he'd stayed, Cord thought. He'd been there.

"You've got a woman who loves you now," Cord finally replied, ignoring the stab in his heart when he once again thought about not being around enough for his own kid.

"I do," his dad agreed. "And I'm grateful."

"You've got an entire family who loves you, Dad."

His dad finally looked over, and Cord could see a mist of tears threatening at his eyes. He'd been through a lot that year, but if one good thing had come from all of it, it was how the family had banded together to be there for each other. To be there for their dad.

"I wasn't a good father," he said.

"You were fine, Dad."

"I . . ." He turned back to the others in the room, and Cord watched as his hand trembled where it gripped his cane. "I wanted to be," his dad admitted. "I truly did. I loved all of you kids with all my heart. I just . . . wasn't good at it. I'm thankful every day, though, that my mistakes didn't push any of you away. At least not forever. I'm thankful you're all so close now."

He took a step back, turning so he faced Cord, and when Cord couldn't find any words to contribute, his dad continued.

"Consider coming home, Cord. Not later, but now. Life isn't about a job. It's about the heart. You're going to be a good dad. So much better than I could have ever been. And you're going to cherish every moment when you're older. I let your Momma walk all over me, son, but that's not something you're going to have to worry about. Don't let this opportunity pass you."

He took another look back into the hospital room before reaching out with his free hand and patting Cord on the arm.

"Next weekend is Christmas. Our last at the house. Bring Maggie with you. Start a *new* life there so you have *good* memories to add to the rest of them. Embrace what life has handed to you."

He walked off before Cord could let him know that he *had* invited Maggie, muttering about needing to check on Dani, and Cord turned back to the room. He hadn't set out to invite Maggie to his family Christmas that morning. He'd still been contemplating the implications of doing so. Would she read the wrong things into it? Was *he* ready to have her there?

All those things, he'd been thinking because he'd wanted to be sure. But as soon as the words had tumbled out of his mouth, he'd known it was the right thing to do. Because he *did* want what his dad had just suggested. He wanted to create a new memory associated with the house. He wanted to start a new life.

The idea still scared him, of course. Everything had moved so fast between the two of them, and he couldn't figure out how to slow it down. Not that he'd done anything *to* slow it down. He'd only added to the speed. But still . . . all the changes frightened him. He didn't know if he was making the right decisions.

Maggie caught him watching, and the gentle curve that tugged up the corners of her lips had a band squeezing around his heart. He could see so much emotion being directed back to him. And he knew it wasn't all due to the baby she held in her arms.

This woman thought he was sweet.

She thought he would be a good dad.

He didn't for a minute buy that she'd really been comparing him to her father while they'd been sitting in the waiting room, but he did believe the other words she'd said. Only, could he live up to her expectations?

He hoped so.

Another lullaby sounded over the hospital's speakers, and Maggie's smile inched higher. And this time, his lips curved with hers. Did that mean Dani had given birth? And if so, had she delivered a boy? Or would he and Maggie soon provide the family's first grandson?

At the thought, he suddenly felt the need for space. He stepped back, out of the doorway.

He didn't go far, just out of sight. And he pulled in a deep breath. He and Maggie would have a baby within a few weeks. He would have a son. He would be a father.

He let the thoughts repeat.

Going there no longer caused stress. The knowledge brought joy instead. But he still couldn't figure out how to do it right. How to make sure he didn't let them down.

Doctor Hamm came around the corner at the far end of the hall, and Cord watched as the older man drew nearer. He'd seen the doctor at the hospital earlier. He was in the building today in an official capacity, but he'd also stopped by the birthing center when he'd heard that Erica and Dani were both there.

"Cord." As Doc Hamm stopped at Cord's side, he offered a smile and a handshake. "Just the man I was looking for."

"Yeah?" Cord returned the greeting. "What can I do for you, Doc?"

Hamm nodded in the direction he'd come, his genial expression disappearing. "Take a walk with me?"

Worry immediately settled inside Cord. Was this about his dad? "Sure."

He didn't ask for details as they moved down the hall. If the doctor had something to talk about that needed privacy, then Cord would wait. But the fear that *hadn't* been in him when he'd been thinking about his impending fatherhood now showed up as fear of the unknown. Had he missed something else with his dad?

Hamm stopped once they'd rounded the corner and had stepped into a small alcove, but when he turned back, Cord didn't see the grim expression he'd expected. Instead, it was happiness that radiated back at him.

"I'm retiring, Cord."

Shock registered, hitting him as if being whacked with a two-by-four, and "wow" was the only thing Cord managed to say. The doc had been a fixture Cord's entire life, and though he'd known the man wouldn't work forever, he also couldn't say he'd ever really thought about him retiring. Doc Hamm was just *there*. Always. "Congratulations," he finally managed to tack on.

"Thanks," the doc said. "It feels like it's time. Annie moved to Chicago a couple of months ago. Her husband was offered a great job, and they just put in an offer for a home. It looks like they'll be staying. So . . . well"—he lifted his hands—"the missus and I miss them, Cord. We miss the grandkids. So, we've decided to move, too."

Another wave of shock reverberated, shifting Cord to the heels of his feet. The doc wasn't just retiring, he was moving away. For good.

Selfishly, Cord wondered who would keep an eye on his dad when he wasn't around. He'd always assumed Doc would be there.

"Of course you'd want to do that," Cord forced himself to add. Doc Hamm had only the one child, and Annie and her husband were raising three kids. Who wouldn't want to be around their grandchildren?

"I knew you'd understand." Doc nodded in the direction they'd come. "You're having one of your own, I hear."

It didn't surprise Cord that word had gotten around. "I am."

The older man's face softened. "Life changes when kids come into play. Life is *good* with kids. With family around."

"Definitely." Cord didn't say anything else because the moment suddenly felt intense. First his dad had given him a talk about being there for his son, and now the doc had pulled him aside . . . and Doc was also talking about kids. About family.

Was the world trying to tell him—

"I'm asking if you'll consider buying my practice, Cord."

Cord gaped at the other man. "What?"

That was not the path he'd have seen this conversation going.

Doc nodded, his mouth pulling taut. "It's hard to walk away from, I'll admit. But the decision sure would be easier to swallow if I were leaving my patients in your hands. In fact, I've been hoping you'd decide to come home for a while now. I know you've done well for yourself. You're in with a group that should make you extremely proud. *I'm* proud of you. But I also can't help that I've always imagined you as the doctor to follow in my footsteps here. I'd love to hand the reins over to you, Cord. It would give me the greatest honor. And I know your dad would love to have you back home, too."

His dad?

Cord's shock skittered to a halt. Why had Doc brought his dad into the conversation?

Had his father put Doc up to this?

Was *that* what his dad's earlier conversation had been leading up to?

He managed to tamp down the spurt of anger—and to keep

himself from saying anything he might later regret—but he also recognized the feeling now flowing through him. This whole thing felt like a setup. It felt suspiciously like the type of manipulation his mother might have once orchestrated. Of course, she would have done so only if it had benefited *her*. But wouldn't *this* benefit his dad? Wasn't Cord coming home exactly what his dad wanted?

"I see I've caught you off guard," Doc Hamm said when Cord forgot to reply. Hamm reached out and clapped Cord on the shoulder. "There's no rush. Give it some thought," he suggested. "If you're not interested, then I'll put the word out. See if I can find another physician looking to move to the area. Let's talk after the holidays, okay?"

Cord managed a cordial nod. "Sounds good."

Doc walked off in the direction he'd originally come, and Cord stood rooted to the spot. Years of anger threatened to surface.

His common sense told him to go talk to his father. To see if he really had put Hamm up to this. His common sense *also* told him that whether his dad had put him up to it or not, it wasn't as if the doctor would retire simply because Cord's father might have suggested doing so could be a way to bring Cord home. This was a legitimate proposition. It was an offer that he *could* consider. If he wanted to move back to Birch Bay.

But, did he?

He needed to find Maggie.

Not to talk about this with her. He had to come to his own decision. Instead, he just wanted to be near her.

Before he could turn back for the hospital room, however, his phone dinged, and he looked down.

Alice Dawn Denton, born 1:13pm, seven pounds thirteen ounces.

The text arrived with a video of mom, dad, and newborn baby.

As he watched the video, everything inside him went still, holding tight as reality set in. Then warmth began to seep throughout his body. He and Maggie were going to have the first Wilde grandson.

Potential fury with his dad or not, he couldn't stop the thrill the knowledge gave him. He hadn't let himself put too much thought into the idea before. He couldn't have imagined none of the other babies wouldn't also be a boy. But now that it was a fact, he found himself unable to stop the grin from appearing on his face. He *had* to find Maggie.

When he turned, anxious to get back to her, he discovered that he didn't have to go looking after all. Because Maggie had already found *him*. She stood ten feet away, her own phone held out in front of her and her mouth forming a little O of surprise. She lifted her gaze.

"We're going to have the first grandson," she whispered.

The kind of pride that Doc Hamm had been talking about earlier enveloped Cord. "We're going to have the first grandson."

CHAPTER EIGHTEEN

MAGGIE STOOD IN THE DOORWAY OF THE BEDROOM CORD HAD BEEN using, her fingers twined together and her hands resting on top of her belly. She watched as the man packed his bag to head back to Billings. "I'm going to miss you this week."

She bit her lip as the words slipped out, and Cord looked up.

A smile gentled his features. "I'm going to miss you, too."

She swallowed, her worries temporarily eased. They'd come so far so quickly, but at the same time, it felt as if things had stalled since they'd gotten back from the hospital the day before. Possibly, they'd even gone in reverse—at least for him. Cord hadn't done or said anything different. Not directly. He was still sweet with her. He still caressed her belly and talked to their son. And he still kissed her as if pulling his lips away was the hardest thing imaginable. Yet he'd been different. Even before they'd left the hospital.

They'd visited with Dani and Alice before heading home, and she'd noticed a distance between him and the others at that point. He hadn't snuggled with Alice quite the same way he'd done with Ivy. He hadn't smiled and joked with Dani as he had earlier with the rest of his siblings. Basically, the wall that had once so prominently sat between him and the rest of the world seemed to have been securely re-erected. And whatever was going on in his head? He hadn't shared a thing with her.

"You're sure there's nothing you need to talk about before you go?" she asked, hoping he wouldn't drive away without opening up first. His altered mood had been bad enough, but worse was wondering what had caused it. Was he second-guessing their relationship? Had being there for Ivy's and Alice's births changed his mind for some reason about wanting to be present for his own child's?

She hoped not. And really, she would find that hard to believe. He seemed too invested in his son at this point. But *something* had happened at the hospital to cause this change.

"I told you, I'm fine." He didn't look at her as he repeated the words he'd used the night before, zipping his bag closed instead, then he exited the room to cross to the small guest bathroom. He didn't meet her gaze as he passed her in the doorway, and when he entered the other room, he left the door open. She could hear the drawer she'd emptied for him being opened and closed.

"Do you still want me to go with you to your family's house next week, then?"

He popped his head back out of the bathroom at her question. "What? *Yes.* Of course, I want you to go with me. Why would you ask that?" Worry creased his brow. "Do you not *want* to go?"

She *did* want to go. But only if he really wanted her there. And the more she'd thought about it, the more the invitation had felt spur of the moment. Had he gotten carried away with kissing her and blurted it out without meaning to? Was that what had been bothering him?

"I just don't want to be in the way," she explained. "I thought that maybe once you'd had time to think about inviting me, you'd—"

He was back in front of her before she could finish her sentence, and as he ran a fingertip along the underside of her chin, he pushed her gaze up to his.

"Mags." The blue of his eyes held more emotion than she'd seen in the last twenty-four hours. "I *want* you to go with me. I invited you because I want you there. I'm looking forward to spending Christmas with you, but I'm also looking forward to you spending Christmas with my family."

That meant a lot to her. Especially since she wouldn't be able to be with her own family. She didn't feel like taking that long of a drive to see her parents, and she couldn't go to Mason's because he would be working. "Then tell me what happened," she tried again. "Because something changed for you yesterday, and you've been different ever since. Admit it."

She stared him down, refusing to back off. And when she said nothing else nor made any attempt to soften her stance, he finally relented.

He blew out a breath. "Okay, yes. Something did happen. You're right. But it's an issue that I need to think through on my own, okay? I'm sorry. I just . . ." He pressed a quick kiss to her lips. "I don't want to talk about it yet, Maggie."

She could deal with that. *Possibly.* Especially given the earnestness of his answer. But she had to know one thing first. "Does it have anything to do with me or the baby?"

"Sweetheart." A hint of a smile touched his lips, and he shook his head as he cupped her face. His eyes smiled along with his lips. "*No.* You and the baby are awesome. You, *me*—and Cord, Jr.—are awesome." He finished with a wink, and she pursed her lips.

"I've not agreed to Cord, Jr." They'd talked about baby names several times, but they hadn't yet settled on anything.

His smiled inched higher. "*Maggie* Jr., then."

"*Cord.*" She fake-punched him. "Stop it. I'm being serious. You're worrying me, okay? I just want to make sure that we're okay. And if this isn't about us, then I'd love to help . . . if you'd let me."

His gaze turned serious as he continued to stare down at her. "You and I are absolutely okay. Trust me on that. This is something with my dad, all right? Something that I need to work through and then probably talk to him about. But I'm going to wait until after the holidays to have that conversation. I don't want it involving others or getting in the way of everyone enjoying time together next weekend."

She wanted to ask what it was again, but she wouldn't do it. She respected his privacy. But if it was serious enough that it might disrupt his entire family's Christmas, then she couldn't help but worry for him.

She reached up and captured one of his hands. "You'll be able to put it behind you next weekend, though? Long enough to enjoy time with your family? To enjoy . . . *our* time together?"

She didn't say out loud that she was talking about them spending the night together, but she could see that he understood. His lids lowered as he took in her mouth, and she caught herself licking her lips in anticipation of a kiss.

"I promise it won't get in the way of our time together," he murmured. Then, thankfully, he fulfilled her desire and kissed her. It was hot and urgent, but it ended way too soon. And when he lifted his head, she could see his expectations for the coming weekend mingling with hers. Neither of them knew if they would do anything more than share the bed together, but whatever happened, it would be the intimacy of being with each other that meant the most.

"I'd intended to invite you into my bed last night, you know?" She told him that because she wanted him to ache a little by knowing it. Like she'd ached when she'd had to go to bed alone. "But you—"

"Stupidly went to bed before you could offer," he finished.

"Yes. You did." It was as if he'd sensed what she'd been about to suggest, and suddenly he'd been ready to turn in. They'd stood from the couch together after finishing a movie, but then he'd kissed her and headed to his room before she could get a word in edgewise.

"I'm an idiot," he confessed. "I shouldn't have let my personal issues get in the way."

"No, you shouldn't have." She gave him the kind of come-hither look that had worked on him back in April, and he groaned out loud.

"Maggie," he whispered before he leaned in and kissed her again, and that time when he pulled back, he shook his head and let out another groan before dragging her down the hallway. "Quit tempting me, woman. I'm going to miss my flight back if I don't get out of here."

They were headed to the front door. "It would be a *real* shame if you had to spend the whole week with me instead."

He chuckled, the sound making her smile because of the sexual frustration she heard in it, but he didn't stop moving until he reached the door. Once there, though, he turned back, and that time he kissed her longer and hungrier than he had before. And *that* time, he had *her* whimpering before he was done.

"You're an evil man, Cord Wilde." She licked the taste of him where it lingered on her lips.

"I'm a *lucky* man." He lifted her hand and kissed her palm, then he let his gaze slowly travel the length of her body. "Do you have any idea how beautiful you are, Maggie?" His eyes met hers. "You were before, but you're even more so now. You're mind-blowing."

A flush washed through her. "You must have a thing for round women."

"I have a thing for gorgeous women." He kissed her hand again. "*This* gorgeous woman."

He'd called her sexy once before, and now beautiful and gorgeous. And if he were lying, then he was the world's best liar. She'd certainly not thought of herself in that way in months, and before that, typically "good-looking" was as far as she'd go. She was more girl-next-door than Victoria's Secret model, and she'd always been okay with that. But when Cord looked at her like he was doing now, she felt as if she could go head-to-head with any long-legged, designer-clothes-wearing woman strutting her stuff.

Of course, she might waddle down the runway instead of strut, but even so, she suspected that Cord would be looking at *her*. This man was good for her confidence.

"Think about me this week," she told him.

He lifted his brows. "I think about you all the time, babe."

Oh, this man was a charmer. She swallowed as he reached behind him and opened the door.

"I'll pick you up Friday?" he asked.

"I'll be here." She hooked her thumb back over her shoulder. "And I'll have the dollhouses ready to go." They'd gone Christmas shopping earlier that day, picking up gifts for the latest two nieces, as well as purchasing gift bags large enough to wrap the dollhouses in. They just hadn't gotten around to doing the wrapping yet.

"Leave them. I'll take care of it when I get here. I don't work Friday, so I'll head out first thing. Snow is supposed to move into the area again next weekend, so I'll drive instead of charter a flight, but I'll still be here in plenty of time."

"Good. I'll miss you until then."

He grinned, the sight top-level toe-curling, then he leaned in and kissed her one more time. When they separated, he stepped backward out of the door. "Let me know what the doctor says about you this week."

"Last week she said that I could have sex if I wanted to."

He looked as if he'd swallowed his tongue. *"Mags."* His entire face flushed hot. *"That* is evil."

She grinned back at him. "That's just me getting you back." She blew him a kiss and stepped back to shut the door. "I'll see you Friday, hot stuff."

After he'd walked toward his rental, she closed the door, and when she turned and leaned back against it, she didn't even try to fight the smile. She was in love with that man. There was no doubt.

Could he be falling in love with her, too?

She hoped so. Maybe that's what he'd give her for Christmas. His love. Because that was the only thing she wanted.

She pushed off the door, intending to go wrap the dollhouses instead of waiting for him to do it, but her phone rang before she could make it to the kitchen. She pulled her cell from one of the deep pockets of her shirt and was surprised to find it was her mother calling.

"Hey, Mom." Most often, Maggie was the one who called, but every once in a while her mother surprised her. And sometimes it wasn't a good surprise.

"Hey, baby. How are you doing?"

Maggie stopped in the middle of the room as relief washed through her. Her mother was having a good day. She could already tell. "I'm doing great, Mom. How are you? You sound good."

"I am good. Your dad and I just got back from buying a new horse. We needed another one since our reservations continue to increase every month." After their first year of getting comfortable owning the ranch, they'd steadily grown the business.

"I can't wait to see it the next time I visit."

"Me either. Her name is Summer. You'll love her." A pause of uncomfortableness briefly hung in the air before her mother asked, "How's the baby?"

Maggie knew that even after all this time it was still hard for her mom to think about unborn babies, much less to talk about them. When Maggie had visited to tell them about her pregnancy, she'd been concerned the news would send her mother into a downward spiral. If it had, though, neither she nor Maggie's father had mentioned it. They didn't always share everything, though.

"He's doing good, Mom." She rubbed her hand over her son. "He's still growing."

"Still kicking?"

Maggie closed her eyes as her mother's question caused physical hurt for the pain her mother had once been through. "He's kicking my hand right now."

"Good. Here, your father wants to talk to you." Her mother was gone before Maggie could say anything else, and the next thing she heard was her father saying her name.

"Hi, Dad." She loved her dad fiercely, but she always got a twinge of regret in her chest if she thought about it too much. She'd once been such a daddy's girl.

"Hi, sweetheart. The baby's still good? You're good?"

She nodded, tears clinging to her lashes. "My doctor says everything is on track."

"And you're still thinking you won't deliver until close to your due date?"

She hadn't exactly said that before. She had no idea when she'd deliver. But there was also no reason to think it *wouldn't* be near her due date. "That's the assumption."

"Good. Your mom and I have our assistant manager lined up to handle things at that time. Once you're home from the hospital, we plan to come visit for a few days. We can stay in the hotel, of course. I know that Cord will be staying with you." She'd talked to her parents the week before, letting them know of her change in relationship status with Cord. "We don't want to step on his toes," he added.

"You won't be stepping on anyone's toes, Dad." And by then, Cord would be sleeping in her room. "The guest room will be available if you decide you want it." She wouldn't push the issue because she didn't know if her mother could handle staying in the house with a newborn. "But Dad," she started, then she couldn't make herself go on.

"What is it, Maggie?"

"I . . ." She closed her eyes and pictured the waiting room as it had been the day before. And again, the way it was when Harper had been giving birth to the twins. She wanted *her* parents to be at the hospital for her. If they couldn't make it in time for the delivery, then she at least wanted them there after. She didn't want to have to wait to introduce them to their grandchild.

She hadn't specifically asked that of them before. She'd always felt it selfish to even think the words. But it had been twenty-two years. Surely her mother could be there for her.

"Mom sounds good," she said, delaying the words she really wanted to say.

"Your mom has been doing really well lately. She's getting more exercise. We got the workout room upgraded and reopened for guests, and she's been using it every day."

Her mother always did better when she stayed active.

"She still cooking a lot?"

"Improved her jalapeno cornbread recipe recently, and now she's talking to the chef about using it in the restaurant."

Maggie smiled. Her mother's jalapeno cornbread was better than the potato soup Maggie had cooked for Cord that first night at the cabin.

"Dad . . . will you please consider coming to visit me in the hospital? I want *my* family there. Not just Cord's family." And she had no doubt that Cord's family *would* be there. They'd all accepted her as part of them, and they'd already been discussing plans for being there while at the hospital yesterday.

"I don't know, Maggie . . . You know your mother."

"I do know, Dad. But maybe it's time?"

She didn't say anything more. It wasn't just her mother's reluctance that bothered her, but her father's too. She'd once been so close to her dad. He'd been her hero when she was a kid. Always there for her when her mother couldn't be. And though the two of them did remain close—as close as the distance allowed, anyway—when he and her mother had moved away, she'd felt deserted.

"I think we'll just wait and visit after you're home."

CHAPTER NINETEEN

Fat snowflakes fell from the sky as Cord shifted into park, stopping his truck beside his sister's SUV. He looked over at Maggie. Light glowed across the fresh snow and into the cab of the truck, coming from the strands of clear globes running the length of the porch. Hanging on all of the front windows and the house's new double doors were pine wreaths tied off with large red bows, and visible through the panes of the front doors was a festively decorated tree. The place looked ready for a magical Christmas.

He reached over and took Maggie's hand. "You ready for this?"

He'd arrived at her place earlier that day and helped fix the side dishes she'd signed them up to bring for dinner. Jaden and Arsula were in charge of the prime rib; his dad and Gloria had taken desserts, and everyone else was on sides.

"I suppose I am." Her breaths were too short, giving away her fib, and Cord tilted his head as he looked at her.

"Why are you nervous? It's not like everyone doesn't already know you."

"I know. I'm just jittery, I guess." She looked out the window, her teeth nibbling her bottom lip, before bringing her gaze back to his. "I'm tired because I didn't sleep well last night. So my emotions have been all over the place today. But also . . . I haven't been to anyone else's family Christmas since I was in college," she confessed, and he totally understood that. It had been since high school for him. Since before his mother died.

"Then how about we be nervous together," he suggested. "This is new for me, too."

He'd had similar thoughts earlier that week but had pushed them aside anytime they'd filtered into his consciousness. Bringing her tonight was the decision he'd made, and it was the route he wanted to be on. However, the speed which things had moved between them continued to overwhelm him. A few short weeks ago he'd thought he would never have a serious relationship, much less a kid on the way *and* a girlfriend. And now . . .

Well . . . the present he planned to give Maggie after they were alone later certainly wouldn't slow things down any.

He leaned across the space, sliding one hand over her belly while slipping the other behind her neck, and pulled her mouth to his. The kiss didn't last long, but he tried to show her through touch that, same as her, he was both scared and excited for this evening. Her returning smile was exactly what he'd been hoping for.

"It's going to be a good night," he whispered.

"I know." Her eyes shone bright as she peered back at him, and the complete faith he could read in their depths relaxed him. It didn't matter what his father might have tried to manipulate him into doing the weekend before. It didn't matter that he still hadn't talked to his dad, nor that he'd decided *not* to talk to him at all. Arguing about his father's actions wouldn't help anything. He and Maggie were good. He and Maggie could be great if they stuck together. And that was what counted.

He kissed her fingertips before pulling away. "Sit tight until I get around to help you out."

She nodded, and as he exited the truck and rounded the front, he refortified himself to go into the house. From the look of the vehicles already parked, he and Maggie were the last to arrive. He hoped that meant they could get on with dinner and then presents without too much small talk. He'd spent the week *not* talking to anyone in his family for fear that he'd let his continuing anger be exposed, and as he'd told Maggie the weekend before, he didn't want his issue with his father to get in the way of their last Christmas in this house. And soon, it wouldn't be an issue any longer, anyway. Because he had come up with a better plan.

He held Maggie's hand as she exited the truck via the step he'd had installed, then he reached into the back seat and passed over the dishes of Brussels sprouts and green beans they'd brought. He grabbed as many of the wrapped packages as he could carry while still leaving a hand free to help Maggie if she needed it, then together, they headed for the porch.

"You good?" he asked as they reached the steps. The six inches of snow that had already fallen had been cleaned from the sidewalk and front steps.

"I've never been better."

She gave him another smile, and this time his heart thumped a little harder. He was glad she'd come with him.

"Maggie!" Megan squealed as she opened the door to the two of them. Megan and Nate had refused to let any of them enter the house since renovations had been completed two weeks before. They'd needed time to have the place cleaned and move in all the furnishings Megan had picked out, as well as let the decorators get the tree and other decorations put up. They'd wanted everything to be a surprise for the whole family. "Come in!"

As Cord stepped across the threshold, he leaned in to give his sister-in-law a kiss on the cheek. "You look happy," he murmured. It was fitting to have Megan greet them at the door since she'd been key in pulling the place together. "Hosting Christmas suits you."

She laughed. "I'm *thrilled*. And I know we don't live here, but after all the renovations we've overseen and picking out every piece of furniture, artwork, dishes, and supplies now in this place, it kind of feels like we do."

"Cord. Maggie." Nate came up the hallway behind his wife.

"Hi, Nate." Maggie's nerves could be heard in the tightness of her voice, and Cord put a reassuring hand to the small of her back.

"Nate." Cord nodded at his brother. "Everyone here already?" He could see several of his family members in the back room, as well as hear even more who were out of sight.

"We were just waiting on you."

Megan took the presents from Cord, and Nate offered to go out to help bring in the rest of the gifts, and just like that, Maggie was swept down the hall, into the crowd of his family. He waited before stepping back outside, watching to make sure she would be okay without him. Her nerves had surprised him. But when she didn't look back, instead quickly disappearing into the throng of people in the other room, his own anxiousness eased.

"We're all thrilled about you and Maggie," Nate said as they headed for the truck. "And if I remember correctly, I think I called it the day of my wedding."

"You called what?" Cord eyed his brother in confusion before remembering the toast Nate had made right before he'd walked down the aisle. He'd pointed out that Cord was the last man standing. The last single Wilde. And he'd implied that could easily change.

Cord hadn't believed that possible.

"Love is good, man," Nate said just before the top half of his body disappeared into the back seat of Cord's truck. "Hold on to it."

"I never said I love her," Cord pointed out. And he didn't love her. He cared strongly for her, definitely. He thought she was wonderful, and he couldn't be happier that it was her having his child. But he hadn't reversed his stance on love. Love and hate were too intertwined, and he wouldn't give anyone the power to use that kind of emotion against him. Not even Maggie.

"You're full of shit." Nate reappeared with the rest of the presents from the back seat. The dollhouses were under a tarp in the bed of the truck. "And I'm not blind, either," Nate continued. "I've seen you with her. You couldn't keep your eyes off her last week at the hospital. And I just watched you again with her. You're protective of her, man. You're head over heels."

Cord grabbed the overnight bags he and Maggie had packed and stacked one of them on top of the presents in Nate's arms before hanging the other over his brother's fingers. "Of course I'm protective. She's carrying my baby."

Nate rolled his eyes. "It's love, idiot. You're just too damned stubborn to admit it."

"It's not love, and it's not stubbornness. It's reality." He pulled back the tarp, not interested in talking about his "love life" any longer, and took great pleasure in seeing the way his brother's eyes widened at the sight of the remaining two gifts.

"What the crap are those?"

Cord grinned. "*Those* are my security in remaining the favorite uncle for years to come."

"That's bullshit," Nate muttered with awe in his voice before turning back for the house.

Cord carried in the dollhouses one at a time, setting each inside the front door and being extra careful not to tilt either one. Maggie had painstakingly added tiny strips of tape between each piece of furniture and the floors of the rooms each piece belonged in, and he'd been given strict instructions not to allow anything to get misplaced. She didn't want a bed to suddenly end up in the kitchen.

Once he had both presents in the house, and by the time he'd shrugged out of his coat and hung it up, word had gotten to Jenna and Haley that he'd come in with something extra special. He picked up one of the gifts, readying to carry it into the other room—the main Christmas tree had been set up in the back—and he took only one step before both girls appeared. They stood at the end of the hallway, their jaws slack and astonishment written across their faces.

"Please tell me those are for us," Haley begged.

Jenna seemed at a loss for words.

Cord grinned. The rest of the family had risen from their seats and filed in behind the girls, and they all wore similar expressions to his oldest two nieces. Also, not a single person spoke. The room had gone eerily quiet. "This one," he began, making a show of looking at the nametag hanging off the side of the package, "is for . . . *Haley.*"

The girl bounced on her toes, a little squee of noise coming out of her.

"And the one Uncle Nate is going to carry is for Jenna."

Jenna's hands went to her cheeks, her mouth still forming a small O.

"Don't tilt it," Cord informed his brother when Nate reluctantly squatted to pick up the other gift. "And hold it by the bottom."

The group of them parted as Cord and Nate made their way down the hall, nothing more than murmurs coming from any of them, and as Cord caught Maggie's eye, he gave her a wink. She was as much a part of these gifts as he'd been, and he loved that they got to share this moment together.

Once space had been made near the tree and everyone had appropriately oohed and aahed over the fact that the gifts were "larger than any other gift ever," both Haley and Jenna turned to him. "Can we open presents before dinner? *Pleeease.*"

DINNER HAD BEEN DELICIOUS, the company sublime, and being included as part of the family in the night's fun was turning out to be one of the best times of Maggie's life. She sat on one of the love seats beside Cord, laughing each time another gift was opened because as soon as the recipient laid eyes on whatever their present was, either Jenna or Haley asked if they could open their gift from Uncle Cord yet. And every time the answer was no.

Without it needing to be said, there had been consensus among the adults that the two girls' presents would be the last ones to be unwrapped.

"Now?" Jenna asked as Harper held up the two onesies she'd just revealed for Emma and Ellie before draping them over the sleeping babies.

Cord's fingers aimlessly stroked along Maggie's back as he chuckled along with everyone else. He'd been touching her all night. "Not yet," he said, and Jenna and Haley both groaned.

"This one is for Maggie," Nate announced. He stepped across several piles of paper and reached over Mia's head, who sat in the middle of another pile of paper. She had new toys and packaging scattered everywhere around her. "It says it's from Dad and Gloria." Nate had been playing "Santa" by passing out all the gifts tonight.

Maggie graciously accepted the present, its glittery silver paper topped off with a shiny green ribbon, and sent the older couple a smile. "Thank you." She'd never felt so welcomed. Or so loved.

"I hope you like it," Gloria said. "Max picked it out."

"I hope it's not another belly casting kit." Jaden shuddered from his position on the other side of the room, and his fiancée elbowed him in the stomach.

"Shut up," Arsula said. "That was a great gift." It was also the one that Arsula had picked out. "She'll forever have a sweet memory of what she looked like just before giving birth."

"Said from a woman who's yet to have everything about her stretched into an unrecognizable form," Dani added.

Harper and Erica both snickered along with Dani, and though Maggie had had a similar thought about the idea of casting her oversized belly into a giant mold, she'd appreciated the thoughtfulness behind the gift.

She opened the present in front of her now to find a gorgeous ceramic table lamp with the phases of the moon cut out around the sides of its cylindrical shape. The cutouts were meant for the light to shine through. "Oh, my," she whispered and held it up in front of her. It was a muted blue color. "It's gorgeous."

Max beamed. "We thought it would work well in the baby's room. It doesn't put off too much light."

"It's perfect." She turned to show it to Cord, but when she found him looking slightly away from the group, his jawline more rigid than usual, she was reminded—yet again—that he hadn't directly spoken to his father all night.

She hadn't been able to catch him alone to ask if he was okay, but she *had* caught looks from several members of his family any time it had been obvious Cord was intentionally keeping his dad at a distance. They'd seemed as confused by the situation as she.

"What did *Uncle Cord* get you?" Jenna asked from the floor. She'd sat down next to the dollhouse present that had her name on it when they'd first started opening gifts and hadn't moved from its side once.

"I don't know." Maggie tossed the girl a what-can-you-do look. Cord had shared that he wanted to give her his present when they were alone later, which worked for her because she'd hoped to save her gift for him until they were by themselves, too. They'd set the two gifts on the dresser in their bedroom when they'd been given a tour of the house earlier. "Maybe he didn't get me anything," she teased.

"That would be *awful*." Jenna scowled at Cord as if the words were the truth, then she glanced back over at her still unopened gift. A furrow formed between her eyes before she said, "I could share mine with you if he didn't get you one," and Maggie's heart fell a little more in love with the whole family.

"Don't worry." Cord curved his hand over Maggie's shoulder. "I got her something. And it's even better than what we got *you*."

Both Jenna's and Haley's eyes widened, as well as Maggie's, and she turned to look at Cord. What could be better than the dollhouses? He stared back at her, the look on his face part secretive and part naughty Santa, and she suddenly found herself ready for the "family" part of the evening to be over.

"I think you should give it to her now," Haley declared.

"You mean *right* now?" Cord looked between the two girls, his movements clear and intentional. "Like...*before* you two get to open *your* gifts?"

Their eyes went even bigger. "Now?" Haley asked in an excited whisper.

"I don't see any more presents under the tree," Haley's dad pointed out from his position next to Dani. Ben passed baby Alice off when Dani held her arms out for her daughter, then he inched out to the edge of his seat. He looked as excited to find out what was in the large gift bags as the girls.

"Uncle Cord?" Jenna begged with her eyes.

Everyone in the room turned to look at Cord, and the pleasure Maggie took in that single moment made the entire night more special. This family was love. They were big and sometimes rowdy, and even knowing that there was something going on between Cord and his father, Maggie couldn't miss what each of them meant to the others. What this night in this house meant to all of them.

Cord scanned the faces, even lingering on his dad's anxious expression for a beat, before giving a decisive nod. *"Now."*

The girls whooped with excitement and jumped to their feet. Maggie kept herself from warning them that they needed to be careful or they might mess up all the cute furniture placement before they could even see it, and as Cord's hand slid down her side and pulled her in close, she turned her face and pressed a kiss into the side of his neck.

"I love you." She mouthed the words into his skin. He wouldn't have heard them, but the words wouldn't stay inside her any longer. She loved this man, and she wanted to be with him forever. She wanted them to make a family and a home with their son.

She wanted them to have what everyone else in this room had.

"Uncle *Cord!*" Jenna and Haley gasped at the same time as they unveiled the dollhouses and took in the three fully customized floors. They dropped to their knees to peer into each room.

"You are the best," Jenna whispered. Her face glowed with the thrill of her gift.

"Still your favorite uncle?" Cord asked.

The child rose and threw herself into Cord's arms. "*Always* my favorite uncle."

Haley piled on as well, lots of giggles coming from the lump of squirming bodies, and as Maggie leaned back to give the kids plenty of room to love on their uncle, a cramp grabbed her in the lower part of her back.

She grimaced, reaching for the spot that ached, but quickly righted her expression and hoped no one had noticed. The cramp, however, didn't let up.

"Are you okay?" Erica leaned forward from her seat behind Maggie and whispered into her ear. "Was that a contraction?"

Maggie turned to look at her friend. "*Shhh. No.* Of course not. It was just a twitch in my back." She wasn't even due for another two weeks.

"Back pains can be labor, too. What did the doctor say this week?"

"Would you stop?" Maggie whispered. She didn't want to take the attention off the girls.

"What's going on?" Cord asked, clueing in, and at his question, everyone else in the room quit talking. Even the girls quieted from their excitement over the dollhouses.

"Is something wrong?" Gloria rose from her seat. "Are we about to have another baby?"

"Are we about to meet my grandson?" Max added.

Maggie couldn't believe all the attention that had suddenly turned to her. And for no reason. "No." She held her hands up, hoping they'd all go back to fawning over the girls. "I'm perfectly fine. Trust me. I'm just . . . *huge.* The extra weight has been causing my back to ache more here lately. That's all."

She kept herself from rubbing her back, but she could tell that

Cord wasn't buying that she was perfectly fine. He knew she was still hurting.

"Do you want to go lie down?" He asked the question for her ears only, and though leaving in the middle of the one moment the girls had been looking forward to all night was the last thing she wanted to do, she suddenly *did* wish to be out of there. Her back had hurt on and off since the night before, which was why she hadn't slept well, but she'd found that stretching her legs out and propping herself up had helped. And she didn't have room to do that down here.

She nodded. "If you don't think anyone would mind."

He took her hand and immediately rose.

"Everyone." Cord had their attention before he even opened his mouth. "Merry Christmas Eve to you all." He winked at Jenna and Haley. "And especially to two of my favorite nieces. But Maggie and I are going to turn in for the night. We'll see you bright and early in the morning."

"To see what Santa brought." Jenna's eyes sparkled.

"Exactly."

Maggie smiled at the girls, the move a silent apology for interrupting the moment—which she doubted they understood—then she assured everyone else when they asked that she really was okay.

"She didn't sleep well last night," Cord shared. "And I think you all have worn her out."

He hadn't let go of her hand, and when he looked down at her again, the concern in his eyes gave him away. He was seriously worried about her. She found herself on the verge of tears just from the distress coming from him and hoped desperately that they could escape the room without her having to say anything else.

"Let us know if you need anything," Megan offered, and Cord assured her they would. Then he led Maggie to the steps, and they disappeared upstairs.

CHAPTER TWENTY

CORD PUSHED THE BEDROOM DOOR CLOSED BEHIND THEM AND turned Maggie to face him. He captured both her hands, looking her over from head to toe. "You're okay?"

"Absolutely. The pain has already started to ease off."

"I think we should call your doctor."

He cringed as she guffawed, knowing he was acting more like a nervous first-time father than the educated physician he was. But he couldn't help it. The way her face had paled downstairs worried him.

"Or I could check you myself," he offered. "You said your cervix had started thinning this week. You could be dilating now."

She stared at him, seemingly aghast. "That is *not* going to happen." Pulling one hand free, she jabbed a finger over her shoulder. "What *is* going to happen is that I'm going to borrow your pillow, as well as take my own, then I'm going to prop myself up in bed like I did last night"—her voice changed then, growing deeper —"and then we're going to have the Christmas Eve we've both been thinking about all week."

Heat spread through Cord as the gray of her eyes deepened along with her voice. "Maggie . . ."

They couldn't have the night *he'd* been thinking about. No way. And he shouldn't have been thinking it to begin with. Not with her being nearly nine months pregnant. But the woman could be such a tease.

He brought her hand to his lips. "How about we just have a nice evening relaxing together. No pressure for anything else." He pressed a kiss to the back of her fingers. "We could exchange presents." He kissed her palm. "I'll go grab us a couple of cups of hot cocoa." He touched his lips to the inside of her wrist. "And we'll sit and watch the snow outside the balcony doors while I hold you in my arms."

Part of the renovations had included adding balconies to all the rooms.

She studied him silently, her head tilted just the slightest amount. "That does sound really good," she murmured. "But how about you give me a back rub first? Then"—she lifted a shoulder in a shrug, and her eyes screamed mischief—"we see where things go."

The woman was going to be the death of him. "We are *not* doing what you're thinking."

"Why not? Afraid of a little pregnancy sex?" Her teeth flashed with her smile, and he forgot his concern for a moment. Instead, he pulled her in and gave her a taste of what she was begging for.

"*Mags*," he whispered into her hair after he forced his lips from hers. "This may not be safe. Your back is hurting."

She didn't immediately reply, and he pulled back to look at her. Her face told the truth.

"That's it." He moved to the bed and pulled the covers back on one side, then he stacked both pillows against the headboard. "Your overnight bag is in the bathroom. You change while I go find us some cocoa, and when I get back, I want you right here in this bed."

Her naughty smile returned. "Yes, sir."

Cord didn't say anything else, just growled in the back of his throat and kissed her on the forehead, then he left the room and headed for the kitchen. He could hear the rest of his family still hanging out together in the main room, and he had one tiny bit of regret that he wasn't in there with them. It *had* been a good night. And this had been a Christmas like none other before. So much had changed for all of them, and there was such a level of happiness in this house now. Not at all like when they'd been kids.

Even so, he'd rather be upstairs with Maggie. And he'd rather *not* be in the same room with his father.

He knew it was unfair not to have had a discussion with the man. Everyone deserved a right to defend themselves. But the more he'd replayed the two encounters in his mind over the last few days, the more he hadn't been able to see how that *hadn't* been a setup. Granted, Doc Hamm did want to retire. There was a perfectly good reason for that. But that didn't mean Hamm had personally intended to seek Cord out. And it *didn't* mean Cord's dad had a right to make that happen. His dad could have come to *him*. He could have mentioned to him that Hamm was retiring. Cord could have reached out to Hamm if that was what he wanted to do.

There were any number of ways things could have played out that involved being upfront and honest. And that was Cord's issue. He didn't allow people to manipulate him. Ever.

He heard a cry come from one of the babies as he ducked into the kitchen, heading for the pot of cocoa Megan had prepared earlier in the evening, and he let the feeling of peace replace the previous annoyance as he thought about the fact that it would soon be his own child he heard crying. And if the night went the way he hoped, he'd be hearing that cry every day instead of just on the weekends.

With a smile on his face and a skip in his step, he prepared a tray with two mugs, two spoons, and two little bowls—one with peppermint chips and one with marshmallows—and he headed back up to the mother of his child. He knocked before entering the room, and at her soft "come in" he cracked open the door and pushed it wider with his foot.

Inside, the room was mostly dark, and Maggie now sat propped up in bed as he'd expected, but what he didn't expect was to find her in a white lacy gown. Her hair had been brushed and drifted into piles around her shoulders. Her bare toes peeked out from the bottom of the full-length gown. And from head to toe, he could see every shadow and curve of her body beneath the almost sheer material.

The soft light coming from the bedside lamp only added to her allure.

"Mags," he whispered. She amazed him. "You're stunning."

She glowed at his compliment. "You make me actually believe those words."

He stepped inside the room. "There's no reason not to believe them. Have you looked at yourself lately?"

He set the tray down on the dresser just inside the room, returning to close and lock the door, then he picked up the small present he'd set out earlier. The one Maggie had brought for him was already lying on the bed beside her.

"Cocoa or gifts first?" he asked.

"I want you to touch me first," she said instead, and his will was shot.

"Maggie." He crawled onto the bed, kicking off his shoes as he went, but he removed nothing else. He told himself that tonight wasn't about making love. He wouldn't let it be. He didn't want Maggie to be uncomfortable in any way, and given she'd been hurting on and off since the night before, he wouldn't risk adding to it. He just wanted to be there with her. Right in this moment.

"Just touch," she told him, as if reading his mind. Then, as he settled in on his side beside her, she took one of his hands and put it over her stomach.

Pleasure washed over him. He'd felt his son move many times by this point, and he'd touched her belly for every one of those instances. But he'd never allowed himself to reach under any of her clothes. He always touched through fabric.

He didn't reach under her gown now, either, but with the thinness of the material, it was practically the same as caressing bare skin. He ran a finger over a long stretch mark. He slid his thumb over her protruding belly button. It had popped out that week, and every time he'd looked at her today, he'd thought about how cute she was.

Only, she wasn't cute. She was beautiful.

"Our son is going to be so lucky to have you as his mother," he whispered as he remained propped up next to her, then he followed his hand by leaning in and kissing her belly. Next, he rested the side of his face where he'd placed the kiss. He could hear gurgling inside, but their son remained still. She was full beneath him, though. Her skin was stretched tight.

"You'll be there to take care of him if I can't?" Her worry made him hurt for her.

"I'll always be there." Cord lifted up to look at her. "As long as you'll let me," he promised. And as he stared down at her, he knew that if it weren't for the promise he'd made to himself so many years ago, he could totally fall in love with this woman. He cupped her cheek with his hand and pressed a kiss to her lips.

It was only a kiss. One meant to show words he would never say, but then her mouth parted.

She groaned as their tongues touched, and she recaptured his hand and moved it back to her body. But this time, it wasn't her belly she covered. Instead, his hand went to her breast.

"Mags."

"Just touch me." Her eyes had closed. "Please, Cord. It's been so long."

So that's what he did. He lifted back to one elbow, and he let his hand and his eyes move over her the way he'd been wanting to do for so long. He traced over every dip and curve. He circled her darkened areolas and nipples. He cupped her heavy breasts. And with every moan and soft breath he heard, he grew even bolder.

One of her hands fluttered up, reaching for him, but he moved it back to her side. This was her night. Not his. He didn't need anything more than to touch her.

"Please," she begged a couple of minutes later, the word barely reaching his ears, and when her fingers began to tug at the skirt of her gown, inching it higher up her thighs, he snagged the material and helped her.

Together, they slipped the gown up and over her head, and in her eyes he saw her nervousness as she bared herself completely to him. But he didn't let her nerves stand. There was no need for them. He kissed her, he stroked her, and he took every liberty of a man who'd seen and loved her body before.

He nipped her behind the ear. He skirted a finger over the outside of her breast.

And when she begged once again, he finally slid his hand lower and slipped his fingers between her legs.

"Cord!" she breathed out his name, her chest bowing upward and her eyes closed tight.

"Hold on, baby." He parted her wider, and it took less than a second to find the spot she so desperately needed him to touch. "This okay?" he asked. Passion had him ready to do anything she asked, but nerves held him back.

Her head jerked in a nod. "Yes. Please. Touch me. Don't stop."

So, he didn't stop. He flicked and tweaked, and he suckled at her nipples while his fingers worked below, and in only a matter of minutes, her entire body began to tighten in front of him.

"Don't stop, Cord," she begged.

He wouldn't stop now if he could.

As he continued to bring her to the edge, he couldn't take his eyes off her glorious body. He'd never seen anything more perfect.

"Now," she whispered, and her body grew even tauter. *"Yes. Yes. Pleeease."*

Cord didn't let up as her orgasm ripped through her. He held her, and he touched her, and when she turned her face to his, he kissed her with both tenderness and passion. He kissed her in a way he'd never kissed another woman. And when her body finally calmed, when she collapsed back to the bed in a heap, it was everything he could do not to let tears leak out of his eyes to match her own.

CHAPTER TWENTY-ONE

Maggie woke sometime in the early morning hours. Her back was hurting again, but she didn't want to move. Cord lay curled up behind her, both of them on their sides, and his heat against her backside felt almost as good as his hand and fingers had felt earlier against her front.

She mentally stretched and purred as if she were a cat. That had been the best orgasm of her life.

She felt slightly bad that the moment had been all about her, but just slightly. They would have other times to do more. And if she didn't feel like doing anything else before the baby was born, then there would be plenty of time after.

"You awake?" Cord said from behind her.

"*Mmm,*" she replied instead of answering. She wasn't ready to move yet.

"You okay?"

She turned her head at the sound of his unease, and when she did, he lifted his head so he could see her better. There was no light on in the room now, but a nightlight from the bathroom cast a glow across the bed. She could see his worry in the lines pulled on either side of his mouth.

"I felt your body tense," he explained. His hand slid along her side and moved around to her back. "Is it your back again?"

"Just a little."

He began to massage her, somehow knowing exactly where to rub, and this time she did purr like a cat.

"That feels good," she murmured.

"I'm glad. I'll do it the rest of the night if you need me to."

She fell silent, enjoying the moment and letting him work out some of the soreness, and once the tightness had eased, she rolled to her back. She'd put her gown back on earlier, but she recalled the way he'd looked at her when she'd been naked. After witnessing that, she didn't know why she'd ever been hesitant to let him see her that way in the first place. Her shape and the many stretchmarks clearly weren't an issue.

"Do you want your present?" She pushed to a sitting position, remembering that they'd never gotten around to exchanging gifts. "Since we're both awake, and since it's officially Christmas now?"

He sat up with her. "I'd love it. And I'd love to give you yours, too."

They took a couple of minutes, both using the restroom and brushing their teeth, and by the time Cord had come back into the room, Maggie had put on a robe she'd pulled from her bag and turned on the bedside light.

Cord stopped in the middle of the room, his eyes lingering on the robe covering her see-thru gown. "Now that's a real shame."

She grinned. "Give me a break. I'm feeling vulnerable."

"*Now* you're feeling vulnerable?" His brows went up. "Not when I had you naked and squirming in my arms?"

"Stop teasing me," she chided. "And come back over here. I want you to open my present first."

"My pleasure." He climbed onto the bed similarly to when he'd returned to the room earlier and found her waiting for him in only her gown, only now *he* wore only a pair of flannel pajama bottoms. She eyed his broad, bare chest and recalled the feel of all that muscle bunching under her hands, but she didn't let herself touch. Again, there would be time for that later.

"You should quit having those thoughts," he told her as he crawled to her side, and when she felt herself blushing because she'd *totally* been having those thoughts, he turned her face to his.

"I love you, Cord."

He froze at her words, his lips only a breath away from kissing hers, but his expression didn't change.

She swallowed. "That's probably too soon to say, huh?" Talk about feeling vulnerable.

She pulled away and reached for the present she'd brought and told herself not to be hurt because her words had made him look so terrified.

"Here." She thrust the gift into his hands. "Merry Christmas."

She looked toward the wall past the end of the bed as he took his time pulling the wrapping paper from the box, and as she stared at the abstract watercolor hanging above the dresser, knowing that she was intentionally avoiding him, she pictured Cord from earlier in the evening. From when she'd tried to show him the gift from his dad and Gloria, and Cord had been intentionally avoiding his dad.

Cord hadn't mentioned anything else about whatever was going on between the two of them over the last few days, nor had she asked. She hadn't wanted it to color this weekend as it had last Sunday. But the subject had certainly crossed her mind. She couldn't figure out what could have him so upset that he'd feared dealing with it might have jeopardized his family's Christmas.

She'd watched Max tonight as she'd once again pondered what could have happened. And she'd seen nothing to indicate that Max even knew there was a problem. He'd seemed as perplexed by Cord's avoidance of him as the rest of the family, and not one time had he come across as upset about anything.

"Cord." She turned back as he ripped through the tape holding the box closed.

"What?" The way he didn't look at her annoyed her. What was

the man's issue? So she'd said she loved him. So what? Was it that much of a surprise?

Irritation had her grinding her teeth together. The man was supposed to be falling in love with her, too, dammit. "Will you tell me what's going on with you and your dad?"

He did look at her then. And once again he stilled.

"I thought talking about it might help." She softened instead of continuing to hold on to her frustration. This was the man she loved. She'd known he might not say the words back to her when she'd blurted them out, but she'd wanted him to know anyway. And she also wanted him to be okay with his father.

The idea of a distance growing between him and his dad—the way it had between her and *her* dad—bothered her. She didn't want that for him.

"Can't you tell me?" she asked.

He lifted the box top off his present, but he never took his eyes off her, then slowly, he nodded his head. "That's what couples do, right? They talk about things?"

Relief rushed through her. "Yes. They do. They rely on each other to help."

He paused only a moment longer before saying, "My dad set Doctor Hamm up to try to get me to buy his practice. Doc Hamm is retiring. He caught me while we were at the hospital last weekend to run the idea past me."

Confusion filled her. This was a good thing, right? He had an opportunity to move home without having to start over.

So, why was he upset?

Her competing thoughts must have shown because he added, "My *dad* didn't mention this to me. He went behind my back and set things in motion."

"Okay . . ." She still didn't get it. He could own his own practice here in Birch Bay. A practice that was already in place with years' worth of patients. And he had to know that the Wilde name would have most of them sticking around to give him a chance.

When he didn't say anything else, she said, "Why would that be so bad, Cord? You'd be here. With me and the baby. *With* a successful practice."

He shook his head as he watched her, and she felt like she was missing something key.

"I won't be manipulated, Maggie. Not by my father nor by anyone. But also, I worked very hard for the job I have. I would be an idiot to walk away from that."

He would be an idiot to walk away and have a life with her?

She began to feel like this conversation wasn't going to go the way she hoped.

Pulling at her robe and retying the belt over the top of her stomach, she lifted her chin. "Does it even matter that I'm in love with you?"

She held her breath as she waited for his response. He hadn't looked away, so she hoped that was a good thing. But he also hadn't given any indication that her love was what he sought.

"Cord?"

"Why don't *you* come to Billings, Maggie?"

"What?" That was the first time he'd even hinted that he might like her in Billings with him.

"Yes." He nodded, and finally his features began to relax. "We could make a family there. You, me, and the baby."

He reached behind him to retrieve the present he'd brought for her, then he placed it in her hands. His hands slipped beneath hers, cupping them—which cupped the square box he'd just given her—and he finally offered her something other than a noncommittal stare. He smiled.

"Marry me, Maggie Crowder. Come to Billings with me. I'll support you. I'll take care of you. I'll take care of our baby." He nodded again. "It'll be good between us."

She sat frozen. Marry him?

That was the last thing she'd expected.

She looked down at the box in her hand, realizing for the first time what must be inside of it. A ring.

An *engagement* ring.

She gulped. Cord wanted to marry her.

As excitement began to build and happy tears started to push their way out, something else screamed at her to hold back. To not let the thrill of the moment seize control. Something wasn't right about this.

"Maggie?" Cord nodded toward the box, his smile still in place. "Open it, sweetheart. I want you to marry me."

He said the words almost as if he were offering her a prize of some sort.

She didn't open the box. Instead, she pulled one hand free of his and lay it gently over the bow attached to the top. She visualized doing something similar with her heart. As if protecting it. Or not letting it be seen by anyone who might want to hurt it. She didn't feel good about this moment.

Lowering her eyes, she let her gaze fall before she replied. And when she did reply, it came in the form of a question. "Do you love *me*, Cord?"

She didn't look back up because she didn't want to see his smile disappear.

"You know that I care for you, Maggie. You have to know that."

She nodded. "I do know that. But do you love me?"

Even knowing that it would hurt, she forced herself to lift her gaze anyway. Because she couldn't hide from this. And what she saw *did* hurt. It wasn't love at all.

"Might you *ever* love me?" she whispered, her voice shaky now.

"Mags." He took the box from her and began to peel the paper from it himself. "We can be good together. You know that. We *are* good. But this is the best I can do, sweetheart. I told you from the beginning that I don't do—" He seemed to stumble briefly before he finished with, "relationships."

The look on his face was apologetic, as if he understood

completely that he was smack-dab in the middle of a relationship, even as he sat there telling her that he couldn't do one.

"Then, what *is* this?" Her patience snapped at the same time that her heart cracked wide open. "What do you think we've been doing for the last several weeks, Cord? Simply playing house? Like those two dollhouses downstairs?"

He reached for her as she moved to rise from the bed, and she smacked his hands away.

"Don't touch me."

He managed to get the box open at the same time she stepped from the bed, and he pulled out the ring box that sat inside. "Here." He freed the ring from its velvety cushion. "This is for you." He thrust the ring at her, but she refused to look at it.

"I don't want it."

"Please, Maggie." He rose from the bed and came around to stand before her, and dang, but the pleading in his eyes almost got to her. He looked like he would be lost without her. "Take it," he urged. "Marry me."

She forced herself to think. Maybe this wasn't as bad as she suspected. Maybe he was just doing a spectacularly good job at botching a proposal.

Maybe this could turn out okay after all.

Pulling in a deep breath, she let herself look down at the ring, and the sight of it took her breath way. With a large diamond in the middle and a ring of baguettes circling it, it had to have cost a pretty penny. But did the cost of it mean anything? Especially if he wouldn't even consider that he could let himself fall in love with her?

She didn't know what to do.

"Maggie." Cord slid his palms over her shoulders and stooped down to look her in the eyes. "Tell me what to do, baby. How can I fix this?"

And just like that, the answer came to her. And she also understood that she likely wouldn't like how this was about to go.

"Answer one question for me," she said, and when he nodded, she went on. "Why would you ask me to marry you if you don't think you can ever love me?"

He swallowed as understanding dawned on his face. He knew she wouldn't like any answer he had to give. "Because it's the right thing to do," he said. "Because I won't be tricked into moving back home, and bringing you to Billings is the only way I can take care of both of you."

That's what she thought. He was doing it only for the baby. Just like their "relationship" had come about only because of the baby.

Good thing she was used to being let down by those she loved.

It was time to go. She took a step back, needing distance as much as wishing she could rewind the last month of her life. It would be better if she hadn't let herself fall in love with the idiot. "I don't need to be taken care of, Cord. Nor do I need someone in my son's life who doesn't want to be there."

"But I *do* want to be there."

A lump formed in her throat. He wanted to be in their *son's* life. Only. "Good," she forced the word out. "I'm sure he'll appreciate that in the years to come."

She'd left her overnight bag in the bathroom, so she moved that way.

"And the other thing I don't need," she said as she reached the open doorway and turned back to him, "and something that I *won't* stand for, is a relationship that's no closer than the one I've had with my own mother over the past twenty-two years. I deserve love, Cord. True love. And I deserve happiness and a life filled with knowing that the man I choose to be with would walk through fire for me."

"I would—"

She held up a hand, halting his words. "A man who would at least *consider* rearranging his life to be with me when the opportunity arose—no matter how that opportunity came about—and a man who didn't offer me a ring simply as a solution to make sure that *he* wouldn't have to do any compromising. You're trying to manipulate *me*, Cord. Exactly as you insist you won't allow to be done to you. And I get it. It's not a nice feeling. That's why I won't stand for it, either."

She stepped inside the bathroom, already pulling up her phone to text Arsula in order to wake her friend and see if she could get a ride home. And as she rummaged through her bag to dig out clothes to change into, the tears that had waited patiently for her to tell the man whom she loved to go take a flying leap finally released.

CHAPTER TWENTY-TWO

DAWN HAD CREPT INTO THE MORNING SKY TEN MINUTES EARLIER, AND Cord remained where he'd been for the last thirty minutes. He stood at the kitchen window that had the best views of both the eastern sky as well as the view of the new parking lot that had been poured for the purposes of the lodge. The SUV he'd bought for Maggie now sat next to his truck. And as his gaze landed upon it once again, the anger that had been building since Maggie had walked out of their room burned even brighter.

He should never have gotten involved with her.

He should never have invited her to this house.

The coffee cup he'd left on the counter beckoned, reminding him that though he'd brewed an extra strong pot when he'd first come down—and had poured himself a mug full of the stuff—he had yet to take a single drink. And though he'd love the hit of caffeine, he decided that he wouldn't waste any more time sticking around. If he got out of there now, before anyone else made it out of their room, they might think it an ass move on his part, but at least he would know he'd left without ruining their last memory of the place, too. He couldn't fake happiness this morning, and he didn't want to risk tainting the joy of Christmas for everyone.

Reaching for the bag he'd set at his feet, he allowed himself a brief good memory of being with Maggie and the rest of his family as they'd opened gifts the night before—before everything had tanked so terribly—then he turned for the door.

Arsula and Erica both stood just outside the kitchen doorway, arms crossed over their chests and fury carving hatred into their faces.

"You are so *done* with her," Arsula declared.

He didn't need to be told that. "You think?"

"What an ass," Erica spat out. "I thought better of you than that."

"Than what?" He played stupid because it fit with his sour mood. Plus, he'd done nothing wrong with Maggie. He'd offered her marriage, and she'd basically spit on it. Nodding toward Arsula, he said, "This one just told me I was done with her. I'm simply agreeing."

Erica looked as if she wanted to claw his eyes out. "You could at least hurt at the thought of it, you jerk. Arsula said Maggie cried the whole way home."

"She's probably still crying," Arsula pointed out.

He didn't want to think about the tears he'd seen rolling from Maggie's eyes when she'd left their room. He'd offered to take her home himself, but she wouldn't even talk about it. He'd tried handing her the keys to his truck so she could get herself home. Still, she'd refused. She hadn't wanted anything more to do with him. Ever, according to her.

"If you're so worried that she's still crying"—Cord kept his features impassive—"then maybe you should have stuck around to console her."

He actually jerked back when Arsula lunged for him. Thankfully, Erica stopped her before she could make contact, but he didn't know how long the restraint would last. And honestly, he deserved whatever either of them wanted to dish out. He knew his statement was cruel. There'd been no need for it. But cruelty beat caring. If he cared . . . his insides might try to break him like they'd tried to do when Maggie had walked out during the middle of the night.

Continuing his act, he motioned back toward the window. "How did her SUV get here, anyway?"

Arsula didn't answer, and Erica only glared.

"Fine. Don't talk. It's no skin off my nose." He made a show of hitching the strap to his bag over his shoulder, and once again, he headed for the door.

Only, Dani showed up this time. She held Alice in one arm, the baby bright-eyed and looking around, and his sister was rubbing her half-open eyes with her other hand. "What's going on in here so early?" She yawned. "I thought only babies woke up at this hour."

"I'll tell you what's going on." It seemed Arsula had found her voice again. "Your good-for-nothing dickweed brother broke our friend's heart last night."

Dani was suddenly wide awake. She looked at Cord. "What did he do?" She asked the question carefully, as if expecting to hear something she would also want to kick his ass over, and though she was looking at *him*, she'd been talking to the others.

Because of that, Cord remained mute. He reached for the now-lukewarm cup of coffee.

Arsula once again crossed her arms over her chest. "He asked her to marry him and to move to Billings so *his* life wouldn't be interrupted."

Dani blinked, her expression looking as if cold water had been splashed into her face, then she addressed Cord. "You asked Maggie to marry you?" She glanced around at the others. "How did this break her heart?"

"Because when he asked her," Erica explained, "he also told her that he didn't—"

"And that he *wouldn't*—" Arsula interrupted.

"—ever love her. He said he'd asked her because he was 'doing the right thing.'"

Dani didn't immediately reply. Instead, she carefully studied

Cord. Cord stared back, not allowing her to read anything he was thinking.

"Is Maggie still here?" Dani finally asked.

"No," Arsula answered. "Jaden and I took her home about three hours ago."

Ah, Cord thought. So, his baby brother had been instrumental in returning the vehicle Cord had bought for Maggie. That sounded about right.

Cord took another sip of the coffee. "Are you three about finished talking about me?"

"Who's talking about you?" Gabe said as he entered the kitchen. At the sight of the three women who stood facing Cord, Gabe's brows rose. "What am I missing?" He pressed a kiss to his wife's cheek and murmured, "Good morning, sweetie."

"Good morning," Erica replied. "Ivy still sleeping?"

Gabe nodded, then he poured himself a cup of coffee and leaned back against the sink. He looked at Cord. "Why are they talking about you?"

"Because your brother is a jerk." Dani spoke for the three women. Alice fussed in her mother's arms, as if picking up on the tension in the room, and Gabe's expression changed to that of boredom.

"This is news?" Gabe peered over his cup at Dani. "Didn't I say as much way back in high school?"

Dani scowled. "He isn't being a take-your-crap-without-asking type of jerk. He's top class now."

"Well, he always did like to aim for the top."

Cord had had enough. "That's it." He set down his cup. "I'm out of here."

"Wait." Gabe straightened, and his gaze seemed to take in the overnight bag hanging over Cord's shoulder for the first time. The lackadaisical expression cleared from his face. "What's going on?" He took in the others, as if open to anyone filling him in. "You can't leave. The girls haven't even gotten up yet. We haven't seen what Santa brought or had breakfast together like we planned."

Cord didn't let himself think about what he'd be missing. What he'd forever miss because he would be all alone in Billings the rest of his life. "You can do that without me," he said. "I'm going back home where I belong."

"What the fuck, man?" Gabe muttered. He turned to Dani, and she shrugged.

"He and Maggie broke up last night," she explained. "She's gone."

"Oh." Gabe once again turned to Cord. "*Shit.*"

Cord did *not* want their sympathy. He shouldn't have even gotten involved with Maggie in the first place. Therefore, he didn't deserve sympathy. He knew how these things worked. He'd been stupid to play with fire.

"It's fine," he said. He made sure not to make eye contact with either Arsula or Erica, both of whom seemed to remain poised to take his head off if need be. "The whole thing was a mistake to begin with."

Arsula growled in the back of her throat.

"You're not going to decide to . . ." Dani paused instead of finishing her sentence, and she glanced over at Gabe, worry marring her face.

And whatever she'd been about to say, Gabe seemed to understand. "No." He shook his head. "He can't do that."

"I can't do what?"

"Have nothing to do with the baby, idiot," Arsula snapped. "How can you be so clueless? They're worried you're going to back out of being a dad and ignore your son. Just like you originally told Maggie you intended to do." She turned to the others, ready to say more, but the rest of Cord's siblings filed into the room. Nate and Nick both seemed confused at the sight of the group of them, while Jaden simply moved to Arsula's side. And even though confused, his twin brothers immediately picked up on the fact that Cord was the focus. *And* that he deserved their anger.

"What did he do?" Nate asked.

"He ran Maggie off," Jaden replied. "We took her home in the middle of the night."

Cord dropped his bag back to the floor and settled in to let them all say their piece.

"How did you run her off?" Nick looked as if the breakup pained him as much as it did Cord.

"He asked her to marry him," Dani said.

"In order to 'do the right thing,'" Erica added, and Nick and Nate both cringed at the words. But then Cord remembered something that might take the attention off him, and he looked at Jaden.

"Wasn't it *you* who told me that I *should* marry Maggie? Because it's 'the honorable thing'?" He air quoted Jaden's words from when they'd had their family meeting a few weeks ago, and he took great pleasure in watching Arsula's ire refocus itself on her fiancé.

"*You* told him to do that?"

"I—" Jaden flinched, knowing he was in trouble. Then he sighed. "It was said in the heat of the moment. I didn't actually mean for him to *do* it."

"Or more likely," Cord interjected, almost enjoying the moment now, "you just didn't mean for me to *say* that to her."

Jaden fumed, the look he fired Cord's way making it clear he would get his brother back. "You're a *moron* for saying that to her."

"Why? She asked me, so I answered."

"Then you're a moron for thinking it."

"More like, you're just a moron," Nate added. "Why didn't you just tell her you love her?"

"Instead, he told her that he *didn't* love her," Arsula shared, and for the first time since she'd come into the room, she sounded more exhausted than angry. Exhausted, most likely, over worrying about her friend. And that small change in her demeanor made Cord even more ready to be out of there.

He knew he'd hurt Maggie. But he also knew that hurting her had never been his intention. Far from it. What he'd wanted to do was to look after her. To come home to her every day. Emotions didn't have to be tossed into the mix. At least, not love. Yet, the one time he'd not only considered asking a woman to marry him, but had been excited at the prospect of it, she'd tossed the entire thing back in his face. It was insulting. And it pissed him the hell off.

Not to mention, while she'd been turning him down, she'd also been accusing him of trying to manipulate *her*. Which was *utter* bullshit. He'd been trying to provide for her. He'd been attempting to give their child the life he'd thought she wanted for him. Two parents! Instead ...

He stood up straighter as a new idea formed. Had *she* been manipulating *him* from the start? The entire relationship had been her idea. Having sex again ... *her* idea.

Getting him to open up. To share things about his life, about his father ... that had all been her. All with the intention of reeling him in. And then she'd gone and told him she loved him. What the fuck was he supposed to do with that?

And of course, "love" had come up right before asking about his dad. Hadn't that been convenient? Had *she* known about Hamm's offer even *before* he'd told her about it? Had she and his dad been in on it together?

He ground his thoughts to a halt. He was aware he could veer toward paranoia when it came to people trying to use his emotions against him. He'd been accused of that more than once in the past. So, he also knew that he needed to take a step back and relook at things once he'd calmed down. Once his entire family wasn't in his face, telling him he'd screwed up.

"I'm going to go," he said again, this time knowing that he wouldn't let them stall him. He picked up his bag. "I hope all of you have a great time this morning, and please, give my apologies to Jenna, Haley, and to all of your spouses for not being here."

∽

As Cord approached the spot where he'd found Maggie on the side of the road only one month ago, he glanced over at it. So much had happened since that night. And so much had happened that he wished *hadn't* happened.

He kept going down the road, not looking back. He wanted to be out of Birch Bay as soon as possible, and he didn't intend to return until his son was on the way. At this point, though, he didn't know if Maggie would call him when she went into labor. He would reach out in a few days to ask if she would still let him know. Just because they weren't a couple anymore didn't mean that he didn't want to be in his son's life—no matter what might have been running through his family's mind. And through Maggie's, most likely. Especially given her parting words.

If you really do want to see your son after he's born, then revert back to your plan of renting a place near me. Otherwise, your time will be limited.

He hadn't expected her to continue welcoming him with open arms after he'd broken her heart, naturally, but the knowledge that he'd spent his last night in her house hurt. He'd liked where they were, and he hadn't seen any reason to change it.

Of course, *he* was the one who'd tried to change it. He'd tried to bring her closer to him so he could have everything he—

He stomped on his brakes, his tires momentarily locking up as his truck slid in the new-fallen snow, then he pulled over to the side of the road. He'd tried to bring Maggie closer to him so he could have everything without having to give up anything.

Had Maggie been right? Had he been trying to manipulate *her*?

Crap.

That hadn't been his intention, but he could certainly see how it might look like that from her point of view. And hell, it looked like it from his point of view, too. He'd offered her a ring, hoping she'd immediately agree because she'd be so dazzled by . . . *what?* The gift of *him*?

He snorted at the thought. He wasn't exactly a gift most days.

And granted, he hadn't offered her the ring only to get her to move. He *did* want to take care of her and the baby. That had always been priority number one. And he would absolutely love having them close enough to come home to every night.

But if he wasn't willing to give her what she wanted—to give her his heart—then why had he ever expected she'd jump on his offer and do his bidding?

Once again, Arsula had been right. His entire family was right. He was an idiot.

He'd asked Maggie to marry him as a last-ditch effort to have everything that he wanted—while also showing his dad that he wouldn't be manipulated. And it had backfired spectacularly.

Idiot.

Moron.

Dumbass.

He was all three and then some. No wonder Maggie had dumped him. He'd deserved it.

He would deserve her never speaking to him again, but he hoped that wasn't what would happen.

Glancing in his rearview to make sure no one else was out on the road on this snowy Christmas morning, he started to pull back out. But then he realized that he had stopped right before going into the curve where his mother had died.

He pushed back down on the brake and stopped. He hadn't looked at the exact location his mother had died since the day it had happened, and he couldn't say for certain why.

Anger?

Hurt?

Guilt?

He shifted into park and turned off the truck, but before getting out, he reached over to the passenger seat and unzipped his bag. Lying inside, and on top of the clothes he'd worn the day before, was the gift Maggie had given him last night. He hadn't laid his eyes on it until after she'd walked out, but when he'd looked into the opened box after she'd gone, his breath had caught.

Inside had been a photo of Maggie. She'd had a pregnancy shoot at some point, and she'd framed one of the shots for him. What was poignant about the picture, though, aside from the fact that Maggie's beauty and loving smile had jumped out at him, was that the photo had been taken by a tree he'd recognized.

When his mother had planned her wreck, she'd chosen one of the most recognizable trees in Birch Bay. There had been an oversized knot on one side of the trunk for as long as he could remember, always making him think of a goiter as a kid. The tree was used as a marker when giving people directions. *Their place is two houses on the right past the goiter tree. If you pass the goiter tree, you've gone too far.*

Maggie had chosen that spot for the picture she'd wanted to give to him, and though he'd been too angry when he'd first seen it to do anything more than want to throw the frame out the window, he had a different view on things now. Had she picked the tree because she'd been hoping to give him a new visual associated with that location instead of the memories he carried?

He hadn't had the dream in a couple of weeks. Not since he'd shared it with Maggie. But even so, failing his mom was always in the back of his mind. And this tree was in the center of his biggest failure.

He took a long look at the photo now, and even without Maggie there with him, he suddenly felt more in control of the past than he'd ever been. Putting the picture down, he zipped his coat and grabbed his hat and gloves, and then he stepped out of his truck.

The road remained silent, and the snow that had started the day before continued to fall. They'd had a good amount of accumulation, but nothing out of the ordinary, and Cord had no problem making it around the curve and coming out the other side. When he did, he stopped and simply took in the view. On the right side of the road was where Bailey had ended up. It was where the cliff that had begun appearing in his dreams had emerged, and where Maggie had slipped over the edge in Bailey's car.

On the other side of the road was the tree.

It was much larger now. Sixteen years hadn't slowed its growth, and the goiter stood out in great detail. He took a moment to picture Maggie as she was in the photo, standing by the tree, her hands cupping the child they'd made together. And then he pictured his mother's vehicle crashed into it.

She shouldn't have died that day. If he hadn't walked away, she wouldn't have.

But then . . . was that the truth?

He'd been only sixteen. Even if he'd stayed with her, when her aorta had ruptured, what could he have possibly done? He wouldn't have even known what had happened.

The ambulance had already been called. He'd had a cell phone on him, and surprisingly, it had worked in that spot on that day. He'd called 911, not thinking that his mother would need medical assistance so much as not knowing if the person in the other vehicle would. He'd called, and the dispatcher had said that police and EMTs were on their way. He'd done all he could do. And then he'd walked away.

What had always sat heavy inside him, though, was the fear that he'd done it on purpose. That he'd let his mother die intentionally. And that thought had been there for one simple reason. Because he'd been relieved she was gone.

He'd failed her, yes. His role and his job had been to save her. And he'd failed.

But had he done it on purpose?

As he looked back on the day now, he could finally answer that question. He'd had no clue she could even potentially die. He'd been a kid. And he'd been traumatized, both by her during his previous sixteen years of life, and on that day when he'd come upon the wreck. He might have both loved and hated her. Or more specifi-cally, he'd *wanted* to love her. And he'd wanted to be loved in return. But no, he had not let his mother die on purpose.

The relief that filled him had him feeling lighter than he could ever remember. He checked the road again before stepping into it and crossed to the other side. Before moving to the tree, though, he looked back. And he thought about the dream that had terrorized him so often. There was no cliff on the other side of the road. Maggie had never been there, nor in jeopardy.

He turned back to look at the tree. It had been his mother's SUV wrecked there. Not Maggie's. Never Maggie's.

Maggie had been in this location only as a vibrant pregnant woman who'd loved him and wanted to give him a special gift.

Warmth oozed through him, and he moved to the tree. He lifted his hand and rested it on the oversized knot. Then he hung his head between his shoulders.

I knew you'd be here. I knew you'd help.

He could still remember his mother's words every time he'd shown up after she'd hurt herself. The woman had been a ruthless narcissist. And it had been a whole lot for a sixteen-year-old boy to deal with.

He lifted his head and looked at the tree. "She's not like you, Mom. She'll never be like you. Maggie is sweet and selfless, and she's having our baby. And no way will she raise him the way you raised us."

Of course, neither would *he* raise their son as his father had raised them. He would never have to worry about being like his dad in the sense that his dad had let his mother walk all over them. But he also wouldn't be like his father because he wouldn't be there for his son. Not every day. And that was on *him*.

I'm asking if you'll consider buying my practice.

Doc Hamm's offer floated into his consciousness. He *could* move home. If he wanted to. And then he'd be able to see his son regularly.

Maggie had been right yet again. He at least had to consider Hamm's offer. It didn't matter how the opportunity had come about; it was a legitimate offer. His life wasn't the same one it had been a month ago. And it would never be that life again. So, he had to consider it.

His heart began to race. He really could see his son on a regular basis. And from the very beginning. He might not be with Maggie, but he *could* be here for his son. He thought about his father's words. *Life isn't about a job. You're going to cherish every moment when you're older.*

Embrace what life has handed to you.

Then he thought about Hamm saying how pleased he would be to leave his patients in Cord's hands. Cord hadn't said anything at the time, but he'd had the thought that if Hamm knew he'd recently let one of his own patients die, he wouldn't be so willing to pass his practice off on Cord.

But *had* he let her die?

He wasn't sixteen anymore, so he couldn't excuse his actions away on his age. But he also hadn't directly misdiagnosed her. He should have taken the time to see her, yes. The office might have been closed, but she'd presented with typical appendicitis. He'd known that the moment the receptionist had relayed the woman's symptoms. But he'd also not fully believed she'd been experiencing such because the woman had come in with made-up issues before. He'd seen so much of his mother in her. Always wanting attention. Always ignoring or flat out crushing her kids' hearts.

He might have passed her off that afternoon, but the crux of the matter was that she'd made her own choices when she hadn't gone to the hospital. Everyone had to be responsible for themselves to some point, and though he'd never again repeat that kind of mistake, he could allow himself forgiveness for this one.

He could also promise himself he'd never again let his own past color how he dealt with any patient.

He patted the knot in the tree and nodded with certainty. "You're finished having a hold over me, Mom. Right now, right here. It's over."

He had to let fear quit driving his decisions. And that's what he'd been doing for so long. Fear that he'd let his mother die on purpose. Fear that he would let someone else stomp on his heart the way his mother had always done.

He might have screwed up the really good thing he'd had going with Maggie, but he wouldn't screw up his relationship with his son, as well. He was going to accept Hamm's offer. He was going to come home to Birch Bay.

The last bit of weight lifted from his chest as he thought the words. He would see his son grow up. He'd be able to be there anytime his son needed him.

And maybe someday he could earn Maggie's forgiveness, too. Maybe he'd even suggest they try again.

His phone rang, and assuming it was one of his family members calling from the house, he didn't reach for it. He shouldn't have left and disrupted the morning they'd all had planned. But at the same time, he needed to be right here. He'd needed to deal with his past.

Turning to walk back to his truck, he made the decision to return and to spend Christmas with his family. The kids had probably already discovered what Santa had left for them, but he could take pleasure in watching them show it all to him. Plus, he could give credit for the dollhouse curtains and wallpaper to Maggie since the two of them had gone up to their room last night before that could be made clear.

He pulled his phone out when it rang a second time, a smile on his face, and picked up his step. Only, it wasn't anyone from the house that was calling. It was Maggie.

He stopped in the middle of the road. Had she changed her mind?

Would she still marry him? Especially if he let her know that he would be moving back to Birch Bay?

He tapped the button to answer the call, but as soon as he spoke, he knew she hadn't called to tell him she'd changed her mind.

"Cord." She sounded frantic. "Something is wrong with the baby. I'm in labor, and the baby is coming too fast. My water broke right after I got home, but I wasn't ready to do this yet, so I didn't go to the hospital. I don't want to deliver him only to find out that he didn't make it, Cord." Her whimper crushed his heart. "I can't do this alone."

"Maggie." He was already running for his truck. "You're fine, baby. The baby is fine. Have you called an ambulance yet?"

He could picture the tears streaming down her face. "Yes. But all the snow . . . They said they'd get here as fast as they could, but—"

"I'm coming. I'm already on my way." He pulled the truck out onto the road without bothering to look first. "I'll be there as soon as possible. Focus on that, sweetheart. Focus on me coming to you."

"Okay," she hiccupped through her tears. "But hurry, Cord. I need you to be here."

He tossed the phone onto the console between the front seats, leaving the call open but needing both hands to navigate the road. And he prayed like he'd never prayed before.

If he didn't get there in time, he might fail yet another person. And this time it would be Maggie he hurt. But he wouldn't allow that to happen. He wouldn't allow himself to even think like that.

Because he would *not* fail the woman he loved.

CHAPTER TWENTY-THREE

First babies weren't supposed to be coming this fast.

Maggie paced the length of her small living room, looking out the front windows yet again. There'd been no sign or sound of an ambulance yet, and Cord still hadn't made it either. Someone had to get there soon, though, or she would be delivering this baby alone.

She texted her brother. He was too far away to help, but she wanted him to know what was going on, and she asked him to let their parents know, too. Now she just had to wait and hope that nothing went wrong.

The baby hadn't moved for several hours—at least, she didn't think so. She'd been so upset after leaving Cord earlier that she couldn't say for certain, and then she'd cried so much once she'd gotten home that baby movements were the last things she'd had on her mind. And then her water had broken.

Still . . . the baby not moving worried her. A lot. And she couldn't help but think about her mother right before she'd gone to the doctor that last day.

"You have to be okay," she whispered to her baby, her hands roving over her tight belly.

Tears marred her face as another contraction grabbed hold and bent her over. Groaning, she stooped, barely holding herself up with a hand to the arm of the couch, and she tried to focus on breathing. She tried to focus on anything other than the pain. But as the contraction continued, all she managed was more tears and a lot of sweat. She wanted Cord there. She shouldn't have left last night.

She should have gone to the hospital as soon as her water broke.

If something happened to the baby, it would be her fault, and she would never forgive herself.

The contraction started to ease up, and Maggie straightened slightly and sucked in several deep breaths. She was panting, and if it weren't for the almost continual pains sweeping through, she suspected she'd be in the throes of a panic attack. But so far, the pain and the focus she was having to maintain had kept her from letting fear overtake her.

She couldn't stay upright any longer, so she headed for her bedroom before another contraction could begin. She'd unlocked the door earlier, and she'd let the dispatcher know the EMTs should come right in. She hadn't told Cord the same, but she had a feeling he'd break the door down to get to her if needed.

The thought had her replaying the night before. The man might have said he didn't love her, but she'd begun to wonder if that was true. Erica had pointed out before that due to his mother screwing with his head, it might take a while for him to admit how much he cared. Was that all that was going on? Or had she read him wrong from the very start?

Another wave of pain hit, and Cord left her mind. Instead, she screamed. She had to be getting close.

"Maggie!"

Cord's voice penetrated before she saw him rushing into her room, and as she lay curled in on herself, every muscle in her body working to produce what nature made her capable of, she sent up a soft "thank you" that she wouldn't be doing the rest of this alone.

"I think I'm close," she forced out. "The contractions are right on top of each other."

"Let's get you out of your pants, and I'll take a look."

He went into the same doctor mode she remembered from the night he'd found her on the side of the road, and the professional and focused voice eased her. She wasn't alone in this. And the man she loved—and who just might love her—was going to make sure everything came out all right.

Another pain hit, and as she worked through it, Cord got her pants off and put clean towels under her, and by the time that contraction eased off, he was stooped at the foot of her bed, his head visible between her knees. A look unlike any she'd ever seen shone back at her.

"We're about to have a baby, sweetheart." If that wasn't love looking at her, then she didn't know what was. "He's crowning, and you're doing amazing."

She smiled. They were going to be amazing.

"Are you ready to push?" he asked.

"Is it time?"

"As soon as the next one hits." He nodded. "You've got this. You're amazing. You're incredible."

"You love me?" she asked, and his face softened into the most glorious smile.

"I love you." He hurried to her side and pressed a kiss to her lips. "I love you," he repeated. And then another contraction hit. "It's time, beautiful. You can do this. You've got this. Bring our beautiful baby boy into this world."

She pushed with everything she had, the fear from earlier completely erased, and as she felt their son leave her body and slip into his daddy's hands, she heard her name being called yet again. The EMTs had arrived, but they were too late. Credit for this delivery would go to Dr. Wilde.

SEVERAL HOURS LATER, Cord still hadn't left Maggie's side. The

EMTs had made it into the house in time to help deliver the after-birth and tie off the cord, and then they'd loaded all of them up and set off for the hospital. Maggie had been amazing. And their little boy?

Well, he wasn't so little.

Arriving at nine pounds and thirteen ounces, Cord could now see why Maggie had looked ready to deliver for quite a while.

"Do you want to try putting him to your breast again?"

Cord had held his son in his arms while Maggie had been dozing. She hadn't gotten any additional sleep after leaving the house last night, so once all the excitement of the delivery had been over and she'd seen that their son was perfect—and his entire family, as well as her brother, had filed in to meet the newest addition—he'd convinced her to take a nap.

"Please." She held out her arms for the baby, her eyes still half-lidded, and as he leaned in to settle their son in her arms, he pressed a kiss to her forehead.

"I love you," he whispered.

She grinned up at him and puckered her lips, wanting more than a forehead kiss. "And I love *you*."

She settled their son at her breast, and as Cord hovered over her, he basked in the knowledge that he most assuredly *did* love this woman. He'd asked Gabe once how he'd known that it was love he'd felt for Erica, and his brother had assured him that when it happened to him, he'd just know. Cord had scoffed at the idea of it ever happening, but he was a firm believer today. And Gabe had been right. He'd just known.

In fact, he didn't know how he hadn't known before.

"We're going to have to settle on a first name for this guy." Maggie spoke softly as she peered down at the baby. She stroked the backs of her fingers over his soft, dewy baby skin, and Cord saw firsthand what love looked like.

"How about Max?" he suggested, and Maggie looked up.

"You want to name him after your dad?"

This was something he'd thought about a lot. They'd discussed a variety of names over the past weeks. Some which held certain meanings they wanted attributed to their son. Others that would represent distant family members on either side. And they'd also discussed naming him Max. They'd waffled several times among several different selections, and though Cord had been annoyed with his dad for going behind his back, he wouldn't let that act define their relationship.

What he'd come to understand in the last few hours was that as their son grew older, even into adulthood, Cord would also want to do anything and everything he could to help the boy make the right decisions. He'd like to think that he wouldn't work in secret to set up opportunities which would be the most beneficial, but at the same time, he *could* say that such situations could arise. And if they did . . . well, the chance was there that he might just take it.

He now understood that what his father had done, he'd done out of love. And he couldn't fault the man for that. His dad had never set out to steer Cord in any direction that was purely for his own benefit. Cord understood that, too. Instead, his dad had only ever tried to be a good parent. Which was all Cord had ever wanted.

"He is the first grandson, after all," Cord pointed out. "After a long string of seven girls."

"True." She turned her gaze back to the baby. "And Max is a good, strong name."

"It means 'greatest.'"

Her grin was soft. "I remember." They'd talked about the meaning of the name when they'd first considered it. She looked back up at Cord. "And we do have the greatest son."

The baby had latched on to his mother's breast, and the two of them made a picture Cord would never let himself forget. "There will never be one greater," he agreed. "Unless you let me talk you into another later."

At his words, her eyes widened. "You already want another one?"

He already wanted about four. "I have a couple of brothers ahead of me already. You don't want me lagging behind, do you?"

She chuckled at his joke, and love filled her eyes. As she dipped her head and rested her cheek against their son's forehead, she kept her gaze trained on him. And he saw seriousness enter their depths. "So, you're thinking of this as a permanent type thing?"

His truck remained at her house, so he didn't have the ring to offer her again. "It's as permanent as you'll let it be. I don't want to rush you, Maggie, but I promise that if you'll have me, I'll never leave your side. I don't know how I didn't see it before, but you're the love of my life, sweetheart. You're the only woman I've ever wanted to spend more than a few days with, and you're the woman I now want to have a baseball team of kids with. I'll be patient, though. I'll be your friend, and I'll be your lover. And when you're ready for more, both *of* me"—he flicked a glance at the baby—"and *from* me, then you can let me know." Her shot her a naughty grin. "I'm here to serve, baby."

Love shone back at him the same way he'd just watched her shower their son with. There were no doubts in her eyes. "Is your house in Billings large enough for a baseball team–sized family?"

Surprise had his jaw dropping open. It hadn't even occurred to him that he'd not mentioned his new plans. "We're not going to be in Billings. Not unless *you* want to. I've decided to accept Hamm's offer and buy his practice. If you're good with that plan, then I'd love to spend the rest of my life right here with you, and with the rest of my family. I'm ready to come home."

NOTHING in the world could make Maggie happier than what she had right now. A baby she adored, a man she loved and who loved her back. But to hear him say that he wanted to come home. That he wanted to embrace the family that was there waiting for him . . . well, her heart was about to explode.

"Yes," she said, and at his raised brow she elaborated. "Yes, I'll marry you. Yes, we can have more kids. Only, can I please have a minute to recover from this one? And *yes*, I want to live right here in Birch Bay. Forever."

Cord lowered to the bed, and he wrapped his arms around both her and the baby. "You're my entire world, Maggie Crowder. I don't want to do life without you."

"Ditto." She smiled, then she tilted her face up and pressed a soft kiss to her fiancé's mouth. "And now," she whispered against his lips. "Don't you think we should *officially* introduce baby Max to the rest of his family?"

Cord grinned. Everyone had come to the hospital shortly after they'd arrived earlier, and though she'd assured them it would be okay for them to return home to finish enjoying Christmas morning, they'd convinced her there wasn't any other place they wanted to be. They'd all promised to stick around until she and Cord decided on the baby's name, and since that had been done, there was no reason to wait. She was ready to get her new family back in there.

As Cord stepped out into the hall to go invite them back in, Maggie did an obligatory straighten of her hair and hospital gown and lifted Max to her shoulder. She'd never get enough of squeezing his tiny body.

Mason was the first one who came back in, and at the sight of his sister, pride filled his eyes. "You did good." He'd told her that before, but she liked hearing it again.

He leaned in and kissed her cheek, and then *all* of Cord's family filed into the room. Even the four new babies. The place was packed, but they made it work. Cord came to stand at her right, one hand reached down to take hers, and Mason stood at her other side, his hand resting on her shoulder. But when she looked up at Cord to see if he was ready to make the announcement, she saw a quick shake of his head.

"Why not?" she whispered.

Mason's hand patted her on the shoulder, as if to get her attention, and when she looked back over, she saw that the hospital room door was opening again. And coming through it this time were her mother and father. And then the tears that had been so much a part of her last nine months reappeared once more.

"Mom," she sniffled. "Dad."

"We're sorry we're late," her dad told her. "Your mom wanted to stop by the gift shop on the way up." He held her mother's hand tight in his, but her mom didn't look as if she needed the support. Instead, Maggie witnessed nothing but love and amazement coming from the other woman as her mother's gaze latched on to baby Max.

She stared at the baby for a moment before shifting her eyes over to Maggie, and then it was pride Maggie saw. "You're going to be an amazing mother."

More tears fell, both from her and her mother, and once the two of them had settled down, Maggie looked up at Cord again. He squeezed her hand. "We have a couple of announcements to make," he said to the group, and Maggie understood that he also intended to share their engagement.

"Three announcements," she corrected. She wanted them to know that he was coming home.

He nodded. "Three. First"—he motioned to Maggie and the baby —"I'd like you all to meet Maxwell Cord Wilde."

The women in the group pressed their hands to their mouths, and Max teared up. "You're naming him after me?"

"He's got to carry on the Wilde name, Dad. Who else would we name him after?"

His dad nodded, as if at a loss for any more words, and Maggie made the second announcement. "Second," she said. She looked up at Cord. "I've agreed to marry this amazing man."

Arsula's and Erica's eyes glistened.

"And third," Cord continued. Maggie noticed that he didn't quite look at his dad at this point, and she squeezed his hand tighter. She was so proud of him for not letting anything his father might have done impact what she and he could have together. "Doctor Hamm is retiring, and I'm going to make him an offer to buy his practice. I'll be moving home to stay."

Shock echoed through the room, and Maggie kept an eye on Max. Max seemed as dumbfounded as the rest of them. He hadn't known that Doctor Hamm was retiring.

"Cord," she whispered, and when he glanced down, she nodded toward his dad.

"I had no idea that Hamm was retiring," Max murmured. "He's been around forever." He looked at Gloria. "Did you know this?"

Gloria agreed that she'd not heard about it either, and as Cord brought his gaze back to Maggie's, they shared a moment that was both a learning experience and a feeling of relief. Cord had jumped the gun about his dad instead of talking to the man directly. But thank goodness he could let that lingering feeling of manipulation go and now just focus on what he *did* have in front of him. And that was everyone and everything represented in that small room with them right now.

EPILOGUE

FIVE MONTHS LATER . . .

THE DAY WAS perfect for a wedding. Cord stood at the open loft door of the barn, overlooking his family's land, as well as his siblings and their spouses, their kids, his father and Gloria, and all of Jaden and Arsula's wedding party and guests. The only people he hadn't recently laid eyes on were Maggie and their son. They were around somewhere, though. She'd walked down the aisle for her friend earlier, dressed in a strapless, short summer dress and cowboy boots, while he'd been on daddy duty. And ever since the reception had started, she'd been flitting in and out of the crowd, having the time of her life.

Part of what she was doing, she'd informed him, was gathering more notes for *their* wedding. Though they already had the majority of their wedding planned—they also intended to marry in the barn, but they wouldn't be sporting a country theme—Maggie claimed that since they would only marry once, she wanted to make doubly certain everything fit both of them to a tee.

As far as he was concerned, they could stand before a judge and he'd be happy. He just wanted to marry the woman that he loved. But he also couldn't deny the appeal of being bound together forever by taking vows on the land spread out before him.

The sky was a clear blue today. The type of sky Montana was known for. The cherry trees were in full bloom. And happiness radiated from every person on the property. He was thrilled for his brother and Arsula. Their own happiness couldn't be missed, and he couldn't wait to share the same experience with Maggie.

Footsteps sounded on the stairs at the other end of the loft, and he turned to wait for the woman of his dreams to ascend. He didn't have to be told it was Maggie coming up to find him. Somehow, he always just seemed to know when she was near.

Laughter from several of the kids came from the grounds below, as well as two distinct baby giggles, and Cord admitted to himself that life couldn't get any better.

"Babe?" Maggie's messy bun on the top of her head appeared before he saw her face, and when he caught sight of her bared shoulders and their adorably sweet son propped over one hip, he fell even more in love.

"Over here," he said before her gaze made it to him.

"What are you doing up here?"

"Right now, I'm just watching you."

She tossed him the kind of look that had first captured his attention and started the ball rolling between them, and he considered suggesting she take Max back downstairs to be watched by one of his cousins so Cord could defile her up here.

The loft doubled as meeting rooms, but the extra partitions had been removed and lights strung throughout as a backup for a reception space if the weather had changed last minute. Thankfully, there had been no need for that, so they currently had the place all to themselves.

"You want to roll around in the hay with me up here?" he asked, and given her brief pause, he thought she just might agree.

"There's not actually any hay *up* here," she pointed out instead.

"Spoilsport." He kissed her cheek as she made it over to him, and together, they both turned and watched the action below. When renovations had been made to the barn to turn it into a meeting space and wedding venue, a railing had been added across the loft door so on pretty days like today, the oversize door could remain open.

"This will be us soon." She tucked her head into the curve of his shoulder as he wrapped an arm around her.

"Not soon enough."

The last five months had been more than Cord could have asked for. After Christmas, he and Doc Hamm had quickly set things into motion for Hamm's retirement and for Cord to take over, while at the same time, Cord had made arrangements in Billings for the remaining partners to buy him out.

Maggie hadn't gone back to work that semester. She would in the fall, but she'd decided to spend the first eight months of their son's life home with him. Additionally, she'd shown no signs of postpartum depression. He thought it helped that her mother came to visit quite often these days, and that the Crowders were already talking about having Max stay with them a few weekends a year until he was older, when they planned to let him spend as much of his summers at the ranch as Maggie and he would allow.

Cord was all for whatever part they wanted to play in his son's life. Family was what life was about. Just as his father had said several months ago. And he still intended to have a very large family with Maggie. In fact . . .

"How have you made it today?"

She smiled up at him. "I only threw up once while helping Arsula get ready, but I managed that without anyone noticing."

Their second baby would be arriving in the world in roughly eight months. "Good."

"But I *did* catch Arsula throwing up."

Cord's brows hitched. "She's pregnant, too?"

"That's what she said. I asked when she couldn't hide what was going on, and she admitted that they're due on Christmas Day."

"They're trying to steal our baby's thunder?" he teased. He leaned in front of Maggie and tickled Max in the belly, making his son squeal while kicking his chubby little legs out in excitement. "I learned something today, as well."

"Yeah?" Maggie's arm snaked around his waist.

"Nate and Megan are expecting, too."

Maggie looked up. "When?"

"January first."

"Wow."

They both turned to look back out at the crowd below, Cord thinking about how a once scattered and broken family were now seven happy couples with babies arriving in rapid succession, and he wondered how they'd all managed to get so lucky.

"Megan is motioning for us to come down," Maggie said.

Megan had moved off in the direction of the lodge, her arm now raised and waving toward Cord and Maggie in a beckoning motion. At the same time, the rest of the family were separating from the wedding party and guests and making their way away from the crowd. They were all headed to the section of orchard that had been designated for the family picture.

The photos, themselves, might be part of Jaden and Arsula's wedding day, but they would signify a much larger moment in time. This photo would be the Wildes. The family no one had ever expected them to be, but who they'd all always dreamed of becoming.

"There couldn't be a better day for a family picture," Cord concluded.

"There couldn't be a better family to be *in* the picture."

Dear Reader,

I hope you can envision the family picture in amongst the cherry trees the way I can. I didn't write the scene itself taking place because I can't begin to do it justice. Instead, what I really wanted to do was to include an actual photo. Because this family is that real to me. So, instead of a final few paragraphs of me showing you all the Wildes standing in the middle of the trees, every single one of them happy and complete, please close your eyes for a moment and imagine that picture with me. And thank you for loving the Wilde family as much as I do.

ABOUT THE AUTHOR

As a child, **Kim Law** cultivated a love for chocolate, anything purple, and creative writing. She penned her debut work, "The Gigantic Talking Raisin," in the sixth grade and got hooked on the delights of creating stories. Before settling into the writing life, however, she earned a college degree in mathematics, then worked as a computer programmer while raising her son. Now she's pursuing her lifelong dream of writing romance novels—none of which include talking raisins.

A native of Kentucky, Kim now resides in Middle Tennessee. You can visit Kim at www.KimLaw.com.